FELIX
GREY

MARIO THEODOROU

For Ελένη and Άβα

Always remember that dreams come true if you have the courage to believe in them. x

It has taken a great deal of effort to bring to mind those things that once occupied my daily life but have since become a collection of distant and vague memories. It is, I suppose, the appanage of time to make people forget the great adventures that have shaped their lives and helped pave the way to their present. It is only now, through fear of forgetfulness, that I sit down to write this account of his time in office for the next generation of Greys to read and hold dear.

It is, though, with a deep sense of foreboding, that I embark on this undertaking, for enclosed in this journal are a collection of secrets that will amaze any person who should have the opportunity to read them. Nevertheless, it is my duty to document his life for his successors, and I shall proceed with care and be mindful of those details that I can freely commit to paper. I write this account in the hope that future generations may have the insight and knowledge to solve the deeper mystery at the heart of this tale.

Anonymous

East India Club

- September 11th, 1904 -

Lord Monteagle stirred and slowly opened his eyes. He was feeling the ill effects of an afternoon spent drinking fine wine and brandy with his associates in Fitzrovia.

'East India Club,' announced a porter, opening the carriage door.

Monteagle heaved himself up from his seat and slowly stepped out of the carriage onto the busy pavement. Mayfair had a reputation for its bustling nightlife but was exceptionally crowded during the long winter months. The constant rain did little to dampen the spirits of those gentlemen who frequented the clubs in the area. They stretched from St James's to Berkeley Square and boasted some of the most beautiful buildings in the city; great Georgian houses spread over five floors of marble and stone.

He had barely straightened his top hat and tie when an elegant, dark-skinned woman approached. She wore a sheer patterned tea gown, and her piercing green eyes shone brightly against her oil-black hair.

'Welcome, my Lord,' she said, in a mild Indian accent. 'My name is Seema Sharma. I am a hostess at the East India Club. Mr Burbage has been anticipating your arrival.'

'Very well,' slurred Monteagle, his breath emanating a strong smell of alcohol, 'let us proceed.'

Seema Sharma led Monteagle up the wide marble stairs towards the double oak doors and the club's reception hall. In the centre of the room, framed by ornate vases, overflowing with wildflowers from the Indian subcontinent, stood a towering sculpture of the goddess Durga sitting on a ferocious Bengal tiger. A representation of the club's past as a base for workers of the East India Company.

They carried on through the hall towards the winding staircase. Monteagle took a moment to study the paintings hanging from the walls, large portraits of past maharajas and British governors of India, all equal in size and splendour.

'Does it surprise you to see Indian maharajas on the walls of a London club?' asked Seema Sharma.

'Nothing surprises me anymore.'

'These pictures are a representation of our combined wealth and power,' continued the hostess. 'They depict what can be achieved by the coming together of our two great nations.'

'Ha!' scoffed Monteagle. 'You would speak of India in the same breath as England?'

'Do you not invest your English wealth in our Indian resources?'

'You forget yourself!' barked Monteagle, affronted by the

hostess's familiarity.

'My humble apologies,' hissed Seema Sharma. 'I did not mean to offend. Please, let us continue.'

At the top of the staircase, the hallway split in two opposing directions. Seema Sharma led Monteagle along the west corridor, accentuated by a vibrant red-and-gold carpet, towards a wooden door adorned with a carving of the elephant god, Ganesh.

'They are just through here, my Lord,' she said, opening the door and inviting Monteagle to enter.

Inside, a group of gentlemen sat around an oval table with neatly stacked banknotes piled in front of them.

Jonathan Burbage, a greying gentleman, well-turned-out with warm blue eyes, rose to greet Monteagle.

'We were about to start without you, my Lord,' he jested.

'I was held up,' replied Monteagle, in his brash manner.

'Well, no bother, you are here now. Allow me to introduce James and Henry Coleridge,' he said motioning towards two finely dressed young men, similar enough in height and appearance to be twins. 'They have just returned from a spell in India where they have established a very successful tea plantation.'

'It is a pleasure, my Lord,' said both men, bowing in unison.

'And here on my right,' continued Burbage, 'is Mr Clement Morris, one of London's premier insurers and a notorious cardsharp.'

'Nonsense!' protested Morris, a middle-aged man with sharp features and cold, calculating eyes. 'Although, I should be happy to cover your losses, for a small premium, of course.'

'Pay him no attention,' warned Burbage, 'he likes to gain the psychological advantage before the game has even begun. Now, how about some drinks?'

'Whiskey,' replied Monteagle.

'Good idea, whiskeys all-round!' called Burbage, waving his hand theatrically at Seema Sharma.

The hostess poured five measures from a tall crystal decanter before adding a single ice cube and handing them out to each guest. Monteagle took his seat alongside the house dealer, removing a large pile of banknotes from his inside pocket and placing them on the table for all to see.

'I was just regaling these gentlemen with stories of our time together in India, setting up your plantations,' said Burbage, addressing Monteagle. 'What days they were.'

'You are a sentimentalist, Jonathan,' replied Monteagle, gulping down his whiskey.

'A man's memories are worth their weight in gold. I know you still reminisce on that time as fondly as I do, even if you do not care to admit it.'

'I certainly do not. I find the Indian heat unbearable, as I do find the people, the food, and the roads.'

'Tell me, my Lord,' entered James Coleridge, 'how do you find working with the locals?'

'We have a straightforward understanding. They are employed to work our lands and if we are unhappy with their day's efforts, they are sent home without pay.'

'That sounds rather old fashioned,' replied James Coleridge.

Monteagle held up his empty glass and motioned towards the hostesses to refill it. 'It guarantees efficiency and ensures a satisfactory return on our investment.'

'Yes, but what about your relationship with your workers?' asked Henry Coleridge. 'Surely, they can't be overly enthused with such an arrangement?'

'If they do not like the conditions of their employment, then they are free to leave. There are thousands more who would readily take their place.'

'That I can account for,' agreed Burbage. 'I have never seen so many people in one place. It's like a giant colony of ants.'

'Such an abundance of labour must have a positive effect on your insurance premiums,' added Clement Morris.

'We can always guarantee production if that's what you mean?' replied Monteagle, taking hold of his newly filled glass from an indignant Seema Sharma, who had listened to their conversation in silent fury.

'Gentlemen,' called the dealer, taking advantage of a small break in the conversation, 'shall we begin?'

'Yes, I think so,' replied Burbage, taking his seat. 'We are all well-enough acquainted.'

The men took up their positions around the table as the dealer shuffled the pack and began to deal the cards.

'The game, sirs, is three card poker, and the starting bet is two shillings,' he said, placing the remaining stack by his side.

A business-like silence fell upon the table as the men gathered their cards, taking a moment to arrange them and decide on their strategies.

'The bet is with you, my Lord,' said the dealer, motioning towards Monteagle.

Monteagle took a second to scan the table and, importantly, his opponents.

'Raise, one pound.' He declared, placing a bank note in the centre of the table.

'That is quite a substantial bet, my Lord,' replied Burbage, tossing his cards towards the dealer. 'Too rich for my blood.'

'And mine,' agreed Clement Morris, placing his cards to one side.

'I should like to test your mettle, sir,' announced Henry Coleridge, placing his bank note on the table alongside Monteagle's.

'I'm afraid I am out too,' said James Coleridge, reluctantly throwing his cards down.

'Two players remaining,' called the dealer, motioning towards Monteagle and Henry Coleridge.

Monteagle took hold of his whiskey and gulped down its contents. He placed the glass on the table and turned to face Henry Coleridge.

'I am unaware of your estates in India; are they in the north?' he asked.

'They are,' replied Henry Coleridge, 'although we cannot call them our own. We lease the land.'

'That is most interesting,' said Monteagle, throwing down two cards to be replaced by the dealer.

'Do you still have many interests in India, sir?' asked Henry Coleridge, replacing a single card with the dealer.

'Some. Although, I own them all, lock, stock and barrel.'

'Then you are fortunate indeed.'

'Your choice, my Lord,' beckoned the dealer, bringing the attention back to the cards.

'Five pounds,' declared Monteagle, pushing his bank notes forward across the table.

'Five pounds?' repeated Burbage, shocked by the scale of Monteagle's bet.

'That is what I said,' replied Monteagle wiping some sweat from his brow. 'It will be five pounds if you wish to continue.'

Henry Coleridge took a moment to consider Monteagle's bet, then reluctantly placed his cards face down on the table. 'Not on this occasion, my Lord,' he conceded. 'I fear my middleweight numbers would not have been strong enough to keep you honest.'

'Very clever, my Lord!' clapped Clement Morris. 'Your questions were merely a ruse to ascertain how much money you thought might be suitable to scare your opponent off the pot. Fortunately for you, Henry gave you all the information you required.'

'Naturally,' said Monteagle, rising from his seat to gather his winnings. 'You must always play the man and not the cards.'

As he reached across the table for his money, Monteagle felt a sudden wave of dizziness come over him. He swayed, gripping the table to steady himself.

'Are you alright, sir?' asked Henry Coleridge, viewing Monteagle with some concern.

'I am quite… well,' replied Monteagle, his voice slower and more laboured than usual. 'I just… need… to…' he stuttered, unable able to finish his sentence.

Suddenly his legs gave way and Monteagle collapsed onto his knees, his eyes vacant.

'My Lord! exclaimed Burbage, rushing to Monteagle's side to help prop him up. 'What is wrong with him?' he squealed, shocked at the peer's limp frame.

'It seems his Lordship has had too much to drink,' replied James Coleridge, taking hold of Monteagle's other arm.

'I shall summon his carriage,' said Seema Sharma, leaving the room.

The men carried Monteagle's limp body out of the card room and down the long, winding staircase towards the club's reception. Having heard the commotion, members began to appear from their rooms to catch a glimpse of the stricken man.

Outside, a carriage waited to receive Lord Monteagle's body. The men carefully placed the peer on the long wooden bench inside, then covered him with a blanket and closed the door.

'Take him home and give him something to sober him up,' called Burbage to the driver, who pulled tightly on the reins, setting the horses speeding away into the dark London night.

It was some hours before Lord Monteagle finally began to regain consciousness. He could feel the early-morning sun on his face as he lay stretched out on the carriage's passenger bench.

He pulled himself up, his head still hazy from his sudden turn, and wiped the long beads of sweat from his forehead. Outside, he could feel the carriage horses running at full tilt and the carriage rocking wildly from side to side.

'Slow down, Jacob!' he shouted with what little energy he could muster. But the carriage only seemed to speed up further, careering through the cobbled streets at a frenetic pace.

Monteagle reached for the window, trying to pull it open and alert his driver, but the latch was jammed.

'I'm quite alright, Jacob. Slow the pace!' he shouted, his voice lacking its usual punch.

Outside, Monteagle could see the London streets passing quickly by the window. The broad pavements and ostentatious Georgian houses that marked out the affluent area around Mayfair were replaced by the rough cobbled alleyways and tall warehouses of the London Docklands. Monteagle took in his new surroundings in disbelief. Why were they here of all places?

The events of his evening at the East India Club came flooding back to him. He could recall meeting Burbage and his guests in the small card room and their poker match. He could also remember winning a large amount of money before feeling unwell. But then there was nothing – just a feeling of utter helplessness. His last image was of the many faces around the table, staring down at him as he knelt on the poker room floor, unable to move. Had he been poisoned?

Monteagle looked around the carriage in shock. He hadn't noticed at first, but it was different from his vehicle. It was much smaller, with narrow wooden benches instead of his comfortable cushioned leather seats. The windows were smaller and had been covered with a dark material to conceal the passenger inside. There were no handles on the doors, only a bar to rest one's arm.

Monteagle leaned against the window and looked up towards the driver. He couldn't see the man's face, but his frame was more considerable than Jacob's, with broad shoulders and a thickset neck, covered in tattoos. Monteagle pulled at the carriage door frantically, but it would not move. It was locked from the outside.

'What is the meaning of this?' he shouted, banging on the carriage roof.

Having used up all the energy he'd managed to gather, Monteagle slumped back in his seat to catch his breath. Suddenly, the horses began to slow, and the carriage eventually pulled to a halt. Through the window, Monteagle could see the driver dismounting. He scanned the carriage looking for anything he might use as a weapon, but the small compartment had been expertly stripped and prepared for his abduction.

Within seconds the man was at the carriage door. He glared at Monteagle through the shaded window, his sardonic smile revealing his black and yellow teeth. He looked like the type of ruffian one would expect to frequent the Dockland's notorious drinking holes and opium dens. He removed a key from his pocket and used it to unlock the door, slowly opening it to reveal a gun pointing at Monteagle's stomach.

'My Lord.' He bowed mockingly.

'Why have you brought me here?' asked Monteagle.

'My employer requests an audience.'

'Whatever he is paying you, I will treble it. Just take me back to my club.'

'Ha! You men of title think everything has a price.'

'Does it not?'

'Not in the eyes of the maker,' replied the driver, pulling Monteagle out of the carriage and placing the gun in his back. 'Now, walk!'

Reluctantly, Monteagle started to walk. First, through a series of narrow side streets and cobbled walkways, before finally arriving at one of the river's many docks. He observed the workers going about their early-morning business, hopeful of alerting them to his situation, however, these were casual labourers, picked up that morning and given a chance to earn some money, which they weren't prepared to risk by accidentally noticing anything untoward.

He could smell the sweet scent of sugar in the air, mixed with the sickly burning smell of rubber, suspecting that they were somewhere between Tower Hill and Wapping, where such products had been stored in recent years.

The area had been renowned for handling the trade in luxury items like wool, wine, ivory and even ostrich feathers. But the increase in vessel size and the lack of railway access saw a sudden decline in its viability, and with less trade in the area came a sharp rise in the flow of illegal goods and criminality. It wasn't uncommon for people to disappear off one of the many piers and jetties that lined the docks around the area, never to be seen again.

As they approached the river, the driver directed Monteagle towards an intimidating black barge, moored on the bank with a narrow rope bridge leading to its deck.

'On you go then,' he said, pointing his gun towards the vessel.

'And if I refuse?' asked Monteagle.

'Then I'm to put a bullet in your back and send you to the bottom of Old Father Thames.'

Monteagle hesitated. He knew that once inside the barge, the possibility of escape, or discovery by the authorities, was limited.

'Get a move on!' snarled the driver, prodding Monteagle viciously in the ribs with his weapon.

Monteagle reluctantly stepped onto the rope bridge and crossed the thin planks towards the long boat's deck. He could still feel the weakness in his legs as the bridge swayed and wobbled, almost causing him to lose his balance. He finally made it across, relieved to feel solid ground beneath his feet again.

At the end of the walkway was a door with a low-lit entrance. Monteagle stepped inside, his eyes taking a moment to adjust to the change in light. He could make out the rectangular shape of the long room with various pieces of furniture dotted around the open space. His eyes suddenly focused on a tall shadowy figure standing at the far end of the room.

'Welcome,' called a low, rasping voice.

'What do you want with me?' asked Monteagle, some authority returning to his voice.

'Only what's owed, my Lord.'

'I have no debt with you,' declared Monteagle.

'Oh, but you do, sir. You have a very substantial debt indeed.'

The shadowy figure struck a match and lit his pipe, revealing a red leather patch covering his left eye.

10 Downing Street

Heavy raindrops dappled the black gates surrounding 10 Downing Street. It had been a wet start to Autumn, and the slow march of feet usually heard outside had disappeared along with the summer sun.

Inside, Humphrey set about lighting a fire for his master, Felix Grey. He placed the heavy logs on top of the tiny embers and fanned the gathering until the flames caught alight, filling the study instantly with heat.

Humphrey stood up, straightening his stiff back. The cold weather had brought on his arthritis earlier than usual, and he was thankful for the fire's warm relief.

Felix had offered to bring in some help, but Humphrey

refused. He'd been with the Grey family for over four decades and had practically raised the young prime minister, ever since the early passing of Felix's mother, Leonora Grey, to cholera. A strong-willed petitioner for women's rights and a renowned suffragette, Leonora had made Humphrey promise to always remain by Felix's side, and he was not prepared to break his oath or see his life's work handed over to a stranger. Besides, he liked to stay active. It was hard work, but Humphrey had seen first-hand what happened to people in semi-retirement; their joints began to seize up, and their muscles wither away, bringing on old age quickly. No, he would continue in his role and keep his strength while he could.

He circled the room, checking everything was in place before allowing himself a moment's rest. He'd barely taken a seat and closed his tired eyes when he heard the door to Number 10 open and the house staff spring into action.

Humphrey let out a long sigh. He was used to the furore that usually accompanied Felix's return from Parliament. It was as though the house itself had awoken from a long rest, with every room and all its staff readied and waiting to receive the Prime Minister.

Humphrey slowly pushed himself up from his warm seat and straightened out his suit. Within moments, the door sprang open, and Felix bounded in, accompanied by his friend and the Home Secretary, Thomas Percy.

Percy was a rotund man, heavily built, with flushed cheeks and a loose suit that made him appear older than his forty-four years. In contrast, Felix looked young for a politician, clean-shaven, with only the odd grey in his neatly combed black hair. He wore a cleanly pressed suit with polished shoes, and a handkerchief rested on the brim of his chest pocket.

'Afternoon, old man,' he said, approaching his steward.

'I am beyond your cajoling, Felix' replied Humphrey. 'The fire is lit, and I am content. How was Parliament?'

'In an uproar, as always.'

'And what pray tell do they have to moan about today?'

'The list is unfortunately both long and infuriating.' replied Felix, pouring himself a large scotch.

Over the past few months, he had become accustomed to its taste and enjoyed a stiff measure or two to wash away the day's cobwebs.

'They have no stomach for reform,' added Percy, lowering his plump frame into one of the seats, facing the fire. 'They like to cling to their to outdated traditions.'

'There is nothing wrong with tradition, Home Secretary,' said Humphrey, 'only its application. Greedy men will find the advantage in any idea, old or new. Now, will you be staying for dinner?'

'Unfortunately, not. I have a mountain of work that requires my immediate attention.'

'I won't hear of it, Thomas!' protested Felix. 'There is nothing that can't wait until you are properly fed and watered. Humphrey, have another place set at dinner, will you please. And let Mrs Hughes know that she will be feeding an extra mouth.'

'Very well,' replied Humphrey, leaving to coordinate matters.

'You do realise that he's wasted here,' said Percy, waiting for the study door to close. 'He should be in the backbenches, whipping the members into shape.'

'He'd have them running for cover,' agreed Felix, amused by the thought. 'He's been with the family ever since I was a young boy. I don't know what I would do without him.'

Felix crossed the room and held his hands over the fire for warmth, it had been a short journey back from Parliament but a cold one. On the mantlepiece sat a picture of Felix, taken on the night of the general election. Crowds had gathered outside Downing Street to welcome their new prime minister. It was a night he would never forget; the clapping and cheering, the warmth and optimism he had felt from the British people.

Having been parachuted into office at the tender age of thirty-two, Felix had become the third youngest prime minister in British history, with only the Marquess of Rockingham, the Duke of Grafton and William Pitt the Younger having been more junior. However, with little experience to draw on and few alliances in both Parliament and his coalition government, he'd found the first two years in office difficult. Many of his reforms had been blocked in the Commons, and Felix was finding it impossible to effect any meaningful change, let alone live up to the public's inflated expectations of him.

Had he known how easily people's opinions could change, how quickly the dissenting voices would appear, he may have held back a little, detached himself from the euphoria that would inevitably fade with time, instead of standing on the steps to Number 10, smiling broadly and waving.

Hindsight would make an excellent companion for any man, but particularly a prime minister.

Felix's thoughts were disturbed by a knock at the study door.

'Come in,' he called.

A young footman in full livery entered.

'Sorry to disturb you, sir,' he began, 'but Police Commissioner Thompson is here to see you.'

Felix looked at Percy, surprised by the news. The commissioner had never visited Downing Street without prior arrangement. He would usually send an officer ahead to make enquiries before arriving in person.

'This is most unorthodox,' said Percy. 'Shall I ask him to come back at a more suitable time?'

'No need,' replied Felix. He preferred to deal with the unknown head-on. 'Send him in,' he instructed the footman.

'Good evening, gentlemen,' began the commissioner, entering the room. He was a short man in his late fifties, with greying hair and a tightly cropped moustache, and his perfectly polished boots and precisely pressed creases were evidence of a time spent serving in the British army. 'Apologies for the suddenness of my visit, but I come with grave news. I thought it best to seek you out directly before you heard the undoubted whispers in Parliament.'

'Go on,' replied Felix.

'At approximately midnight last night, Lord Monteagle was abducted from the East India Club while playing poker with his associates. The perpetrators drugged him with an organic compound known as ethoxyethane, a common anaesthetic, colourless and easy to mask when poured into a person's drink. They then switched carriages so that his associates delivered the stricken man directly into their hands before disappearing with him into the night.'

'What cowards!' Exclaimed Percy.

'Indeed, sir. The men were clearly organised and had been planning the abduction for some time. They knew of his Lordship's arrival and had made the necessary arrangements to extract him swiftly and with minimal fuss.'

'Military men?' asked Felix.

'It's a possibility, Prime Minister.'

'Have they issued any demands or asked for a ransom?'

'No,' replied Thompson, reaching into his pocket, and taking out a small envelope. 'They did leave this, however,' he said, handing the envelope to Felix. 'We found it in one of the dark backstreets, lying on the cobbles alongside the limp body of Monteagle's driver, Jacob Moore.'

Felix opened the envelope and took out a small rectangular card, no bigger than a half-pound note. It was light in weight but rigid to the touch and had a series of strange markings on both sides. He turned the card over in his hands, noting the odd shapes and symbols.

The first, an image of a common five-pointed star, had been crudely drawn and was faded and out of shape. Felix had seen many like it in the history books and encyclopaedias at Number 10, and on the walls and paintings of his Mayfair club. The second, however, was less obvious to him. The image seemed to depict a giant goat's head with four horns pointing in opposite directions, surrounding by a cluster of stars with fire and smoke swirling around them. The goat's face was strikingly human, and its black, marbled eyes seemed to stare back at Felix from off the paper.

'Are you familiar with these signs, Prime Minister?' asked Thompson.

'No, unfortunately not,' replied Felix placing the card back inside the envelope. 'I've only a basic knowledge of semiotics, and this is way above my limited understanding.'

'Pity,' said Thompson, 'no one at the station can make head nor tail of it.'

'How is your questioning coming along?' asked Percy.

'We've interviewed the club staff, but no one seems to have seen or heard a thing prior to his Lordship's sudden turn, and the hostess has sworn on record that the whisky bottle Monteagle had drunk out of that evening was opened in the room and could not have been tampered with. We've taken statements from each of the guests in attendance, all of whom were dismayed to hear that Lord Monteagle had been poisoned. We also took the liberty of looking into their whereabouts immediately before and after the abduction, and their alibis appear to stand-up.'

'And his family?' pressed Percy.

'They are just as bewildered as we are,' replied Thompson.

'And what of his driver, this Jacob Moore fellow?' asked Felix.

'According to Mr Moore, he'd been on the carriage awaiting his master's return when he decided to rest his eyes for a few hours. That was the last thing he remembered. Our officers found him some hours later, curled up on the wet cobbles with a bloodied scalp and the envelope resting beside him.'

'And do you believe his account?' asked Felix.

'His injuries are consistent with his explanation.'

Felix took a moment to ponder the information. It had been a clean and well-planned abduction, but it had been carried out in plain view of the public and inside one of London's most famous and busiest member's clubs. How was it possible that no one knew anything about it?

'Have the press been made aware?' asked Percy nervously.

'Not yet,' replied Thompson. 'I'm confident that the matter is still contained, although stories of this nature tend to have a short lifespan before they are leaked out. I would say twenty-four to forty-eight hours at most.'

'Then time is of the essence, Commissioner,' said Percy. 'Have your teams interview the East India Club staff again. If they had been planning this abduction for months, then there is a strong chance there was someone on the inside. We need to find the cracks in their stories. Also, check into Monteagle's affairs, his business associates, his finances, his mistresses. There must be a reason why he was the target.'

'We are doing everything we can and more,' replied Thompson, a hint of irritation in his voice. 'We have experts engaged in all manner of modern scientific and forensic analysis, including our new Fingerprint Bureau at Scotland Yard who are looking for any unexplained fingerprints on both the whiskey bottle and the player's glasses. We also have officers checking the rivers and backstreets for any sign of his Lordship's…'

Thompson suddenly stopped, reluctant to say the word *body* and tempt fate.

'Understood, Commissioner,' said Felix reading Thompson's thoughts. 'Do keep us informed of any developments. I should like to know how things progress.'

'Very well, sir.' replied Thompson, turning to take his leave. 'Oh, I almost forgot,' he said, spinning around to face Felix. 'The evidence, if you will, Prime Minister.'

'Ah yes, the card.'

Felix looked around his desk for the envelope, but it was nowhere to be seen. He glanced over at Percy, who shrugged his shoulders, equally bewildered. Confused, Felix checked his pockets, only to find that he had inadvertently slotted the envelope, with the card inside, into his suit jacket.

'My apologies,' he said, embarrassed. 'I must have placed it in there without realising.'

Felix held out the envelope, ready to return the evidence, when, without warning, he snapped his hand back before Thompson could take hold of it. Something about this case had piqued his interest and made Felix suddenly reluctant to part company with the mysterious card.

Before trying his hand at politics, Felix had carved out a successful career as a lawyer, following in the footsteps of his father, grandfather, and great-grandfather before them. It was this instinct; this need to scrutinise a piece of evidence and unravel the case that had been suddenly reignited in him.

'Prime Minister?' questioned Thompson, pointing at the envelope in Felix's hand.

'If your team is having trouble identifying the marks, perhaps I could be of assistance?' offered Felix.

'How so?' asked Thompson, confused.

'I have a close acquaintance at Oxford University, an ex-collegemate who is somewhat of an expert in semiotics. I would be happy to present the card to Professor Woodruff for review?'

Thompson took a moment to study Felix. It was most unusual for a prime minister to offer his assistance in police matters, but how could he refuse.

'Very well,' he said, 'but I must insist that the card is dispatched to Scotland Yard immediately on your return. It is after all, the only evidence we have.'

'Naturally.' agreed Felix, slowly feeding the envelope back into his jacket pocket.

Having concluded his business, Commissioner Thompson departed for Scotland Yard, leaving the men to their thoughts, and the warm fire.

'What do you know of Lord Monteagle, Thomas?' asked Felix, his mind alive with questions.

'Not a great deal,' replied Percy. 'He likes a drink or two, and clearly likes to gamble. Perhaps he'd become indebted to someone? There are some very unsavoury people around these poker tables, you know.'

'Yes, but why abduct him in such a manner? Why not wait

until he was in his home or somewhere less public? And the card…' continued Felix, rubbing the small paper object in his pocket. 'Clearly, they wanted people to know what they were doing.'

'Best to leave it to the authorities, Felix,' warned Percy. 'You've got enough on your plate.'

Felix nodded, trying to reassure his colleague, even though he'd already begun making plans for the trip to Oxford in his mind.

The men were disturbed by another knock at the study door. Felix barely had time to answer when the thick wooden partition swung open and Mrs Hughes, a stout woman in her mid-fifties and wearing a cook's uniform, came barrelling in, followed by a distressed-looking Humphrey.

'Prime Minister…' she began, clearly annoyed.

'Apologies, sir,' interjected Humphrey, 'but Mrs Hughes insisted on speaking with you in person.'

'What is it, Mrs Hughes?' asked Felix.

'This old buzzard,' she replied, giving Humphrey a sharp look, 'has just informed me that we will be entertaining the Home Secretary this evening.'

'That's correct,' replied Felix.

'But, as usual, he has omitted to ask our guest the pertinent questions that would enable me to do my job to the best of my ability and to the level this house has come to expect.'

'Has he indeed?' asked Felix, eyeing Humphrey with amusement.

'Indeed, he has,' replied Mrs Hughes. 'We have a little saying up north, *Tha meks a better door than a winder.*'

'And what in heaven's name does that mean?' fumed Humphrey, unamused.

'It means that you're always getting in the way.'

Mrs Hughes turned to face Felix.

'If I could just have a minute or two with our esteemed visitor, Prime Minister, I'll be able to get all the information I need.'

'Please, be my guest,' said Felix, motioning towards a nervous-looking, Percy.

'If you would kindly follow me, sir,' began Mrs Hughes, leading the Home Secretary towards the study door. 'The kitchens are just this way. We can discuss your dietary requirements as we walk. You might also want to start with washing your hands, the facilities are just down the hall here…'

With the strong-willed head cook marching Percy out of the room, and Humphrey departing to continue with his dinner preparations, Felix turned his attention to the study window, peering out at the world on his doorstep. The heavy rain had finally ended, and people were beginning to reappear on the streets. How quickly life returned to normal, he thought. Life, however, had been anything but normal for him, not since he'd won the general election and become the British Prime Minister, and, perhaps, it would never return to normal for Lord Monteagle either, not unless the peer was found soon and in one piece.

Corpus Christi

It took all of Felix's considerable willpower to sleep that evening. Thompson's visit had filled him with a nagging curiosity, and he could think of nothing else as he prepared to settle in for the night. He paced the large room, recounting every detail of their conversation, hoping to uncover even the slightest clue he may have missed or overlooked. As with any crime of this nature, there would have to be a strong motive, a compelling reason behind the action, and Felix was determined to uncover it. However, having turned over the facts in his mind for hours and exasperated by his lack of progress, Felix finally retired to his bed, determined to renew his efforts the following day.

Felix arose to the sound of activity. Under Humphrey's close inspection, the house staff were busy preparing Number 10 for a month of state dinners and had overwhelmed the building with their enterprise. It was a rare chance to see the house put to its full use and the staff wasted little time dressing the state rooms and polishing the fine silver. Felix made his way through the hustle and bustle towards the dining room. He had decided the previous evening to make enquiries into the symbols on the card and was keen to make an early start.

After a quick breakfast of eggs and spinach, Humphrey summoned the car for their short journey to Paddington Station, where the necessary arrangements had been made for their safe but surreptitious journey to Oxford and an audience with the Dean of Corpus Christi, Professor Woodruff.

The train carriage was small but agreeable. The staff had fitted the long wooden benches with comfortable leather cushions and had placed a large pot of tea alongside the day's broadsheets. Humphrey poured the tea while Felix took the opportunity to catch up on the morning headlines. He had always considered the newspapers a sound measure of public opinion. He flicked through the tall pages, folding each neatly as he passed, moving from one article to another in search of anything that might grasp his attention and distract from his obsession with the Monteagle case.

At first glance, there seemed to be little to hold his interest. The pages were full of the usual, stale, political and economic commentary, including a detailed account of the rapidly growing German manufacturers sat alongside a list of Britain's largest factories, to give the readers a like-for-like comparison. The top spot, noted Felix, was held by Bryant and May, a match-maker's site in the East End of London.

There was some light relief, however, in the form of Captain

Scott's expedition to the Antarctic and a report on his time with the emperor penguin colony at Cape Crozier and the dizzying effects of snow blindness. But any feelings of contentment were short-lived as Felix turned the page to reveal a most-concerning headline.

'Tragic accident or avoidable manslaughter?' he muttered under his breath.

Felix sat up a little straighter, focusing his attention on the article in front of him.

Tragic accident or avoidable manslaughter? These are the questions surrounding the tragic death of Arthur Jenkins, a young miner from the Rotherham district of South Yorkshire. Mr Jenkins, 22 years of age, had worked in the Birchwood Colliery for over five years and, in that time, had witnessed first-hand the site's old and malfunctioning machinery. As a union man, he endlessly petitioned the company directors about the need for investment, often warning against inevitable accidents and possible deaths.

It is then, with a sense of heavy irony, that on the day of our Lord, Friday, September 10th, 1904, Mr Jenkins met with his tragic and untimely end at the hands of the faulty equipment he had so feared during his time at Birchwood, crushed under the weight of a collapsed rig. In memory of Mr Jenkins' death, the miners of Birchwood have sworn to strike until the company directors agree to make significant assurances on investment.

Opposition leader, the Right Honourable Milton Cavendish, has called on miners of all counties to petition the government on what he has described as 'a systematic failure to protect the great working people of this country'. The enquiry into the death at Birchwood continues.

Felix placed the newspaper to one side. He knew that this young miner's story, however tragic, would be seized upon and used as a weapon against him. Arthur Jenkins' sudden and avoidable death represented everything that was wrong with the system, and it was this sense of injustice that his opponents would twist and manipulate for their political gain. There was no such thing as 'off-limits' in politics, no moral code when it came to Westminster. Every story had value, and this unfortunate miner's tale was worth its weight in gold.

Felix contemplated returning to London, but with the news already out, there was little he could do. Instead, he dispatched a letter of condolence to the Jenkins family in Rotherham and prepared a short statement for Parliament calling for an enquiry into the happenings at Birchwood. Felix tried to reassure himself that he was doing this out of a sense of moral duty rather than political obligation, but in truth, it was increasingly difficult to distinguish between the two since coming into office. For now, his letter would bring the family some small comfort and him a little time to find out what he could about the abduction and the symbols on the card.

It was late morning when the train pulled into Oxford Station, and Felix and Humphrey finally stepped down from their carriage onto the platform. Felix spotted a tall, gangly figure dressed in a leather pilot's jacket and pastel trousers and sporting a driving hat and smoke-covered goggles.

'Professor Woodruff!' he called out.

The professor's appearance hadn't gone unnoticed among the crowds either, who quietly whispered to one another as the gawky scholar bounded past them to greet Felix.

'My dear Felix, how long it has been,' said the professor removing the hat and driving goggles, revealing a tangle of braided auburn hair and bright green eyes.

'A female professor at Oxford?' exclaimed Humphrey, shocked.

'Yes, although we don't like to publicise it. You know how worked up these stuffy old newspapers can get. They're clearly not that impressed with our ability to birth all human life on this planet, including them.' replied the professor, the slightest hint of Texan in her accent.

'Amelia, allow me to introduce my rather tactless and old-fashioned steward, Humphrey.' entered Felix, shooting Humphrey a hard look.

'Yes, of course,' replied Amelia, taking Humphrey's hand. 'The roots beneath the great oak.'

'We do what we must,' replied Humphrey, averse to her brash American manner, and mindful of the gawking public.

'Never mind the locals,' said Amelia, sensing Humphrey's uneasiness, 'they like a good old stare. It reminds me of a visit I once had from a young sultan. He travelled with a large entourage, including his thirteen wives. It caused quite a stir; I can assure you.'

'Nevertheless, I think it would be a good idea for us to leave, before we attract any more unwanted attention,' pressed Humphrey.

'Fear not. I have my car waiting outside. It might be a touch overcrowded, but it will see us to our destination,' said Amelia.

'I'm sure it will be adequate,' replied Humphrey, prompting them forward.

Outside, a gentle frost had set on the flat Oxfordshire fields. Amelia led the men to her waiting car, a cast aluminium vehicle in British racing green with a two-person cushioned bench, a small steering wheel, and a soft retractable roof.

'The Rover 8,' she announced proudly. 'A great feat of British engineering. Although, not quite a Ford, but hey-ho, it'll do.'

Felix helped Humphrey into the car. His arthritis had been fine on the train, but he'd felt its presence the moment they stepped out into the cold Oxford air. Fortunately, Amelia carried a large flask of hot tea with her on journeys, and she poured Humphrey a small cup with a nip of whiskey for good measure. With her guests seated, Amelia wound the vehicle crankshaft, firing up the engine. As is coughed and spluttered into life, the exhaust kicked out a plume of black smoke for the station onlookers to see, much to Humphrey's annoyance. Undeterred, Amelia hopped into the car, squeezing herself between the two men and took hold of the steering wheel.

'All snug?' she asked cheerfully, crunching the car into gear and causing more disturbance before finally pressing on the accelerator and pulling the vehicle away from the station.

The journey to Corpus Christi was largely uneventful. Humphrey enjoyed the vast areas of natural beauty, particularly the rolling hills of lavender, which he found a soothing contrast to the chaotic exuberance of the city, while Felix and Amelia took the opportunity to reminisce on their time together as students at Oxford University. It was a much-needed distraction from the pressures of leadership, and Felix enjoyed the temporary reprieve as much as his focused mind would allow.

Corpus Christi College was small by Oxford standards. The beautiful main quad with its central tower, dining hall, library and adjoining chapel had stood for over five hundred years and showed few signs of ageing. The famous Pelican Sundial stood in the centre of an open court with its majestic golden bird looking out over the vast Oxford grounds and beyond.

Amelia guided the car through a large stone archway and into the cobbled square. As she brought the vehicle to a standstill, the engine let out a loud bang, announcing their arrival to the entire campus. Suddenly, several young faces appeared in the line of windows above them, curious to see the identity of the professor's visitors.

'Nothing to see here!' shouted Amelia, as they climbed out of the car. She'd witnessed first-hand how quickly news could travel on campus and did not want a repeat of the furore that had accompanied the young sultan's visit. The timid prince had barely set foot in her office when hordes of students filtered in to get a look at their exotic visitor, inadvertently blocking the exits and trapping the sultan inside for hours.

Amelia hurried Felix and Humphrey through the square into a warren of charming lesser buildings, stopping outside an old cottage with a thatched roof and an antique oak door.

'We have landed,' she breathed, taking hold of the brass knocker, and hammering it.

Within moments, the door creaked open to reveal Hopkins, a diminutive, grey-haired woman dressed in a dusty steward's uniform, straining to focus on the people in front of her.

'One second,' she called, fumbling in her pockets for her spectacles. 'My glasses are here somewhere. I was just using them.'

'No need, Hopkins, it's only me,' said Amelia stepping past her steward and leading the men through the main hall.

'Righto, Professor,' replied Hopkins, finally locating her glasses on the top of her head. 'Would you like me to prepare some tea and sandwiches?' She asked, placing them on the bridge of her nose, only to see that the professor and her guests had disappeared.

The professor's office was small and cramped, with several bookshelves overflowing with novels and encyclopaedias. At first glance, Humphrey mistook it for a poorly kept library, but the messy desk in the centre of the room littered with the professor's papers quickly revealed its true identity.

'Please, do make yourselves comfortable,' said Amelia, burrowing into a small box of odds and ends, looking for something.

Felix and Humphrey searched the room for a space to sit down, but even the chairs were covered in the professor's files.

'There you are!' announced Amelia rising out of the melee, holding a brass magnifying glass. 'Now, let's take a look at this card of yours, then.'

Felix reached into his pocket and removed the envelope, handing it to Amelia.

'This is our only scrap of evidence. I would like to take it back to London in one piece.'

'You have nothing to fear, I assure you' said Amelia, removing the card from the envelope and holding it up to examine the symbols. 'And, you say it was found at the scene of crime?'

'Yes, in a cobbled alleyway, along with Monteagle's unconscious driver.'

'How interesting.'

'What do the symbols mean?' asked Felix.

'Well, they could mean any number of things, depending on who you are and what you choose to believe.'

'No speaking in riddles,' cautioned Felix.

'Very well. For the laypeople in the room, there are many organisations, past and present, mythical, and actual, who would lay claim, or not, to the symbols on this card.'

'Professor…'

'Sodalitas!' exclaimed Amelia, holding up her magnifying glass to emphasise the point. 'Secret societies to the outside world.

Men and women, but mostly men, with fancy rings and clever handshakes. But, to those who know, groups and fellowships of very powerful and very dangerous people. Although, I confess, I have never seen these symbols appear together in such a manner.'

'Do you think Monteagle was involved with one of these secret societies?' asked Humphrey.

'It is possible. He is, in many ways, just the kind of man you would associate with these types of organisations. Wealthy and powerful. It would not be unrealistic to assume his involvement or even membership with one of them.'

'But what would make an organisation turn on one of their own in this way? What possible offence could he have committed that would lead to such a reaction?' asked Felix.

'It is hard to say. Codes of conduct vary significantly between each group and are as secretive as the organisations themselves. However, what is clear, is that trust is essential to their existence. It's their very lifeblood. If one link were to break, it could have far-reaching consequences for the entire chain. They have been known to deal with weaker links swiftly and with a savage brutality to preserve the group's integrity.'

'Perhaps Monteagle was on the verge of breaking rank and exposing the organisation?' suggested Felix.

'That would account for his abduction,' replied Amelia.

'And the card?' asked Felix.

'A show of force, perhaps. A message to their members that they had dealt with the situation. The card was clearly left to serve a purpose.'

'But by which group?' asked Felix.

'The key is in the combination of the symbols,' replied Amelia, placing the card on the table for Felix and Humphrey to see.

'Let us start at the very beginning. The five-pointed star, or the pentagram, as it's more commonly known, represents the five elements of nature: earth, fire, water, air, and the spirit. It is pagan, but also a prominent emblem within freemasonry. Though its significance, like most, is concealed behind a smokescreen of secret society ambiguity.'

'Good heavens,' said Humphrey, taken aback by Amelia's revelations. He had known several masons over the years, including members of his own family and had seen the organisation as nothing more than a social club for gentlemen. He'd never have imagined it being associated with such dark and shadowy affairs.

'There are many faces to these organisations, not merely the common ones you may be familiar with,' said Amelia, observing Humphrey's reaction. 'Think of them as icebergs. Only a small fraction is visible above the water, but there are entire mountains beneath, hidden from view.'

'I had no idea,' said Humphrey.

'And what of the other symbols?' asked Felix.

'Well, they are altogether more revealing, particularly the goat's head.'

'I was certain I'd seen it before,' said Felix.

'You will have come across it, no doubt, in relation to the medieval knights. You may remember the deity more clearly by his name, Baphomet?'

Felix took a second to think about the name. It was familiar, but he had not read much on the knights since leaving Oxford, just the odd piece here and there in the rare moments he'd found time to pick up a book.

'The knights were accused by Pope Clement V and King Phillip IV of France of worshipping Baphomet during their trials.

Many were executed for their supposed offences. The knights have a long and shadowy association with freemasonry and Baphomet, who interestingly appears in many of their rituals and initiations.'

'So, you believe there is a credible link to the masons?' asked Felix.

'It's certainly a thread worth pulling on,' replied Amelia. 'But this is no ordinary branch of freemasonry. In all my years of study, I have never come across these symbols displayed as they appear on your card. I think an audience with the masons may set us on the right track.'

'Do what you can, Amelia, but I don't want you placing yourself in any unnecessary danger; this is a matter for the police, we are merely trying to assist where we can. We're certainly not trying to be heroes of any kind.'

'You worry too much, Prime Minister,' replied Amelia, trying to mask her excitement.

But Felix had seen the same mischievous look in his friend's eyes before. The impetuous Texan had a reputation for bumbling her way in and out of hazardous situations, and this case had undoubtedly piqued her interest.

Electric Sparks

'Go on then, give it a try,' urged Lord Cecil, observing his son William's reluctance with growing impatience.

The young boy had been staring at the newly fitted light switch for some time with no hint or suggestion of any action. Since hearing about his family's conversion to electricity, William's classmates had teased him daily about the effects of electric sparks, and he had grown fearful of this strange new power source.

'It really is very safe. You will feel no ill effects,' pressed Cecil, imploring his son forward.

William peered up at his father's stern face, searching the deep lines and weathered skin for any signs of uncertainty.

'You are sure, Father?' he asked, hesitant but eager to prove his courage.

'William, you have nothing to fear but fear itself,' replied Cecil, resting a reassuring hand on the boy's shoulder.

If William's classmates' stories were to be believed, the merest touch of one's skin against the soft metal switch would be enough to send a lethal surge of electricity through the body, causing a person to blackout or even worse, die.

William reluctantly reached out and took hold of the small brass toggle, pinching his fingers around its smoothly curved head. To his amazement, there was no shock, no surge of electricity or anything else, he was still standing upright and in one piece. He took a deep breath, swallowing back his fear, and flicked the switch, casting a brilliant light throughout the large study. The effect was intoxicating. William watched as the light's energy danced around the room, reflecting off the ivory walls and crystal chandeliers into the tight corners and tiny nooks that had only ever known shadow and darkness. He'd never seen a room so brightly illuminated; it was as though someone had lit a thousand candles all at once.

'You must never allow fear to be your master,' said Cecil, crouching down to meet his son's eyes. 'It is only an excuse for those who lack heart.'

William felt a burst of pride swell in his chest. He had overcome his fears and his friends' apish warnings.

Cecil studied his son. He remembered when he was a boy, unsure of himself and his position, desperate to prove himself. He wanted to hug William, to tell the boy how proud he was of him, but as a father, he'd learnt to hide his emotions, barricade them behind a wall of conduct and protocol. He'd seen too many boys of privilege growing up with dark pride and arrogance in their hearts and was determined to raise his sons to be men of substance, even at the expense of his own feelings.

'We had better get washed up for dinner,' he said, slowly rising to his feet, 'or your mother will give us both something to fear.'

The dining room was enormous, with an elaborately carved wooden ceiling and newly papered white walls that added to the brightening effect of the new lights. Beneath the hanging chandeliers sat a long dining room table covered in ornate China plates overflowing with vegetables and roasted game.

The staff placed the remaining garnishes and condiments on the table before charging the family glasses with wine. It had been a longstanding tradition for the head of the house to make a toast before dinner, and Cecil was not a man to challenge family customs.

Lady Cecil kept a close eye on her two sons. At fifteen, Peter had been permitted to taste wine at the house toast before, but this was William's first time, and she was determined to keep his consumption in check.

'Wait for your father, please,' she said as the boys reached excitedly for their glasses.

'Just a sip, Mother,' appealed Peter, 'so that William can become accustomed to the taste.'

'That is precisely my worry, that either of you should ever become too accustomed to its taste,' replied Lady Cecil, waving the boys back into their seats.

After what had seemed like an eternity to the boys, Cecil finally rose to deliver a few words, allowing them to take hold of their glasses.

'We have much to be thankful for,' he began, holding his glass with purpose. 'Land, wealth, security. All the luxuries afforded to a family of our position and status. But it is all for nothing if we allow ourselves to fear the unknown. We must always remain tall in the face of adversity.'

Cecil paused for a moment, fixing his eyes on William.

'I would like to toast to our courage, fortitude, and indomitability, for those are the qualities that make us who we are today.'

'A fine speech!' called a rasping voice, cutting through the warm atmosphere.

Cecil turned to see a large, hooded figure standing in the shadow of the dining room doorway.

'Who are you?' he asked.

The man stood upright, revealing his broad shoulders and full intimidating height.

'Just a messenger,' he replied.

Suddenly, a gang of similarly hooded figures entered the room, spreading out to cover its full width. Cecil looked from the dark figures to his family. He could sense the fear and anxiety building around the table.

'What is the meaning of this?' he asked, trying to mask the concern in his voice.

'Afraid, my Lord?' mocked the figure.

'I am not the one who hides in shadows,' replied Cecil.

'Ha! You have spirit. I'll give you that,' said the figure, 'but I am tempted to strip you of that foolish highborn pride of yours.'

'If it is money you seek, none is kept here on the premises. Take whatever else you desire and leave.'

The figure stepped forward, his dark frame seeming to grow with every stride until it felt like he would consume the entire room with his presence.

'My employer requests an audience,' he said, finally moving

into the light, revealing his scar-ridden face and a red eyepatch covering his left eye.

'And if I refuse?'

'Then you shall be removed against your will.'

Cecil's gaze drifted away from the intruder back to his family. He was tempted to test this criminal's mettle but would never forgive himself if any harm were to befall his wife and children, not while he could prevent it. His eyes suddenly caught the glimmer of light reflecting on metal. He turned to face William, noticing his son's hand wrapped tightly around the table knife and a wildfire burning in his eyes. Cecil placed a gentle hand on the boy's, feeling the calm return and his grip on the knife slowly release.

'Then I shall come freely,' he called out, embracing his sons. 'Look after your mother,' he whispered to them, his eyes gleaming with pride.

Cat and Mouse

It was early evening when Felix and Humphrey returned to Downing Street, the journey back from Oxford had been slow, and neither man had managed to get much rest on the train.

Humphrey set straight to work. It was the middle of September, and as was the custom, the doors to Number 10 were to be opened to Felix's fellow politicians for an evening of food, wine, and conversation.

Buoyed by Amelia's revelations, Felix made his way to the study to document his thoughts. As a lawyer, he'd learnt to make detailed notes on all his cases, on the off chance he'd need to reference a small detail or recall a name some months or even years later. It had been a worthwhile exercise and a skill that had proved beneficial during his time in office. The human brain could only commit so much information to memory, and there was a limit to the amount Felix could heap on Humphrey's sharp but ageing mind.

The study was warm and well-lit. On his desk, Felix found a copy of The Times newspaper opened on the centre pages, with a handwritten letter placed on top. Curious, he unfolded the note and read its contents.

Felix, I've managed to obtain an early edition of tomorrow's newspaper. Unfortunately, Lord Monteagle's abduction has gone public. The miner's story is also gathering pace. We must do what we can to appease the workers, or we may see widespread striking. Cavendish has the look of a cat that has just eaten all the cream. Percy

Felix placed the note to one side and picked up the newspaper. There was a small article detailing Monteagle's abduction, but, to his surprise, much of the double-page spread focussed on the young miner's death at Birchwood. The bold headline, *Murder In The First Degree*, sat in large type above a grainy, black-and-white photograph of Arthur Jenkins, with his dark, ink-blotched eyes staring hauntingly back at Felix from off the page.

Felix took a moment to consider the image. The poor quality made it hard to take in the scene, but he could make out a pier in the background, and a young woman stood beside Arthur, holding a single rose. It was the kind of scene that would have melted even the hardest and most unsympathetic hearts. A young couple with their whole lives ahead of them, the promise of adventure in their eyes. There was something innately British about it.

The more Felix studied the picture, the more he realised how far and wide the impact of this young miner's untimely death could spread. Percy was right; the situation needed addressing before it gathered any more pace.

Felix removed his pocket watch and checked the time. It was close to nine o'clock, and soon Downing Street would be overwhelmed with politicians and their parliamentary staff, all discussing Monteagle's abduction and the miner's death. His eyes followed the mechanical hands as they marched around the watch face, willing them to stop, but even the prime minister could not control time, however much he longed to.

The state dining room was as grand in splendour as any of the political houses in Europe. The staff arranged the guest's places at the long table, each with a set of silver cutlery and two large crystal glasses for wine and sherry.

Felix took the opportunity to greet his colleagues as they arrived. The men looked smart in their dinner suits, bow ties and finely polished shoes, and the ladies wore gowns of all colours and styles from notable French, Italian and American designers. The best-dressed competition was as fierce as the clamour for Number 10, with the competitors communicating their contempt for one another through a series of subtle looks and veiled gestures, mainly curt smiles, and friendly nods.

Thomas Percy made his way through the dining hall towards the smoking room, where several men had gathered to discuss their affairs, out of earshot of the women. Among them were Barnaby Shaw, the pompous shadow chancellor and old Etonian, and the leader of the Conservative Party, Milton Cavendish, a tall, middle-aged man with sharp features and cold, calculating eyes that gave off a weasel-like appearance.

The men were familiar and at ease in each other's company, but as with any gathering of close rivals, there was a dangerous edge in the air that could be felt by all.

'What is on the menu for this evening, Humphrey?' asked Percy, rubbing his heavy hands in anticipation.

'Always thinking with your stomach,' mocked Shaw, in his thick Yorkshire accent.

'A large appetite in life is no bad thing. Perhaps if your appetite were more considerable, you'd know how it feels to be in government rather than continuously sitting on the periphery.'

'I believe the main course this evening is duck, Home Secretary,' replied Humphrey, stopping Shaw from responding.

'A fine choice,' replied Percy.

'And how does the Prime Minister's mood fare after the day's big revelations?' asked Cavendish.

'What revelations are you referring to?' questioned Percy.

'Why the abduction of course. Surely the news has reached him by now?'

Percy looked around the room at the amused faces.

'Well, I would say his mood is...'

'Much the same as yours, Milton,' replied Felix, entering the room, 'saddened, but determined to see the guilty parties brought to justice.'

'I am sure you are making every possible enquiry.'

'Indeed, we are,' replied Percy, 'and when we find the culprits, I will ensure they feel the full force of the law.'

'Do you have many leads?' asked Cavendish.

'It's still early in the investigation, but we've had one or two developments,' replied Percy, embarrassed to admit that there had been little to follow up on since the abduction.

'Rumour has it, Monteagle had some very significant gambling debts. I should start your enquiries at some of the member's clubs he liked to frequent,' suggested Shaw.

'I wouldn't pay too much attention to rumours,' replied Percy.

'There is no smoke without fire, Home Secretary.'

'And not all fires are lit with malicious intent.'

Felix observed his opponents' interest in the case with growing uneasiness. The abductors, whoever they were, had been clever enough not to leave any trace or line of enquiry aside from the card, and even that morsel of evidence was shrouded in ambiguity. Percy's subtle remonstrations would not hold his questioners at bay for much longer, not now that the story had gone public. He would need to back up his claims with hard evidence sooner or later.

Felix's thoughts were disturbed by the sound of the house bell ringing. Humphrey waited for the chatter to subside before announcing dinner and directing the parliamentarians and their partners to the dining room.

Felix sat at the head of the table, flanked by Percy, eagerly anticipating the first course. It wasn't long before the conversations resumed, and Felix found himself engaged in several debates around the table at the same time. They ranged from global economics to simple housekeeping at Number 10. Rarely had he spoken to so many people in such a short space of time about so many things. Rather than feeling exhausted by the experience, however, the interactions had left Felix feeling surprisingly upbeat, proud even, to have presided over such a successful event.

'Prime Minister,' said Percy in a low voice, leaning in close to Felix, 'we must discuss this Arthur Jenkins affair. The miners at Birchwood have begun their strike, and there have been murmurs of strikes in other mines, up and down the country.'

Although spoken quietly, Percy's words had not gone

unheard among the guests. Instead, they had been picked up by the alert ears of Milton Cavendish, who had expertly positioned himself a few places down the table, far enough to be overlooked but still within earshot of their conversations.

'Yes, do tell us, Prime Minister,' said Cavendish, directing the table's attention towards Felix. 'What are you going to do about this miner's death, and the impending strikes?'

Felix took a moment to consider the question. With so many watching colleagues waiting to jump on his every word, he did not want to say the wrong thing.

'We'll speak with their union and reassure them that we're carrying out a full investigation into the death of Arthur Jenkins, alongside a review of their working conditions.'

'Spoken like a true politician,' mocked Shaw, raising his glass.

'Come now, Prime Minister,' replied Cavendish, 'We're not in Commons. I think your colleagues would be interested to hear your true feelings on the matter.'

To most around the table, Cavendish's jibes could easily be mistaken for the customary horseplay between parties, but both men had been engaged in a game of political cat and mouse for some years now, and Felix had become well-accustomed to his opponent's subtle but calculated attacks.

'Very well,' said Felix, observing the growing interest around the table. 'I believe working people were fed up long before this tragedy occurred. Arthur Jenkins' death just made them realise it. I also believe they deserve a far greater say in how their communities and working environments are shaped. Those are not unreasonable requests.'

'That's a very progressive stance. And how exactly do you propose we appease these dissenters?' asked Cavendish.

'Their discontent is the result of a system that only rewards those in power. There is very little chance to better oneself in modern society. It's a regrettable legacy of an old system, which needs reforming.'

'Tosh. What nonsense!' barked Shaw. 'There has always been a battleground over which the gentleman has fought with the lesser classes. It is no different now than it has ever been. Of course, they will moan and kick up a fuss, but they'll soon fall back in line when they realise it could cost them their livelihoods. They always do. A firm hand is all that is required.'

It was clear from the approving nods that many around the table agreed with Shaw's summation. Most politicians had a vested interest in the system and were against social reform of any kind. It was this deeply rooted unwillingness to change that Felix had encountered time and again since becoming prime minister and one that had marked the first two years of his time in government.

'If you think this problem will simply disappear under the weight of a few veiled threats, then I'm afraid you have sorely misjudged the situation and the British people.' said Felix.

Shaw opened his mouth to respond when he was stopped in his tracks for a second time by Humphrey appearing at Felix's side, holding a small white envelope.

'An urgent message, Prime Minister,' said the old steward, ending the conversation.

Felix rose from his seat and made his apologies before departing for his study to read the note in private. Once inside, he broke the seal and opened the envelope, unfolding the letter. It didn't say much, and was as direct and to the point as Commissioner Thompson had been in person:

A second abduction. Lord Cecil, from his home. No damage or signs of a struggle. Another card left at the scene. Still no demands. Thompson

Felix felt his stomach take a jolt. A second peer abducted in less than twenty-four hours, and another card left at the scene of the crime. There was now no question of this being merely a personal matter between Monteagle and this group or organisation. It was something far more significant. But what did these peers have in common?

One thing Felix was sure of was that these abductors, whoever they were, must have influence at the highest level to orchestrate the abduction of two lords with such ease and precision. They would need to know their daily routines, comings and goings, public duties, and personal commitments. They would need to know someone close to them, someone, they trusted.

Felix's head was swimming. He placed the note inside his desk drawer and returned to the dining room to see out the remainder of the evening. He circled the room looking for Percy when he was stopped in his tracks by a stocky man in a miner's uniform and wearing the red sash of a labour unionist around his torso.

'I am here representing the working men of this country, who are sick to death of the exploitation that is so rife throughout this land,' he bellowed in a thick Yorkshire accent, bringing the event to a standstill. 'We are at the end of our tethers with this government and seeing as you have been so intent on ignoring our pleas, you've left us with no choice but to deliver this document to you in person.'

The miner handed Felix a long scroll of paper covered in petition signatures.

'How did you get into my house?' asked Felix, brimming with anger.

'Ne'er you mind that, what are you going to do about our demands? We will strike, you know. All up and down this land. Don't test us. We're ready for it.'

Felix stepped forward, occupying a small space of no more than five inches between himself and the miner, showing that he would not be intimidated.

'If you wish to speak to me, invite me to one of your meetings, and we can talk like civilised people. But do not break into my home like a common thief and embarrass me in front of my guests. Such actions are beneath us both.'

Whereas men like Shaw had dismissed the worker's demands as nothing more than a passing gale, Felix had been greatly alarmed by their growing discontent. The sudden appearance of this unionist at Number 10 had proven that any house was accessible and any man reachable.

'Move aside! Coming through!' shouted Percy burrowing his way through the watching crowd, followed by two police officers. 'Escort this man to the nearest police station and see that he is charged at once.' he roared. 'We will not tolerate this sort of open rebellion.'

'That won't be necessary, Thomas' objected Felix, the calm returning to his voice. 'Take him to the kitchens and see that he is well fed, then return him safely to his lodgings.'

'Are you sure?' asked Percy.

'It was just an error of judgement,' replied Felix turning to face the miner. 'There are ways to have one's voice heard, and this was not one of them.'

Felix nodded to the officers, and they escorted the man out of the dining room.

With the commotion finally over the guests slowly returned to their drinks and conversations. Felix poured himself a large scotch when his eyes caught the sharp, satisfied gaze of Milton Cavendish watching from across the room. Cavendish lifted his sherry glass, evidently thrilled with the dark shadow that had been cast over Felix's evening. Felix raised his glass in return, acknowledging his opponent's victory, but suddenly suspicious of Cavendish's part in the disturbance.

Old Pye Street

A day is a long time in politics, or so it had seemed to Felix over the past twenty-four hours. If he had been winning the battle over dinner, he was most certainly losing the war by the time his guests left, and he returned to his study to brood on the night's events and his unfortunate encounter with the miner.

On the surface of things, it looked harmless enough. A disagreement between a union representative and a politician was hardly uncommon. Barely had there been a time in their short history when the unions were not upset by one government policy or another. But something about this unionist's demeanour struck Felix as different, something in their short but heated exchange had made an impression on him. He tried to recall the man's words, but his mind was still overwhelmed by the day's revelations.

However, one thing Felix was now sure of was Cavendish's involvement in the miner's sudden appearance. Such acts were consistent with his opponent's single-minded desire to become prime minister. But how had Cavendish managed to gain the union's trust and convince them to carry out such an openly rebellious act? What had he promised them in return for their support?

Felix felt his stomach lurch for a second time; he could sense the political wind changing. How had things become so strained so quickly? Only as recently as a year ago, his cabinet had been widely praised for their far-reaching reforms and modern approach to government. They had passed a record number of acts through the great houses, most of which they had fought tooth and nail to deliver. But if a day was a long time in politics, then a year was quite simply an eternity.

There was also the pressing matter of Lord Cecil's abduction to consider. Felix opened his desk drawer and removed the commissioner's note, scanning the words for anything he may have overlooked, some subtle clue or detail that could shed some light on the mystery.

'A second abduction. Lord Cecil, from his home.'

Hearing the words out loud seemed strange, as though voicing them somehow made the event more real. But why Cecil? Felix had occasionally dealt with him in the House of Lords and found him to be a man of substance. Quite rare in the halls of Westminster, usually teemed with ruthless ambition. Surely there was nothing sinister lurking behind his cordial and well-respected manner. But then, nothing was ever certain in politics, nothing entirely as it seemed in the corridors of power, where great careers were often forged on rickety foundations. The only constant was time, and time had a way of unveiling even the most expert of disguises. Perhaps there was more to Cecil than met the eye?

'No damage or signs of a struggle. Another card left at the scene. Still no demands,' continued Felix, thinking on each word as he read them.

The lack of any criminal damage or even a struggle suggested to Felix that there might have been some level of familiarity between the abductors and Cecil. Could Cecil have been expecting them? Or perhaps, even more alarming, could he have welcomed them into his home with open arms? That would mean it could have been someone he knew or even trusted. It would answer for the lack of any action or reaction to the events inside the house.

Felix's head was wild with theory and speculation. Determined to quiet his mind, he crossed the room to pour himself another scotch. As he rushed past the open fireplace, Felix stepped awkwardly on the hearth, throwing himself off balance. He scrambled to regain his footing, but his body had passed the point of no return, and he tumbled headfirst towards the marble mantelpiece, landing with a heavy thud.

The impact left Felix sprawled out on the study floor, barely conscious. His head throbbed violently as he lifted his hand to his temple to assess the damage. Fortunately, there was only a tiny lump and no sign of bleeding.

Felix forced himself off the floor and back onto his feet. He cursed himself for drinking too much and allowing himself to fall in such a manner. It was another hammer blow to his confidence, and despite being alone in his study, Felix felt a deep sense of personal humiliation wash over him. Perhaps he wasn't the right man for the job after all. Maybe it was finally time to cash in his chips and clear the way for a better man to take the reins.

Felix took a moment to allow his body to readjust. He was still dizzy from the heavy bang on his head and did not want to risk another fall. As he leaned against the mantelpiece for balance, he noticed something odd. One of the decorative corbels had been turned ninety degrees and was now vertical rather than horizontal like the others. He looked down, realising that the dark coal-stained panel that usually glimmered in the glow of one of Humphrey's large fires was no longer there; it had vanished, revealing what seemed to be a long tunnel, dimly lit by lamps hanging from either side of its narrow walls.

Felix felt his head again, wondering if he was concussed and seeing things. He reached both hands out towards the large fireplace, expecting to feel the missing panel at any moment and return to his senses, but instead, slowly moved forward, one step at a time, without obstruction, until he passed through the fireplace entirely and was standing in the tunnel on the opposite side.

He looked around the thin walkway in disbelief. The tunnel's light pastel walls, with floral designs of freesias and lilies, were as beautiful and elegant as any he had ever seen, and a vibrant green carpet ran the length of the tunnel's floor. Felix was aware of the notorious secret passages and tunnels in Europe's great castles and palaces, but he'd never heard of anything like that at Number 10. He couldn't understand why it was here or what purpose it served.

Resting high on the tunnel wall beside the entrance was a curious-looking lever with the parliamentary crest on it. Felix pulled hard on the lever, and the fireplace's missing panel began to judder back into position, sealing off the path back to his study. Felix turned and followed the tunnel, unsure whether he was awake or still on the study floor, unconscious and dreaming. As he moved forward, the path began to curve away slowly. Felix counted his paces, estimating that he had walked over half a kilometre by the time he saw another door coming into view ahead of him.

Felix cautiously opened the door and stepped into a crooked hallway. It was the type one would expect to find in an old cottage or workman's house. He followed the exposed floorboards through another entrance, eventually entering an oval-shaped room dimly lit by a few struggling wall lights.

Inside, Felix noticed a large oak desk with an array of documents, maps and charts splayed untidily across it. Beside the desk were rows of shelves overflowing with books and encyclopaedias covering all types of subjects, from *Human Anatomy* to *How to Change a Motorised Wheel*. On the walls, in gilt-edged frames, hung portraits of past prime ministers. Felix recognised the faces of Sir Robert Peel, Viscount Palmerston, Benjamin Disraeli, William Pitt the Younger and Arthur Wellesley, the Duke of Wellington. Just below the Iron Duke's portrait sat a gold plaque with something inscribed on it. He crouched down to read the words.

'Old Pye Street. Built for only the most curious, benevolent, and adventurous of prime ministers.'

Felix ran his hand across the plaque in astonishment. He could feel his senses tingling. He began to think about the other past prime ministers who might have found this secret room during their time at Number 10 and all the meaningful moments in history they might have orchestrated from inside it. He thought about the many battles and treaties, the foiled plots, and the high-profile arrests. Could they have planned Napoleon's exile to Elba here? Or uncovered the identity of Jack the Ripper? After all, the mysterious Ripper murders had ended just weeks after William

Gladstone's election and arrival at Number 10.

Drunk on adventure, Felix's thoughts suddenly turned to his mother, Leonora, and what she would have made of the room and the message on the gold plaque. This was a place where prime ministers served not for personal gain or to further their careers but simply out of a duty towards the people they represented. It alluded to the promise of something more meaningful, higher almost than the role of prime minister. He was sure Leonora would have approved. Tales of her time campaigning with the suffragettes were legendary. She had once marched into the Tower of London and smashed the display case holding the Crown Jewels earning herself the nickname, the Tower Suffragette.

Felix could feel his mood lightening. A giddy, almost childlike excitement had replaced the self-doubt he had been wrestling with in his study. He spun around to investigate the rest of the room. Standing proudly against one of the walls was an old, run-down telephone switchboard with hundreds of telephone lines, cords and jacks. Felix leant forward to study the connections. All the major cities were listed and set out in alphabetic order: Bath, Birmingham, Bradford, Brighton and so on, followed by the major European cities and then notable cities from around the world.

Felix continued past the switchboard towards a large clothes rail laden with workers' uniforms, overalls and coats, all colours, shapes, and sizes. Alongside the rail was a tall wooden stand covered in hats of all styles: flats, derbies, fedoras, boaters, bowlers, trilbies, and top hats. Beneath the hat stand sat an even more comprehensive collection of shoes, complemented by a selection of canes and umbrellas.

Felix removed a few hats, trying them on for size before

placing them back on their pegs. He could barely concentrate on a single item for more than a few seconds before his eyes caught sight of something else in the room. This time it was the presence of a small electrical generator hidden in one of the room's dark corners. Felix approached the generator and curiously flicked the switch, turning it on. It took a few moments for the dusty old engine to turn over and for a cluster of bulbs in the centre of the room to finally come to life, emitting a dull light and revealing the most breathtaking sight of them all.

In the centre of the room, beneath the struggling lights, sat a full-scale model of London. It stretched from Buckingham Palace, through Westminster and the City of London, to the Tower of London on one side of the river, and then from Vauxhall, through Waterloo, London Bridge, and Southwark, and into Bermondsey on the other. It was almost five metres long and three metres wide, with almost life-like detail. Each building had been replicated with a deftness of touch that only an artist at the top of their profession could have created. St Paul's Cathedral sat at eye level, dominating the London skyline, while beneath the palace at Westminster, even the narrow London sewers and back alleys had been included.

Felix found himself wondering how long it must have taken to complete, how many months or years of painstaking sittings to produce such a work of beauty? He was almost scared to touch it for fear of damaging any of its features.

As he leant over the towering masterpiece, taking in its majesty, Felix felt a cold draft kiss the back of his neck. He turned to see a small corridor leading away from the room in the opposite direction. Unlike the splendour of the tunnel leading to Number 10, this one was narrow and bleak, with crumbling walls.

Felix stepped inside the unwelcoming corridor. He could feel the cold breeze pouring in through its warped and cracked walls. At the far end was another door. Felix continued forward, determined to see where it led, and the journey finally ended.

He took hold of the handle and carefully opened the door, stepping out onto a dark stretch of cobbled drag. The smell of raw sewage and vermin filled Felix's nostrils as he took in a derelict terraced street set back from the affluent city. Scarred by years of neglect and poverty, it housed some of the poorest people in London: beggars, invalids, and alcoholics, keeping them hidden and out of sight of civilised society. Those who couldn't afford a roof over their heads slept rough, battling the cold and disease. Felix saw a group of them lying in the gutters like mice, gathered for warmth and safety. Above them, in the fading light, he could barely make out the ageing street sign.

It read, *Old Pye Street*.

Freemasons' Hall

Freemasons' Hall was a large imposing building on Great Queen Street, with Holborn to its east and Covent Garden to its west. It had been the central meeting place for the masons since the mid-eighteenth century. Attached to the Freemasons' Hall was the Freemasons' Tavern, a remnant of the original cluster of buildings and a social gathering place for its notorious membership.

Amelia looked up at the famous masonic buildings in awe. She had studied the organisation for years, first from her home in America and then from her base at Corpus Christi, but she had yet to see the secret society's London headquarters in person. It was everything she'd anticipated and more. A glorious collection of buildings reflecting the mix of power, elegance, and supremacy she had come to associate with the masons and the British Empire from her many long nights absorbing their history.

Freemasonry was said to have dated back to the Middle Ages and the stonemason's guild. However, like most stories connected to the masons, even that tiny piece of history was open to debate. What was known, however, was how quickly the organisation had grown and how far its influence and power had spread. Its members comprised some of society's most influential people: judges, landowners, politicians, even royalty. It was said that George Washington was a mason and that Benjamin Franklin had served as the head of a fraternity in Pennsylvania before his death. This combination of power, mystery, and notoriety attracted Amelia to their story as a young woman and still intoxicated her to this day.

Amelia allowed herself a moment to take the building in and reminisce on the excitement she had felt travelling to London from America as a young student, desperate to see such sights. She'd spent much of her childhood in the Texan countryside surrounded by cattle and bison, two of the state's major exports. Although academics, her parents had left the city to take over the family business, exporting hides and furs across the continent. For a young woman brimming with adventure and aspiration, leaving the thriving metropolis was like turning one's back on life itself. She could never quite understand his parents' decision to leave, nor how they had managed to adapt to the mundanity of their existence in the semi-wilderness.

To pass the time, Amelia lost herself in books. She spent days on end reading about the great cities of the world and the many adventures that awaited her outside the confines of their small farming community. The old European cities were at the centre of her dreams: Paris, Athens, Madrid and Rome, the great hubs of history, art, culture, beauty, love, and intellect. However, rising above them all was the great city of London, the apotheosis of the civilised world. Amelia loved reading about its cobbled streets, crooked walkways, meandering rivers, high castles, ancient universities, and renowned temples of law. She would gorge herself on tales of London's infamous scientists, philosophers, artists, villains, politicians, and bloody monarchs. She even read about the notorious printing houses, taverns, members' clubs, and secret societies.

However, Amelia had not come to gawp at the city's famous architecture, nor had she come to fulfil a childhood affinity with London's opulent displays of history and power. She had come to question the masonic hierarchy on the strange cards left at the scenes of Lord Monteagle's and Lord Cecil's abductions.

As women were unwelcome in the Freemasons' Tavern, Amelia had no choice but to arrive at her destination disguised as a man. She used an old makeup trick to age her skin and give off the appearance of facial hair and replaced her usually colourful clothes with the masonic white bow tie and tails, hiding her long auburn hair under a top hat. She approached the main entrance, joining the steady stream of gentlemen flowing towards the Freemason's Tavern, slipping into the throng with the rest of the members.

The Tavern was a vast room, well presented with high ceilings and Tuscan columns running the length of its long walls. Thick wooden beams made up the serving area, and several tables and chairs filled the open space.

Amelia noted the sheer volume of masons present. It was as though the entire membership had decided to descend on the building on the same day. They were all immaculately dressed in white bow ties and top hats and had gathered in groups to discuss all manner of topics, from modern agriculture to the rise of automotive transportation and everything in between. It was said that some of the world's most remarkable feats and scandals had been hatched in the Freemasons' Tavern, and Amelia could not help but feel the touch of history on her shoulder.

She walked around, carefully listening to the members' conversations, trying to get a measure of their tone and how they addressed one another. If she wanted to fit in, she would need to act appropriately and be convincing as both a man and a fellow mason. It had a relatively low chance of success but was incredibly high in adventure.

Amelia took up a spot at the bar and ordered a pint of ale in her best male voice. As she listened to the cacophony of conversations, she began to make out several foreign accents among the crowd. It wasn't until she overheard a group of Dutch members discussing the annual masonic summit that she realised she had snuck into the organisation's yearly assemblage.

Like a lioness stalking her prey, Amelia scoured the room looking for lone masons on the periphery of a group she might target and engage in conversation with, but it wasn't easy. The sheer number of members and their sea of white bow ties and top hats made it almost impossible to decipher where one group ended, and another began.

Fortunately for Amelia, an older gentleman broke free from the herd and approached the bar beside her. Amelia noted his educated tone and grandiloquent manner as he engaged the barman.

'A bottle of your finest Italian wine.'

'I'll have to go to the cellar,' replied the barman.

'Very well.' Barked the Mason.

With the barman departed and the mason waiting, Amelia

seized her opportunity.

'What treasures must be stored in that cellar,' she said, attempting to draw the mason into a conversation.

'Indeed,' he replied, stealing a disgruntled glance at her.

'Abe Woodruff,' she proclaimed, stepping forward to introduce herself.

The mason took a small step back, shocked at being addressed so informally.

'Oh, of course! My apologies,' said Amelia, immediately realising her mistake.

She quickly grabbed the mason's hand, attempting an elaborate secret society handshake, only causing him to recoil further.

'I'm newly joined,' she continued, in her most charming Texan drawl, 'we do it a little differently back home, in the States.'

Amelia smiled at the mason, who quickly gathered his wine from the bartender when he returned and hurried off back into the sea of gentlemen.

Annoyed with herself, Amelia turned back to her ale when she felt the presence of someone standing behind her. She spun around to see another well-turned-out mason. Only this one was tall, with broad shoulders and a thick neck.

'There's no need to get heavy. I was just leaving anyway,' she said, finishing her drink.

'Professor Woodruff?' asked the mason.

Amelia looked up at the mason, shocked, 'depends on who's asking.'

'We've been expecting you.'

'Who is we, exactly?'

'Please, follow me.'

The well-built mason turned and strode off through the busy

tavern. Amelia hesitated, considering the risk, then placed her glass on the bar and quickly followed.

'Where are we going?' she asked, struggling to keep up.

'I shall be escorting you to one of our meeting rooms. Once inside, you'll sit at the table and wait to be addressed. You may only ask a question when invited to do so.'

'Sounds fun,' mocked Amelia.

The mason led Amelia through the tavern and into a long corridor. They paced through a collection of halls and up various staircases, burrowing deeper and deeper into the building's complex warren of floors.

Amelia took a mental note of her surroundings, hoping to sketch a map of the building in her mind. However, after following the mason for over 20 minutes, Amelia realised she'd been walking around in circles. A clever trick to confuse the mind and save the masons from having to put unwelcome blindfolds on all their guests.

After what had seemed like an age, the mason finally stopped.

'We have arrived,' he said, facing a white door with the red-and-white St George's Cross hanging from it.

Amelia looked at the cross curiously. She'd not seen it on any of the other doors they'd passed. Perhaps this was a new wing of the building, or had they just added the cross to one of the original doors to confuse her further? Either way, the tactic had worked. Amelia was no clearer as to the layout of the building or her whereabouts within it than when they'd first set off.

The mason opened the door and ushered Amelia inside. The room was small and dimly lit, and it took a few moments for Amelia's eyes to adjust to the low light. She could make out the silhouettes of five figures sitting around an oval table in complete stillness. An empty chair was already pulled out, welcomingly, in front of her.

'Please, do sit, Professor,' called a voice.

Amelia stepped forward and slowly lowered herself into the seat. She scanned the room, trying to take in as much information about her surroundings as possible, but there was very little data available in the semi-darkness. Once her eyes had become accustomed to the room, Amelia could clearly make out the figures gathered around the table. To her surprise, they were all dressed in black hooded capes with intricately detailed animal masks covering their faces.

At the head of the table was a rotund figure wearing a male lion's mask. Amelia could deduce from the figure's drooping shoulders and poor posture that he was a man, probably in his late fifties. To his right were two more men, both somewhat younger and sturdier. One of the men was wearing a ram's mask, not too dissimilar to the ram's face on the abduction card, while the other was wearing a far more sinister-looking mask depicting a crow. On the left of the lion, Amelia could make out the shape of a woman, probably in her late forties, wearing an eagle mask, next to another middle-aged man in a laughing monkey's mask.

'Welcome, Professor,' said a voice.

'Thank you for joining us,' said another.

Amelia looked around the table, unsure which mask the voices had come from.

'How did you know I was coming?' she asked.

'Our eyes and ears are everywhere,' replied a voice.

'In that case, an invitation would have been nice.'

'We are not in the habit of drawing attention to ourselves,' said the voice. 'We prefer to work in the shadows.'

'Evidently,' replied Amelia.

'Do you have the card?' asked another voice, disorientating Amelia further.

Amelia looked around the group of masons, weighing up her options. She hadn't come this far to leave without any answers. She reached into her pocket and pulled out the card.

'One of yours?' she asked, placing it on the table.

There was silence as the man in the monkey mask reached down and picked up the card, studying it. He passed it to his female colleague in the eagle mask, who also considered it before passing it on again. The card eventually made its way around the table, finally returning to the space in front of Amelia.

'A rather interesting collection of symbols, don't you think?' asked Amelia, trying to invite a conversation despite the mason's warnings not to ask questions until invited.

'How well do you know your history, Professor?' asked one of the many voices.

'Ask my students.'

'I don't mean the stuff you read in your books at Corpus Christi, nor am I referring to the watered-down narrative the establishment serves up to keep its students complicit with the system. What do you know about real history?'

'I know about Baphomet, your goat god. I also know a bit about the pentagram and its links to freemasonry.'

'Then you will also be aware that we have fought off attacks of this kind many times throughout our history.'

'Attacks?' scoffed Amelia.

'Of course,' entered another voice. 'Surely a scholar of your intellect can see that we are being deliberately implicated in this crime?'

'Sounds like the kind of thing I would say if I wanted to distance myself from the card.'

'Ask yourself this, Professor,' said another voice, 'why would we go to the trouble of leaving a card?'

'Perhaps to let your enemies know the consequences of crossing your organisation?'

'We have more sophisticated ways of making a point, most of which do not implicate us in criminal activity. After all, how do you think we learned of the abductions and your impending visit?'

'You know people in high places,' conceded Amelia.

'And how do you think those people would react if they believed we were involved in abducting two lords?'

'That depends on your motive. What if it was necessary? What if Monteagle and Cecil were masons and had put the organisation at risk? In that instance, these high-profile people you speak of may have approved, even ordered the abductions themselves?'

'You're fishing for information, Professor,' called another voice. 'You know very well that we cannot confirm or deny the identity of our members.'

'Then I cannot discount your motive.'

'Then it seems we have arrived at an impasse,' said another voice. 'We thank you for your time.'

Amelia felt the atmosphere in the room change immediately. Within seconds the figures had returned to facing forwards with their backs straight, and chins held up high, a formidable display of discipline and control.

'Is that it?' she asked. 'Surely there's more to discuss. If you are being set up, at least help me find the people who are framing you.'

Amelia's words had no impact on the figures or their cold wall of silence. She glared at them in disbelief when she suddenly noticed the well-built mason standing across the room speaking to something or someone in the darkness. She squinted to get a better look. She could make out the form of a sixth figure sitting in the shadows. She watched as the mason crouched down low, close enough for the figure to lean forward, revealing his owl mask as he whispered something into the mason's ear.

The figure quickly returned to the shadows, and the young mason made his way around the room, approaching Amelia.

'This way, Professor,' he said, motioning towards the door.

Amelia slowly rose from her seat, her eyes fixed on the silhouette of the sixth figure in the corner of the room. There was still so much she wanted to know, so many unanswered questions. If anything, this brief encounter had presented more complications than solutions. Amelia looked back over her shoulder at the silent figures sitting like statues around the table. She contemplated asking a parting question but knew it was pointless. They had offered only the tiniest morsels of information, things they had wanted her to know, nothing more.

Once outside the room, the mason led Amelia on another maze-like journey up and down flights of stairs and through various corridors until they arrived back at the Freemason's Tavern. Frustrated by her lack of progress, Amelia was about to take her leave when the mason pulled her to one side.

'One final thing, Professor,' he began. 'The type of paper your card is printed on is called bleached hemp with rag fibres.'

'Excuse me?' said Amelia, taken aback.

'I am reliably informed that bleached hemp is an old printing material from India, rarely used on the presses nowadays. Only one remaining printer in London still has a stockpile.'

The mason held out a slip of paper and handed it to Amelia.

'And why should I trust a man who sits in the shadows? He didn't even get to touch the card. I watched it the whole time, and it never left the table.'

'He didn't need to touch the card, Professor. Let's just say his family are very well acquainted with the printing trade,' replied the mason, before turning and departing.

Amelia stepped out of the Freemason's Tavern and onto the bustling streets of Covent Garden. She walked for some time, crossing through Piccadilly and onto Charing Cross, before allowing herself to stop and look at the slip of paper. If her meeting with the masons had taught her anything, it was that you never knew who might be watching you at any given time. She slowly unfolded the note and quietly read its contents to herself, her eyes shining with the promise of further adventure.

House of Commons

The early morning dew had begun to lift from the famous walls and arches lining the River Thames along Embankment. The streets, although quiet, were starting to show signs of life, and it would not be long until the calm serenity was replaced by throngs of Londoners on their busy morning commute.

Inside Parliament, the Commons was preparing for an early start. There had been much to fill the newspapers of late, and the members were determined to cover it all before the short autumn recess. The doors opened promptly at 7 o'clock, allowing the members to filter into the chamber. It was the usual hustle and bustle of rushing feet and clashing elbows as ministers hurried to secure a seat on the famous green benches before the start of the morning session. Those arriving after the rush were forced to gather by the doors or in the gangways hoping to hear all that was said and debated without the luxury of viewing their counterparts as they spoke. It was one of Westminster's remarkable peculiarities, to have a members' chamber with too few seats to accommodate its members.

Fortunately for Felix, he did not have to compete for his seat. As prime minister, his place on the front bench was always assured.

Felix made his way through the crowds towards the centre of the house. Rarely had he seen it so busy. The benches were full, and members were already crowding the standing spaces, eager to secure an unrestricted view.

As the crowds continued to build, so did the anticipation. Felix felt a little flutter of nerves twist in his stomach. It was common for politicians to feel nervous before the start of a parliamentary session, particularly the last before a recess. There was always so much to be said, and many voices desperate to be heard and elevated. The scales were finely balanced, and for every person who managed to claw their way up a few rungs of the political ladder, there was always someone else haplessly slipping down to fill their void. Success was never assured in politics, it was fickle, and a politician required broad shoulders to withstand the constant slings and arrows.

'It's a full house, Prime Minister,' said Percy, rising to greet Felix.

'So, it seems,' replied Felix.

He could feel his heart racing and the sweat building on the palms of his hands.

Across the dispatch box, Felix watched Cavendish holding court with his colleagues. He moved from one member to another, whispering instructions to each and patting them reassuringly on their backs. There was an easy confidence between them. They didn't look like men about to engage in a bruising political battle but instead seemed like spectators at the theatre or a football match, preparing for some form of sport or entertainment. The newspapers had once described the House of Commons as a modern-day Colosseum. As Felix nervously watched his opponents, he couldn't help but feel like the gladiator, standing in the great arena, waiting for the gates to open and the lions to be released.

With the ministers finally seated, the Speaker entered the house, followed by the clerks and the Sergeant at Arms, who laid the mace down on its perch to signify the King's presence over proceedings.

'Questions will be taken,' began the Speaker, bringing the low murmur of conversations to a prompt silence, 'but I would ask that the honourable members keep to one question and that replies be of a reasonable length. I am determined that we make good progress through the order paper today before we break for a well-earned autumn recess. Mr Edward Stanley...'

The Speaker pointed to a large man with a round face and a bulging waistline.

'Prime Minister,' bellowed Stanley, in a thick West Country accent, 'it had been well documented, long before Arthur Jenkins' death, that the conditions in many of the mines, factories and plants up and down the country were below working standards, and you've done nothing about it. Even now, with this young man's blood on the chamber's hands, nothing is being done. So, I ask you, how many more young men will have to die before you act?'

'We are working on several reforms that we are readying for

the house. We are also assessing some of the conditions first-hand to publish a report on the matter.' replied Felix, rising from his bench to answer the question.

'A report?' repeated Stanley. 'The need is an immediate one, sir. These company directors have been banking their profits for years while running as lean an operation as humanly possible.'

Loud jeers greeted Stanley's words. Many of the members were the very same directors he was referring to.

'As a consequence,' continued Stanley over the clamour, 'much of their equipment is unsuitable for work, and there is a very real danger that unless this is addressed, there will be more tragic events like those that occurred at Birchwood. You mark my words.'

Stanley returned to his seat to a chorus of boos.

'Mr Henry Huffington!' called out the Speaker, pointing to an elderly politician sitting on the upper backbenches and wearing a dark suit with a collection of military honours hanging from the breast of his jacket.

'Codswallop!' shouted Huffington, rising to his feet, assisted by members on either side of him. 'The people are work-shy; they only want reform to satisfy their idle malingering. If we don't keep the collieries and plants running at full tilt, we'll fall behind the emerging German and American economies. What does the Prime Minister plan to do about that?'

A wave of cheers from both sides of the chamber greeted Huffington's question. Felix waited for the members to settle before addressing the house. It was clear which side of the debate held favour, and he used the time to think of an effective response.

'What is the benefit of having the world's largest economy if we cannot use it to better the lot of our people?' he asked defiantly.

'This house's primary duty is to maintain the strength and

endurance of His Majesty's empire!' called out Huffington to a second round of approving grunts and nods.

'I cannot agree, sir!' said Felix. 'This house's primary duty is to its people, and we must strive to provide them with a better standard of living, both at home and at work.'

'What standard of living will we have when we are forced out of our own Empire?' called a member from the backbenches, causing a further eruption of approvals.

'Order! Order!' called the Speaker, 'Mr Milton Cavendish.'

A silent anticipation fell over the chamber as Cavendish rose from his bench to address the house.

'It should come as no surprise to this house to see our Prime Minister once again hide behind the plight of the British people. Our Empire is under attack, our rivals continue to build their capabilities, and a new power rises out of the ashes of our old colony across the Atlantic. But still, our Prime Minister does not have the backbone to compete. Rather his reformist nature and lack of steel are further opening the door to our enemies.'

'Here, here!' yelled members, waving their order papers with approval.

'It is not a case of backbone or steel,' replied Felix. 'How can we compete with our rivals if we cannot solve the growing problems we face here in our own back garden?'

'You see,' growled Cavendish, 'he is not fit for the fight! These new powers will take control of our seas and cut into our trade. It is little surprise that the workers are restless. We need a firm response. We need firm leadership!'

A cacophony of noise and waving order papers filled the chamber for a second time.

'Order!' bellowed the Speaker. 'Order!'

After what seemed like an eternity to Felix, the noise finally subdued, and the members grudgingly began to settle back into their benches.

'We are in a dog fight, Prime Minister,' observed Percy, wriggling in his seat.

It had been this way ever since Felix's government had come to power, the constant struggle for change, the battle lines formed between maintaining the old and paving the way for the new. To Felix, the mandate from the British people had been clear: reform those institutions that needed reforming, bring the cost of living down to an acceptable level and do your utmost to improve the lives of ordinary people. But for most in the house, these goals were secondary to the constant improvement of the Empire and Britain's standing in the world.

Felix took a moment to gather his thoughts. He knew that Cavendish would have prepared his attack meticulously and that, like a well-trained conductor, he would be driving his audience towards the big crescendo. But what could he do to stop him? Cavendish had the ear of the chamber.

Felix stepped up to the Table of the House. He looked around the room at the many dissenting faces staring back at him, each ready to jump on his every word. He thought about the missing lords and their families, Old Pye Street with its portraits of previous leaders, that inspiring plaque on the wall, and his mother, Leonora, and everything she had endured in her brief but purposeful life. He felt a surge of energy rush through his body. This was the Colosseum, and like a gladiator, he wouldn't go down without a fight.

He stood tall, about to speak, when he noticed something seesawing in the corner of his eye. Felix turned to see the Speaker waving his arm in the air, trying to get the chamber's attention. He was holding a white slip of paper aloft, which his clerk had just handed him moments earlier.

'Something urgent has occurred,' he began, still waving the slip of paper in the air. 'It will require the immediate attention of the Prime Minister. We shall reconvene after the autumn recess.'

Roars of disapproval met the Speaker's announcement, members reluctant to let Felix off the ropes. But there was little they could do. Felix returned to his seat, thankful for the reprieve. He quickly gathered his papers and departed for the Speaker's room.

The Speaker's room was a small box shape, richly decorated with high, oak-panelled ceilings and large portraits of past incumbents. In the centre of the room sat two red armchairs on either side of a charcoal grey fireplace with gilded roses running along the top.

'Mr Speaker?' called Felix, entering the room.

He looked around, but the Speaker was nowhere to be seen. 'How bizarre,' he whispered.

'Isn't it just?' replied a voice from behind him.

Felix spun around to see Amelia sitting in the Speaker's chair with her feet on the desk.

'What on earth are you doing here, Amelia?' asked Felix in astonishment.

'Saving your hide by the looks of things. It was turning into a massacre in there.'

'The wolves are well and truly at the door. But where is the Speaker?'

'You mean, the right honourable James Creswell?' said Amelia in a mock British accent. 'Don't mind him. We're old friends. I simply slipped him a note asking him to bring proceedings to an end so that we could talk in private.'

'Amelia, you can't just call an end to Parliament?'

'I've been to see the masons…'

Felix stopped. He took a seat at the desk alongside his former college mate. 'And?'

'And the plot, it appears, seems to thicken greatly. Of course, by the time I arrived, they had already been expecting me. They knew all about the abductions and the cards. In truth, there was little they did not know. Their people are everywhere, in the palaces, the courts, the police, even in there!' said Amelia, nodding back towards the House of Commons.

'What did they say?'

'They're claiming a case of misdirection.'

'Misdirection?'

'They are concerned that whoever is behind these abductions is trying to frame them. They quickly reminded me that they had suffered these attacks before, from the knights, the French nobility, even the Pope. Let's just say they are more than familiar with the pattern.'

'And did you believe them?'

'It's hard to say. It's possible they were telling the truth. On the other hand, it's just as possible they were saying whatever they needed to in order to throw me off the scent.'

'But they knew of your arrival, which means they must have been watching you.'

'Either that or someone in Oxford spotted us and reported back to them. Most of my students come from the types of families you'd imagine have ties with the masons. I wouldn't be surprised if some keen young canary followed us.'

Felix took a moment to process the information.

'Well, if not the masons, then who?'

'I got the sense they weren't entirely sure themselves. The symbols on the cards are masonic but they were arranged in a way that I don't think even they had seen before.'

'So, we're no closer?'

'I wouldn't say that, exactly. The meeting did produce something of interest.'

Amelia reached into her pocket and removed the scrap of paper the mason had given her.

'What is it?' asked Felix.

'There was an elderly gentleman present at the meeting with a comprehensive knowledge of the printing industry and its varied materials. By all accounts, his family were rather big in the trade. As fortune would have it, he was able to spot bleached hemp with rag fibres from across a large and dark masonic room.'

'What are you talking about?'

'This chap was very intrigued by your little card. Apparently, the bleached hemp paper it's printed on is produced in a little place called India. Only a handful of printers in the city still work with bleached hemp, and only one still stockpiles it.'

Amelia handed Felix the folded paper. 'I suspect they chose this type of paper as they knew it would be hard to trace. Near on impossible, in fact.'

Felix unfolded the slip of paper to reveal a name scrawled inside in pencil.

'Houlston and Sons of Fleet Street.' He read.

'A small holding.' Said Amelia.

'You know it?'

'I may have passed by to take a brief look. Will you send in the police?' asked Amelia.

'Not while we are unsure of their dependability. We have a lead, the last thing we want to do is alert our enemies to that fact. The police can be of no use to us at this stage. In the meantime, we shall do some discreet digging of our own.'

'Where to next, Prime Minister?' asked Amelia, rubbing her hands.

'For now, I need you to return to Oxford and your students. We don't know whose attention your investigations may have attracted, and I would not put you in harm's way.'

Amelia raised her hand in objection, but Felix swiftly cut her off.

'You can still be of service to me from the college. Keep digging into the symbols on the cards. It's key that we understand their significance. I shall follow up with Houlston and Sons and see what information can be gathered.'

'What about your enemies in there?' asked Amelia, reminding Felix of the barrage he had just received inside the Commons.

'I'll have Humphrey set up a meeting with the unions. I want to know what Cavendish has offered them in return for their support.'

'I could do a lot more from here,' pressed Amelia.

Felix checked the time on his pocket watch.

'If I recall, the train to Oxford leaves at ten minutes past the hour. That gives you just over thirty minutes to get to Paddington Station.'

Houlston and Sons of Fleet Street

It was with great surprise that Humphrey opened the door to Number 10 to find Felix returned from Parliament early. He was used to the Commons overrunning and ruining his many well-laid plans but was yet to hear of it adjourning prematurely for any reason.

'Is the building on fire?' He asked jovially.

'Not physically, but metaphorically perhaps,' replied Felix.

'Don't tell me; someone got a member's constituency name wrong again?'

'Cold,' replied Felix.

'Someone lost the key to the wine cellar?'

'They wouldn't dare. Still cold.'

'Someone snuck a woman into the chamber?''

'Warm,' replied Felix.

Humphrey stared at Felix, studying his expression. 'Oh dear, it has something to do with Amelia, doesn't it?'

'Hot!'

'Amelia, is the reason you're home early?'

'Positively scorching!'

'And what pray tell has she been up to this time?'

Felix took a moment to explain the furore he had faced in the Commons, the growing anger and resentment on all sides and Amelia's timely intervention before retiring to his study to document the day's events. As was customary, Humphrey lit a large fire and fetched a tray of sandwiches and a pot of tea from the kitchens.

'Will you be needing anything more?' he asked.

Felix took a moment to think. He was determined to make the trip across London to Fleet Street to investigate the printers on the slip of paper the masons had given Amelia. 'Do you have your spectacles with you?' he asked.

'My spectacles?' Questioned Humphrey. 'Do you have a problem with your eyes?'

'No, I just need something to mask them. If I recall correctly, yours were a little weathered and bent out of shape?'

'They're not weathered and bent out of shape, thank you very much. They're just well used,' replied Humphrey reaching into his pocket and taking out a long rectangular case, reluctantly handing it to Felix.

Felix opened the case and removed the spectacles. They were old and misshapen, with a small crack on the bridge held together with string. He placed them on his face, manoeuvring them into position.

'Very fetching,' said Humphrey. 'Now, will you tell me what this is about, or will I have to follow you around like I did when you were a mischievous child?'

'I have a lead in the case, nothing concrete, but a line of investigation. I need to disguise my appearance to carry out some research.'

'That is a job for the police, not the Prime Minister?'

'I'm not entirely sure we can rely on the police in this matter,' said Felix, repositioning the spectacles.

'What do you mean we can't rely on the police?'

Felix turned to face his steward. He could sense the concern in his voice. 'Amelia has been to see the masons. Someone has been leaking information to them.'

'Surely you don't suspect…'

'I don't know,' said Felix, cutting Humphrey short, 'and therein lies the problem. The police, like the rest of the establishment, is well known to have ties to these secret societies, which makes them hard to rely on.'

'But Felix, think if you were to be discovered?'

'I will take every care. Now, I must get back to work. Inform the staff that I do not wish to be disturbed and tell Mrs Hughes I'll take a late supper this evening.'

'Very well,' said Humphrey, taking his leave.

Felix waited for Humphrey's footsteps to fade, then made his way over to the fireplace and carefully doused the fire. He turned the corbel ninety degrees and watched as the back panel began to retreat, unveiling the secret passage. Felix stepped into the tunnel and followed its ornate curved walls away from his study towards Old Pye Street.

Inside the secret office, Felix approached the giant model replica of London to plot his journey to Houlston and Sons. The most obvious path from Old Pye Street was along Westminster, through Charing Cross and onto the Strand, leading directly onto Fleet Street. But it was risky. The chances of being seen increased dramatically on London's main roads, and as Humphrey had warned, Felix could not afford to be discovered under any circumstances. Instead, he studied the dark backroads and alleyways along the river Thames, mapping out an alternative route.

There was also the small matter of his appearance. Felix had already secured Humphrey's spectacles, but they alone would not be enough to hide his identity. He would need a story, a believable justification for questioning the printer on his business affairs.

Felix pulled one of the encyclopaedias off the dusty shelf, *The Complete Guide to Occupational Exploration.* He flicked through the long list of alphabetically arranged jobs, looking for one that might offer a plausible backstory. He scanned the a's reading the descriptions for an accountant, actor, aircraft engineer and architect, before moving on to the b's and the specifics for a barrister, beekeeper, and biologist. Having only progressed to the c's and a description of a carpenter, after a full hour, he finally decided to turn his attention to the collection of uniforms hanging from the clothes rail instead. He sifted through each disguise, wearing every conceivable tradesman's uniform, but none gave off the impression of a man legitimately interested in, or sanctioned at, looking into a company's accounts.

Exasperated by his lack of progress, Felix finally turned his attention to the messy pile of documents on the desk, a chaotic collection of scribbles, bills and letters previous prime ministers had mulled over while hidden away in Old Pye Street. Among them, Felix found a letter addressed to the Downing Street tax clerk with the royal crest sitting prominently at the top of the paper. He quickly gathered up Humphrey's spectacles, a top hat and a cane and set out towards the front door and the narrow, cobbled streets beyond.

Felix emerged from Old Pye Street to the sound of silence. The winter rains had cleared the streets of people, leaving only the poor and destitute huddled together in small dry nooks around the city. It was a sight he had become accustomed to and promised himself he would rectify once in government. However, every time he'd tried to address the issue of London's needy in Parliament, it had been pushed aside in favour of a more politically agreeable cause, like increasing the navy's wage or providing better equipment for his Majesty's army. No politician in his right mind would agree to spend money on the homeless, not when it could be spent on the military. The dispossessed were of no use to anyone, whereas the Empire could always use more ships.

Felix made his way towards the Embankment, keeping to the back streets along the Thames before cutting up through Temple and finally onto Fleet Street. He could hear the roar of the printing presses all around him and taste the sewage rising off the Fleet, the largest of London's subterranean rivers. As a lawyer, Felix had spent many evenings in the area dining with colleagues at the Temple Inns. He had always known the printing houses to be small, overcrowded spaces bustling with energy and enterprise. However, over the past decade, Fleet Street had blossomed into the nerve centre of the world's news and information, and new buildings were being raised every year, each taller and more spectacular than the last.

Houlston and Sons, by contrast, was a small family holding

set back from the main road, overshadowed by the expanding Fleet Street skyline. Felix noted how withered and unwelcoming the building looked. Its once-vibrant green-and-gold family sign had faded and was barely legible, and the slatted wooden facade was weathered and bent out of shape. There was something eerie, almost improper, about its continued presence on Fleet Street. How had this old relic stayed afloat for so long, entombed in the shadows of this sprawling metropolis? It was like a mosquito wedged into the neck of a lion.

Felix approached the dilapidated building. The smell of dry ink and grease stung his nostrils as he pushed the door open and stepped into a large open-plan room full of old, rickety printing presses working at full tilt, spitting out smoke and oil. It was a far cry from the new, state-of-the-art printing houses with their specialist printing rooms, almost like stepping back in time.

Felix walked across the factory floor towards a small desk at the far end of the room, surrounded by newspapers packed in bundles and ready to be delivered. He noted the array of foreign-language titles printed on various coloured and textured papers. It was clear that Houlston and Sons had come to specialise in rare overseas publications as a way of competing. He lifted one of the newspapers to study the paper it was printed on when a boy, no older than fifteen, with a pockmarked face and dark ink stains on his hands approached.

'Can I help, sir?' he asked.

'What is your name and position here, boy?' asked Felix.

'I'm Alfred, Mr Houlston's apprentice.'

'Then run along and fetch your master for me,' said Felix, flashing the document with the royal crest on it, 'tell him I have come from His Majesty's Tax Office and would like to discuss his accounts.'

'Yes, sir.' stuttered the young apprentice scurrying off to the back of the shop to fetch Mr Houlston.

Within moments an older man, far beyond retirement age with grey hair and thick glasses slowly emerged, aided by the young apprentice.

'That's the man, Mr Houlston, sir,' said Alfred, pointing in Felix's direction.

'Thank you, Alfred,' said Mr Houlston, carefully pulling up a stool, 'fetch our guest a seat, will you.'

Alfred pulled up another stool and Mr Houlston motioned for Felix to join him.

'You must excuse me, I am old, and it takes me an eternity to do most things, even walk across my own shop floor. What I wouldn't give for a pair of younger legs.'

'That's quite alright,' said Felix, taking a seat and placing his cane to one side.

'How can I be of assistance?' asked Mr Houlston.

'We are carrying out routine checks on all the printing houses on Fleet Street, to ensure your accounts are up to date and to see if we can assist in any way.'

'We had our accounts audited less than two months ago?' said Mr Houlston. 'I doubt our rich neighbours are scrutinised half as often as we are?'

Felix felt a sudden pang of guilt. 'I can assure you, we show no favour to any business, large or small. We'll be moving on to the others as soon as we're finished here.'

'You know, we've been on Fleet Street for over eighty years,' continued Mr Houlston. 'We may be small, but our roots here are deep.'

'If you could just have your books brought up, I'll be out of your hair in no time,' pressed Felix.

'I know what they're trying to do,' said Mr Houlston, eyeing Felix with suspicion. 'They want me out, but I refuse to go. I will not be intimidated by them or their chums at Westminster. I served my country, you know.'

Mr Houlston stopped to catch his breath, the slightest exertion of emotion disrupting his already laboured breathing. Felix watched as the older man took in a cluster of large inhalations, eyeing him defiantly.

'What department did you say you were from again?' he spluttered.

Felix felt a wave of anxiety wash over him. He looked down at the document in his hand. His entire cover story depended on the small royal crest at the top of the page. It would not stand up to any scrutiny from the stubborn printer. All Mr Houlston had to do was ask to see his appointment letter, and Felix would be entirely exposed.

'I'm not in cahoots with your competitors if that's your concern,' he said, leaning forward. 'In fact, I think it takes great character to fight them off the way you have.'

'You do,' replied a shocked Mr Houlston.

'It's not fair these big corporations squeezing the city's smaller, family-run businesses. I applaud you for standing your ground. I'd be tempted to go a step further and invest in a new shop front and refurbish the old family sign.'

'A show of defiance? Perhaps I'll invite them to a grand opening party and play them at their own game. It would be worth the cost just to see the looks on their faces.'

Felix nodded in agreement. He could hear the cogs turning in Mr Houlston's mind and see the plans forming in his old calculating eyes.

'But to do that,' continued Felix, 'we need to ensure that

your books are all above board for his Majesty's Clerk.'

Mr Houlston's eyes flickered from Felix to his printing presses and back as he weighed up his options and his guest's sincerity.

'Very well,' he conceded. 'Alfred, fetch my accounts.'

'Yes, sir,' replied Alfred, darting off into another room.

'There is nothing in there of any significance,' said Mr Houlston, slowly rising from his stool. 'Let his Majesty's Clerk feast his eyes on our dwindling profits; perhaps it will disturb his sleep much as it has mine. Although, I doubt he has such a conscience.'

It took Alfred only a short time to return with the company accounts, large, dusty old journals dating back over eighty years, as Mr Houlston had said. Felix organised each book by date, searching the most recent first and working his way back. It was more complicated than he had anticipated, with orders from all over the world and an array of exotic client names; Wong, Singh, Goldberg, DuPont, Garcia, Nakamura and Sequeira. They covered thousands of miles from the Americas to the Indian Subcontinent and all the countries in between.

Alongside each order were the names of the products Houlston and Sons had sold over the years, linen, cotton, pulp and slow fibres. But there was no reference in the books to the bleached hemp the senior mason had recognised during Amelia's visit to the Freemasons' Tavern.

Felix continued to study the pages, increasingly aware of the growing length of his visit. The longer he lingered, the more suspicious it looked, and it wouldn't be long before the old printer would start to question his motives again. He turned from one page to another, quickly scanning the product names, when it dawned on him that perhaps he was looking for the wrong thing or the wrong word at least. Like most tradespeople, printers liked to give their products memorable titles rather than market them solely on their material components. Felix hurriedly skimmed back through the pages examining the orders again. This time he noticed a series of catchy brand names alongside some of the entries.

'That's strange,' he announced loud enough for Alfred to hear.

Since bringing the accounts up, the young apprentice had turned his attention to an old printing press that had begun grinding its gears and spitting out smoke.

'What's that, sir?' he asked, looking up from the faulty machine.

'There seem to be several oddly named products listed here and there,' said Felix. 'What exactly do they refer to?'

Alfred shot Felix a worried look. He was about to turn and hurry off to fetch Mr Houlston when Felix stepped forward, stopping him in his tracks. He preferred to question the young apprentice rather than his wily old master, who would doubtless query Felix on his sudden interest in their products.

'Here, see for yourself.' said Felix.

Alfred used the rag from his belt to wipe the grease off his hands, then buried his head in the book. After a short silence, he emerged, looking utterly confused.

'Well?' asked Felix.

'Sorry. I don't read,' replied Alfred, his cheeks burning with embarrassment.

Felix thought for a moment. It was a delicate situation. He didn't want to disturb Mr Houlston but having come so far, he was reluctant to leave without making a meaningful breakthrough.

'What if I were to read the orders out to you?' he asked. 'Do you think you could explain what they are?'

'Most of them,' nodded Alfred. 'But I've only been Mr Houlston's apprentice for eight months.'

'Let's give it a try.'

Felix took the book in his hand, ran his finger down the list and began reading out the names. 'Classic Brown,' he started.

'That's our wood pulp paper. Most of our customers use that one. It's our best seller.'

'Elegant White?'

'The White is our premium paper. It's made from cotton fibres and lasts longer than our other products. It keeps the inks well too.'

'Rare Green?'

'Rare Green?' repeated Alfred. 'That doesn't ring any bells.'

'The Green is a hemp paper from India,' said Mr Houlston, appearing from the back of the shop. 'We used to bleach it to remove the colour, many years ago now, when it was still in production.'

'But there is a recent sale here?' said Felix, pointing at the entry in the accounts.

The old printer approached the service desk, clutching its frame for balance. 'Alfred, they serve some rather nice scotch at the George, be a good lad and fetch us a bottle,' he said, shooting his apprentice a reassuring look.

Felix watched as Alfred turned and scuttled out of the shop.

'He does worry about my well-being,' said Mr Houlston, following Felix's gaze. 'It's hard to find such honest folk these days, particularly in light of our recent struggles.'

Felix turned to face Mr Houlston. He was sure his cover had been blown but couldn't understand the old printer's sudden hospitality. Mr Houlston extended his hand, holding out a slip of paper.

'What is it?' asked Felix.

'It's a bill of sale for a pair of ninety by sixty-millimetre cards printed on aged Indian bleached hemp, as per the order in the book. You will see that the customer also purchased the press, the plates and all the inks associated with the job.'

Felix took the bill of sale, lifting Humphrey's glasses away from his eyes to get a better look. He could barely believe what he was reading. At the top of the bill was a name.

'Tom Fellows?' he read lightly.

'A rather intimidating lump covered head to toe in tattoos and constantly reeking of alcohol, like every other crook from the Docklands. We contemplated sending him away, but his business was too valuable for us to turn down. Sometimes in life, we do what we must rather than what we would like.'

Mr Houlston stopped to take another deep breath. Felix noticed him subtly remove an object from the desk drawer and quickly place it in his pocket. Was it a gun or a knife, perhaps? Suddenly Felix realised why Mr Houlston had become so agreeable, offering up fine scotch and free information. The wily old printer was stalling, keeping him occupied just long enough to recover his weapon and hold Felix there until Alfred returned with the cavalry. Probably the same villainous group of people who had ordered the cards and abducted the two peers. Felix cursed himself for being so naive. Did he really think he could just walk into this man's family business and demand to see its most valuable secrets without arousing suspicion? How could he be so foolish? Now with his cover blown and his life potentially in danger, all he could think of was Humphrey's disapproving words and the potentially crushing newspaper headlines if he were to be exposed or, even worse, killed.

'Please, take a seat,' said Mr Houlston, directing Felix towards one of the stools. 'Alfred won't be long.'

Felix hesitated, looking around the room for the nearest exit, but the only way in or out of the factory was the main door located all the way across the factory floor. He contemplated running, but it was too far, and he was unwilling to take the risk without knowing what the old printer had removed from the draw and placed in his pocket. Instead, he reluctantly lowered himself onto the stool.

'Was it active service?' he asked, hitting on a strategy.

'Excuse me?'

'Earlier, you referred to your time in the army. I was just wondering if you were engaged in active service?'

'Of course,' replied Mr Houlston, puffing his chest out, 'ten years in the Fusiliers, including tours of India, South Africa and Burma.'

'And now you're in another battle, to keep your business afloat?'

'This business has been in my family for generations. I won't be remembered as the failure that closed its doors. Not if there's even the slightest chance of saving it.

'But at what cost?'

'At any cost! We just need a few more clients, and then we can start to build up a head of steam.'

Felix looked out over the factory floor and the old printing presses, including the rickety one Alfred had been attempting to fix.

'And what about your presses? How are you going to replace them?'

'They would've been on the scrap heap years ago if it weren't for young Alfred. The boy's a miracle worker.'

'He won't be able to keep them running forever.'

'Perhaps not,' conceded Mr Houlston, 'but at least we'll still be in operation while I'm alive.'

'So, you're holding out for death?' Asked Felix.

'Something like that.'

'Then what does it matter if you lose the business now or after you're gone? Either way, it's the same result: the doors will eventually shut.'

'I promised my father on his deathbed that I would fight off these corporations, these vipers trying to put us out of business. They were the same reptiles who drove him to an early grave, and I will continue to fight them until the day I…'

Mr Houlston spluttered, struggling to finish his sentence, the emotional exertion leaving him gasping for air. With the old printer momentarily incapacitated, Felix sprung up from his stool and grasped the lever on the broken printing press, pulling it as hard as he could. The machine began to turn over, grinding its gears together and coughing up fountains of ink and thick plumes of smoke, slowly engulfing the shop. Amidst the chaos and confusion, Felix darted past Mr Houlston, sprinting between the printing presses and across the factory floor towards the exit, finally making his escape.

Outside, the streets were busy with rush hour traffic, the day was ending, and the vast Fleet Street workforce was turning in their pens and inks for the evening. Felix welcomed the crowd, slipping into the herd's safety and out of sight. He could feel his heart racing. He was lucky to have escaped unrecognised and in one piece. Any longer, and Alfred would have returned with reinforcements. The thought squeezed at the pit of his stomach. He knew just how close he had come to losing everything.

Felix turned to leave when another thought materialised. Should he stay and wait for Alfred to return so that he might get a look at these men Mr Houlston had sent for?

He scanned the street, looking for a spot with a clear view of Houlston and Sons when he noticed several members of the public stealing glances at him. He patted himself down, concerned he may have covered himself in ink or grease fleeing across the factory floor, but his face and clothes were clean. Suddenly it dawned on Felix that the large workforce he was using as camouflage was also the group of people who wrote and distributed the news globally. Unlike most civilians, they would undoubtedly know what the prime minister looked like, even in his elaborate disguise. It was only a matter of time before he was recognised. Remaining in Fleet Street was too high risk, even with the opportunity of identifying potential suspects on offer. Besides, Felix had the bill of sale and, with it, a name. It was the breakthrough he had hoped for and the first shred of meaningful evidence they'd received since the case began.

With little option but to leave and thankful to be alive, Felix lowered his head and disappeared back into London's dark backstreets and out of sight.

Sailortown

The clatter of breakfast trays woke Felix from a deep sleep the following morning. Having navigated his way along the River Thames to Old Pye Street from Houlston and Sons, he followed the secret tunnel to his study in Downing Street and made his way straight to his bedroom, collapsing on the bed with exhaustion. With everything that had happened, he was desperate for rest and passed out the second his head touched the soft sheets. Felix looked up from his bed to see the curtains drawn, and Humphrey stood over the bedside table, preparing breakfast.

'Should I address you by another name this morning or are you resuming the role of Felix Grey today?' asked Humphrey.

'Felix will do just fine,' replied Felix sitting up.

'Well, seeing as you're back to playing prime minister, I suppose I must inform you that the Home Secretary is here to see you.'

'What time is it?'

'Almost nine o'clock.'

'Why didn't you wake me?'

'A man who falls asleep fully clothed is probably in need of additional rest.'

Felix looked down, embarrassed to see that he was still wearing his suit from the previous evening.

'Now, will you want butter on your toast or strawberry jam?' Asked Humphrey. 'Mrs Hughes has made a fresh batch.'

'I can take it from here, thank you, Humphrey,' replied Felix, stepping out of bed. 'Inform the Home Secretary I'll be along in a few minutes.'

'Very well,' replied Humphrey taking his leave.

Felix took little time washing his face, brushing his hair, and changing into his suit before making his way to the study. He entered to find Thomas Percy drinking tea and eating scones.

'Apologies, Prime Minister,' he said, brushing the crumbs off his chin. 'Mrs Hughes insisted, and well, I hear her scones are somewhat of a speciality.'

'Is there news?' asked Felix.

'I'm afraid not. However, there has been another incident. This time at a printing house on Fleet Street.'

Felix felt a wave of anxiety wash over him.

'A fire at one of the smaller, family-run businesses,' continued Percy, 'a firm called, Houlston and Sons.'

'A fire?' questioned Felix.

'The flames ripped through the old wooden building in minutes, destroying everything in their path. A blazing inferno.

As you can imagine, the unions are up in arms. They've put it down to more faulty machinery and blame us for doing little to help the ailing printers modernise. I have sent word to the union expressing our regret and willingness to co-operate.'

Percy paused.

'What is it, Thomas?' asked Felix.

'They found the body of the old owner, in the ashes.'

Felix felt his legs go weak.

'He had his arms wrapped tightly around one of his old printing presses,' continued Percy. 'The firemen said it was almost like he was hugging it. Like he had chosen to burn with his beloved family shop. He'd worked there ever since he was a boy, you know.'

'How awful,' replied Felix.

'The fallout from this will likely be significant and drawn out. The unions and the opposition will use it as a further stick to beat us, regardless of the horror.'

It took Felix a few moments to absorb Percy's words. He found it difficult to process the terrible nature of Mr Houlston's death. How had this happened? It had been less than twenty-four hours since he had spoken with the old printer and escaped from his shop. Had turning on the faulty printer started the fire? It was spitting out lots of oil and smoke by the time he fled. Perhaps Mr Houlston didn't have the strength to work the lever with Alfred gone. It was made of heavy cast iron, after all. Suddenly it dawned on Felix. Mr Houlston wasn't hugging the old printing press out of some misplaced sense of loyalty or nostalgia; he was trying to turn it off.

'Are you alright, Felix?' asked Percy, noticing a change in him.

'I'm fine, thank you, Thomas. Just not sleeping very well,

what with all that's happened. Is that everything?'

'Almost,' replied Percy. 'I've been in touch with Commissioner Thompson. His officers have questioned everyone at The East India Club for a second time but have made no further progress. They have also investigated Lord Monteagle's affairs, and it appears his Indian businesses were bringing in a steady income, far above his expenditure.'

Felix looked back at Percy blankly. He had barely heard a word of the Home Secretary's update, his mind still swimming with the news of the fire and Mr Houlston's death.

'Thank you,' he said, turning to leave. 'Humphrey will see you out.'

'We will catch them, Prime Minister,' said Percy, sensing Felix's melancholy. 'We will right this wrong.'

The walk back to his private chambers was a lonely one. Never had Felix felt so utterly discouraged. Not only had he failed in his attempts to solve the case, but his impetuousness had directly resulted in the death of an older man and the destruction of his family business. He no longer felt fit for the job. The correct course of action would be to hand himself to the police and face trial for his part in the fire and Mr Houlston's death. The only thing holding Felix back was his reluctance to see his and Amelia's hard work evaporate into thin air and for the case to grind to a shuddering halt. With the police making little progress finding the missing lords or their abductors and the masons distancing themselves from the cards, Felix's undercover work was the only line of enquiry bearing any fruit. He would have to continue or hand his information over to Thompson and his officers, but having heard Amelia's warning, he could trust nobody, not even the police commissioner.

Felix's mind was spinning as he tried to balance the correct moral path forward with the most rational one. Mr Houlston was dead, but it made no logical sense to allow his tragic demise to impact the potential lives of the missing lords. They were still in danger, and Felix was obliged to help them if he could. He would not simply give up the search and condemn them to whatever fate their captors had in mind based on his own failings. Whilst there was still a chance to save them, he would push on with the case, resolved to hand himself over to the authorities once the peers were found and their abductors put behind bars. That, at least, would go some way to paying back the debt he now owed concerning the old printer's death, or so he hoped. In the meantime, he would set about finding Tom Fellows.

It was late when Felix eventually set off for London's notorious Docklands. He had spent the entire afternoon concocting a plausible story to address his target, should he find him. He considered taking the guise of a priest out to save the drunk and condemned souls of the Dockland's sin-strewn bars and brothels, but if Tom Fellows had played any part in the abductions, he would likely have little fear in the perceived wrath of God. He also considered playing the role of a police officer investigating a mistaken identity case, a lawyer looking to discuss a secret inheritance, and a property agent needing information to resolve a long-standing family land dispute. However, each character posed more problems than they solved.

After hours spent pacing around Old Pye Street, Felix finally decided the most palatable identity would be an illegal trafficker attempting to move illicit goods in and out of the docks and offering enormous rewards for any assistance. Fortunately, there were several pages of information on *London's Docklands* and *Britain's Untameable River Trade* in the giant encyclopaedias at Old Pye Street. Felix gathered as much knowledge as possible, reading about the type of boats the traders used, the cargo they were permitted to carry, and the required licences. He removed a flat cap from the Old Pye Street store, a merchant's jacket and rubber boots and used the full-scale model of London to plot his course.

The journey to the Docklands was uneventful. Felix flagged down one of the new Herald petrol cabs, guiding its driver through a warren of quays and wharves along the Thames to a notorious drinking hole the old seafarers had affectionately nicknamed, Sailortown. A ramshackle area centred around Wapping, Shadwell and Ratcliffe, Sailortown boasted a dingy array of pubs, opium dens and brothels. Many men had lost their fortunes and their minds in Sailortown, but it hadn't stopped the nightly stream of visitors arriving to indulge in the district's dark pleasures.

Felix stepped out of the Herald and onto the grimy Docklands pavement. He paid the driver double to linger for a few minutes, hoping to get noticed and create the illusion of wealth. If there was one thing that attracted the eyes of sailors and merchants alike, it was the prospect of making easy money. Felix noted the number of drunk and destitute figures already sleeping rough as he made his way towards the Prospect of Whitby, a lively-looking pub bursting at the seams with customers and chaos. He bustled his way through the crowded entrance securing himself a table by the bar and ordered a large bottle of rum. It didn't take long for his presence to attract the interest of two thirsty sailors who pulled up chairs alongside him.

'You know, it can be awful lonely drinking a bottle of rum on your own,' said the elder of the two sailors.

'It can even be considered rude in some cultures,' continued his younger mate.

Felix took a moment to consider his strategy. He needed to

show a level of hospitality but also make it clear that his company and, importantly, his rum did not come free.

'I suppose it is enjoyed better when shared with others,' he agreed, signalling for the maid to bring two more glasses.

'Best social lubricant there is,' said the older sailor, licking his lips greedily.

'However, I find a drink tastes better when it has been earned rather than given. Wouldn't you agree?' asked Felix.

'What are you after?' asked the older sailor.

'Information,' replied Felix.

'We don't have any information,' spat the younger sailor, rising from his seat.

'Not so fast,' growled the older sailor, pulling his companion back to his seat. 'That's just his inexperience speaking,' he said, turning to reassure Felix. 'What do you want to know?'

'I'm looking for someone to help me smuggle in a large shipment of goods,' said Felix.

'That should be easy; the Docklands are full of men.'

'Yes, but I'm looking for one in particular,' continued Felix pouring the men a drink. 'He has come recommended.'

The younger sailor looked around the bar nervously, cradling his rum. 'What's this shipment then?' he asked.

'The contents of the shipment are of no concern to you,' replied Felix, raising the bottle of rum temptingly.

'I suppose they're not,' agreed the older sailor, knocking back his drink and lifting his glass for another measure. 'What's this man's name then?' He asked.

'Tom Fellows,' replied Felix.

There was a moment's silence. Felix could sense the name had struck a chord, particularly with the younger sailor, who quickly gulped down his drink, hopeful of leaving.

The older sailor, however, hesitated.

'Do you know him?' asked Felix.

'We know him alright,' he replied. 'The man you want is landlord at the George Inn.'

The older sailor leant forward to claim his prize, only for Felix to snatch the bottle of rum off the table. There was more he wanted to know before giving up his best bargaining chip; how long had they known Tom Fellows? Had they ever met the missing Lords? Were they ever seen in the Prospect of Whitby or the George Inn? But it wasn't that simple. The mere mention of lords or any men of title in the Docklands could have severe repercussions. Where there was wealth and privilege, there was also the law, and the law was not welcome in Sailortown.

'Which George Inn?' asked Felix, aware that many of the pubs in London had the same or similar names.

The old sailor looked Felix up and down.

'Limehouse,' he said, leaning over the table and gripping the top of the rum bottle. 'Though, I'd stay away from it if I were you.'

Felix released his hold on the bottle, and the sailors whisked it away to a dark corner of the pub, determined to enjoy the remaining rum and lose themselves for the night.

Outside, Felix hailed another Herald. He gave the driver his destination, and they set off through Sailortown towards Limehouse and the George Inn. Felix used the time to question the driver on his knowledge of the pub and its clientele. He explained how the George Inn was once a prominent destination for royal navy officers and wealthy merchants before falling into disrepair as the punters and their money began to move along the docks to the more buoyant areas around Wapping. In the last few years, there had been a sizeable drop in customers requesting to be taken to the pub; unless it was late in the evening and heavily drunk, they desperately needed somewhere cheap to rest their heads.

True to the driver's words, the area around the George Inn was eerily quiet and run down when they arrived. Even though the journey had taken less than a few minutes, the contrast between Limehouse and Wapping was stark. It felt as though they were in a completely different city, one suffering the fallout of a long war or a crippling epidemic. Limehouse had previously been one of the most important ports along the Thames. Its thriving trade and bustling nightlife had attracted commerce from all over the continent. But several outbreaks of cholera, and the newly constructed ports further west, along the Thames, had led to it becoming increasingly unpopular. In the last few years, several Chinese communities had moved in, further decreasing its value, and filling the area with tea houses and opium dens.

At the centre of Limehouse, standing as a symbol of its past wealth and sudden decline, was the George Inn. Felix stared in disbelief at the pub's vast frame and high structure. It was a towering building compared to the inner-city pubs, particularly those around Downing Street and the Square Mile, and although in need of repair, it retained a decadent elegance that stirred in Felix a desire to see it restored to its former glory. Perhaps, if the George Inn rose like a phoenix from out of the Limehouse ashes, it would generate some interest in the area and possibly bring back some much-needed trade and investment.

Felix stepped out of the cab and approached the faded pub door. He could see through the window that the lights were off, and the pub was no longer in use. He knocked gently and waited. Realising that anyone upstairs would have little chance of hearing him, he banged harder, sending a loud, echoing rumble into the silent Limehouse night. But there was still no answer.

Suddenly, Felix felt the glare of someone's eyes on his back and a presence move in the shadows behind him. He spun around, trying to catch a glimpse of whatever he had sensed in his peripheral vision, but there was still nothing there, only darkness. He scanned the area meticulously, but with no signs of life inside the pub or out in the street, and with the hour increasingly late, he finally returned to the cab, resolved to continue his search for Tom Fellows in the daylight.

The George Inn

Tom Fellows struck a match and lifted the flame towards his old lamp, casting a dim glow over the room he kept above the George Inn. It was late, and he had only just returned from a night of running errands.

He threw off his wet coat and sat down, happy for a moment's rest. He took hold of the satchel by his feet, carefully untying the knot. There wasn't much inside, a hunk of bread and half a bottle of whiskey to keep the cold and hunger at bay. It had been months since he'd eaten a proper meal, and he longed for something hot to warm his bones. He tore into the bread, washing each piece down with a large gulp of whiskey, then leant back and closed his eyes, willing on sleep, when a loud bang on the cellar door disturbed his peace.

'What now?' he muttered, agitated by the intrusion.

Tom forced his weary body up from the chair, his bones creaking with every movement, and made his way down the crooked staircase towards the pub.

The old barroom was faded and run down, and the smell of stale beer hung in the air, hovering between the few tables and chairs that still rested on the inn's broken and uneven floorboards. The elegantly tiled walls and long wooden beams hinted at a time when the inn had been popular and bustling with life. But Tom's drinking and gambling had hit the inn's profits hard, and he'd struggled to maintain the George, allowing it to slip into disrepair. It had since become a halfway house for sailors and merchants looking for a cheap place to sleep before going out to sea. They would often turn up drunk, looking for a warm bed or shelter from the rain, much to Tom's annoyance.

Tom carried on through the barroom towards the cellar. It was a damp room with a low ceiling and scores of beer barrels lining the walls and stone floor. Each barrel had a strategic part to play in the event of a raid on the George or an unwelcome guest showing up. The barrels stacked by the door were to block an intruder's entrance, whereas those stacked by the stairs were to cover Tom's escape, should he need to be away on his heels.

Three more loud thuds shook the cellar door. Tom hesitated for a moment. Something about them seemed off. They weren't as erratic as usual. They didn't follow the chaotic pattern of a drunk banging on the door, hoping for some respite from the cold. They were too considered, too equal in tone, and spread out to give him enough time to hear them. Tom felt a wave of anxiety wash over him. Something about this visitor made him nervous. He hoped it was just another down and out in need of some shelter, but it was earlier than usual, and deep down, he knew that to be wishful thinking.

Over the past twelve months, Tom had struggled to pay his bills and had turned to the Docklands underbelly to try and make ends meet. It had been easy work in the main, picking up and dropping off packages to other links in the chain, but recently things had become more dangerous, and the last few jobs had involved some muscle work, a practice that made Tom feel very uncomfortable.

His father had always warned him about the dangers of dishonest work. He would say, *don't go upsetting people because, one day, someone might just remember your face and catch you unawares.* It was a piece of advice Tom had taken to heart, probably the only advice his father had ever given him that resonated. The Docklands were large, and there was a constant stream of people coming and going, but it was still easy to bump into familiar faces, and the last few jobs had left Tom feeling vulnerable.

'Who's that then?' He called out.

'Ezra!' came the reply.

The name sent a shiver down Tom's spine. He quickly placed his lamp on one of the barrels and reached for his keys, unbolting the door.

Ezra Fox was a large man, tall with a barrel chest and bulging arms. His long grey-streaked hair covered most of the scar that stretched along his cheek to the top of his forehead. But the red patch that covered his left eye was harder to conceal, and Ezra paraded it proudly as a badge of honour. He had lost his eye in a street fight with a drunken merchant when he was only sixteen. The encounter had brought him widespread fame and notoriety, which he'd used over the years to significant effect, governing the Docklands and building his criminal network. He stepped forward; his large frame barely able to squeeze through the narrow cellar door. Tom took a few steps back. He had never seen Ezra in person; he usually received orders from one of his lackeys but not the great man himself. Ezra's presence meant one of two things; either Tom was in grave danger, or he was about to be in over his head.

'Are you alone?' asked Ezra, his good eye boring into Tom, probing him for any hesitation or signs of deceit.

'Yes,' replied Tom nervously.

'Good. I have a special delivery for you.'

Ezra raised his gnarled fingers to his lips and whistled loudly into the night. Two beams of light cut through the darkness, growing brighter as a motorised van approached, stopping outside the cellar. The driver opened his door and stepped out, followed by a crew of men dressed in overalls.

'Where do you want them?' he asked.

'Put them in the corner, out of the way,' replied Ezra.

The driver signalled to his men, and they began unloading the van's cargo, several large wooden barrels.

'What's all this?' asked Tom, trying to hide his anxiety.

'I need you to store some ale for me,' replied Ezra. 'It's not for drinking mind. I want it well hidden and out of the way. Understood?'

'Of course.' replied Tom.

Ezra turned his attention to the cellar as the men rolled the barrels in and began to stack them. He took a moment to inspect the cargo, checking each barrel for the correct markings, occasionally rocking them to listen to the sound the contents made. Tom quietly sank into the shadows, hoping not to draw any more attention to himself, but Ezra didn't take long to set his gaze back on the errant landlord. Like most predators, Ezra could smell fear, and Tom's was everywhere. He stepped forward, reaching into his pocket and removed a leather wallet.

'For your trouble,' he said, placing a handful of banknotes on one of the barrels. 'And be thankful for that. If I had my way, you'd be doing this out of the goodness of your black heart. But my employer insisted you be paid, to keep you honest.'

It was the first time Tom heard mention of anyone above Ezra. He assumed that the pyramid of crime in the Docklands ended with Ezra at its apex. He wondered who this employer was and how formidable his character must be to have such a notorious figure under his control.

Tom took the money and placed it under his shirt. He knew that any hesitation or reluctance would be seen as a sign of weakness or distrust and could have grave consequences. Ezra's ruthless streak was legendary. Tom had heard countless tales in the pubs and inns around Sailortown of people disappearing or, even worse, their bodies showing up on the banks of the Thames. He did not want to become the next pub story, or the next body, bloated and swollen, floating down the river. Instead, he rolled up his sleeves and set to work, helping the men move the remaining barrels. It was tiring work, and he struggled to push the large wooden containers across the uneven stone floor. But with Ezra looking on, he summoned whatever strength he had and drove the barrels forward, stacking them with the rest of the cargo.

With the last barrel in place and Ezra satisfied, Tom finally sat down to catch his breath. His nose filled with a heavy and unfamiliar scent as he inhaled the dank cellar air. He looked around but couldn't sense where it was coming from. It didn't smell like beer or ale, nor did it smell of the cellar. It was musky and burnt his nostrils and throat the more he breathed it in. He subtly eyed the markings on the barrels. The lettering was foreign;

German, he thought, but unsure, he was reluctant to press Ezra on the matter. It was clear that whatever was being stored in the barrels wasn't ale. But the more he knew about his mysterious delivery, the greater the risk. It was far safer to be kept in the dark than to ask questions and try to understand.

Tom covered the barrels with a large sheet.

'They'll be safe here. You have my word,' he said.

'Your word!?' mocked Ezra. 'What good is the word of a drunken wretch? I prefer to have your fear.'

Ezra stepped forward, raising himself to his full intimidating height, forcing Tom to take a step backwards, nearly losing his balance.

'If anyone asks,' he growled menacingly, 'we were never here.'

'You were never here,' replied Tom, shaken to his core. 'None of you were!'

Ezra waited for the last of his men to leave. He reached for the lamp and curled his fingers around the flame, pinching the wick and extinguishing the light.

In the black silence, Tom heard the cellar door close and the motorised van pull away, leaving him alone in the dark, covered in fear and the smell of burning air.

Confidence Vote

The sun had barely risen the following day when Felix set off from Downing Street for the short walk to Westminster. Having called an impromptu cabinet meeting to discuss the mounting pressure on his government, he'd decided to work out of his parliamentary offices for the day rather than Number 10, hoping a change of scenery might lift his spirits.

Naturally, Humphrey had protested, aggrieved that Felix should leave so early without a warm breakfast in his belly or enough time to read the day's newspapers. But Felix liked to walk when he had things on his mind. It allowed him to work through his problems with a clear head. He'd covered several miles over the years and, in that time, solved many challenges.

However, today, Felix had more on his mind than usual. Having traced Tom Fellow's whereabouts to the dilapidated George Inn, he had missed the landlord and the opportunity to question him on the printers and the card. Unwilling to give up the chase, Felix had paid the cab driver extra to stake out the George Inn and inform him the moment Fellows returned. A deal the driver was all too eager to accept and one that Felix could only hope he would honour.

Felix arrived at Westminster to the sound of silence. He made his way through St Stephen's Hall on the western front of Parliament towards Central Lobby, a lofty octagonal stone room with an intricately tiled floor and mosaic-covered vault; the crossroads at which the Lords, Commons and Westminster Hall met. He had planned to continue through the Commons Corridor moving east towards the Cabinet Offices when he was intercepted by Thomas Percy.

'Thomas?' He said, a little startled. 'You're at it early this morning.'

'Unfortunately, so,' said Percy, the strain of recent events beginning to show. 'I erm…'

'Can't sleep, either?'

'It's been almost a week since the lords' disappearance, and our leads are drying up. I'm at a loss as to what to do next.'

Felix placed a consoling hand on Percy's broad back. He could sympathise with his colleague's despair; it was a feeling he had become used to of late.

'We will catch them, Thomas,' he said, echoing the Home Secretary's consoling words the previous day. 'We will right this wrong.'

Percy nodded his thanks.

'Better dash, I've a meeting with the Speaker, probably

another hour discussing the correlation between lunchtime drinking and falling standards in the house. Wish me luck!' He chimed, trying to muster some of his usual zest, before turning and disappearing back through Central Lobby towards the Speaker's chambers.

Felix continued in the opposite direction towards the Cabinet Offices. He'd decided the previous evening to address the complaints and criticisms he'd faced in the House of Commons the day before. He began to write a detailed response to the question of the British military and its constant need for money in light of the emerging American and German forces. He also wrote about the British Empire as a beacon for democracy and social welfare. Naturally, this led to addressing the conditions in the mines and factories and the continued plight of the working class, a topic that resonated now more than ever, given the tragic deaths of Arthur Jenkins and Mr Houlston.

The more Felix wrote, the more heartfelt his words became, and his document began to take the form of a personal statement rather than a manifesto. It felt liberating. With everything that had happened over the past few days and with little left to lose, he was suddenly free of the constraints of his position. It was unheard of for a prime minister to take a moral stance on such matters. To speak directly from the heart was seen as a weakness, a political suicide of sorts, but to Felix, it was progress and something that had been simmering in him long before the abductions.

Filled with a renewed sense of purpose, Felix waited anxiously for his colleagues in the cabinet to arrive. He watched the clock, eagerly counting down the minutes. The promise of decisive action made him feel like a child again, eagerly waiting for his parents to return home to tell them about the day's adventures and share his stories. Fortunately, he did not have long to wait before the office doors swung open, and cabinet members started to filter in. He watched as they took their seats, noting their gloomy faces. He would take great pleasure in turning that negativity on its head.

Among those entering were senior cabinet ministers James Henry, the Chancellor of the Exchequer, Charles Joyce, the Lord Privy Seal, and the Secretary of State for Foreign Affairs, Francis Wood, followed by their undersecretaries and assistants. They quickly took to their seats, making minimal eye contact with Felix as they entered.

With barely half the table complete, the steady stream of members entering finally stopped. Felix looked around, confused. His eyes questioned those present on why half his cabinet had chosen to snub his request for a meeting, but none of his colleagues would meet his gaze. He waited a few more minutes in the vain hope that perhaps they were running late or had been caught up, but it was evident from the mood inside the room that this was wishful thinking; they were not coming. Felix's ambition burst like a parachute, yanking him out of his lofty hopes and bringing him back to Earth with a thud. What good was a prime minister if he couldn't even form a cabinet?

The uneasy tension was broken by Percy's sudden arrival.

'Sorry I'm late,' he said, slightly out of breath, 'my meeting took a bit of an unexpected turn.'

'At least you're here, Thomas.' said Felix soberly. 'As you can see, most of our colleagues didn't even manage that.'

'Yes. Unfortunately, that comes as no surprise,' said Percy, the promise of more bad news written on his face. 'It appears the members have tabled a motion of no confidence in your leadership.'

'They mean to vote me out,' replied Felix, taken aback.

'Supported by some of our members, and cabinet.'

The news hit Felix like a sledgehammer to the temple. Never in British political history had a governing party and its cabinet turned on its leader in such a manner. It was beyond damning. Felix looked around the room at the handful of cabinet members present. How many of them had been tempted to join the conspiracy? How many of them could he really trust?

'We have a week before the vote to build our case with the house and win back favour.' continued Percy. 'It's not long, but it's something. We still have a fighting chance.'

'A chance?' questioned Felix. 'There is only one sensible course of action available now.'

'Think of the odds, Thomas,' said Henry James.

'Clearly, the odds are stacked against us. But opinions change quickly in the house,' said Percy.

Once again, Felix had left it to the Home Secretary to encourage and reassure everyone. How many times had his loyal friend propped up his ailing premiership over the years? He deserved so much more, thought Felix; a knighthood, no, a sainthood, not the daily stream of problems that continued to land on his desk.

'Here,' said Felix, sliding his work across the table.

'What is it?' asked Percy.

'An honest account of where we are as a country and plans for the future, for what they're worth. Do what you will with them. Show them to our supporters and even our enemies. They may make a difference, although I doubt it very much.'

Felix turned to leave.

'Where are you going?' asked Percy.

'I have something pressing to attend to.'

'More pressing than this?'

'Speak to our members, Thomas. Make a list of who we can rely on and who we have lost. We'll review it tomorrow.'

The journey back to Downing Street seemed longer than usual. Felix noticed every horse, cart, flower and falling leaf. He even paid attention to the mischievous squirrels and swans cautiously following each passer-by, hoping to be fed. Time was such an odd concept, he thought to himself, reflecting on the past few days; it hurries by so quickly when you need it but has a nasty habit of lingering when you don't.

Back at his study in Number 10, Felix grabbed a bottle of scotch and a tumbler and disappeared through the secret walkway towards Old Pye Street. He sat at the desk, opened the bottle, and poured himself a large glass lifting it to his mouth, ready to drown his sorrows and lament his failures, when he noticed the portraits of former prime ministers hung on the walls. Felix studied the stern, determined faces of Sir Robert Peel, Viscount Palmerston, Benjamin Disraeli, William Pitt and the Iron Duke. How had he followed in the footsteps of these great men? How had he walked the same halls, worked at the same desk, and occupied the same great seat of power? The more he thought about it, the more absurd it felt.

Felix's soul-searching was suddenly disturbed by a sound at the Old Pye Street door. He sprang to his feet quietly and crept into the narrow hallway towards the front of the rickety old building. Through the small stained-glass window, he could see the silhouette of a man snooping around outside. Although anxious, Felix remained completely still, eager not to draw attention to his presence. The figure approached the door and lent down, slipping a folded note underneath. Felix waited for him to leave, then grabbed the paper and unfolded it, reading the message:

The landlord has returned to the George Inn.

Felix stared at the words in shock. He'd been so overcome with the no-confidence motion and his self-doubt that he'd forgotten entirely about his deal with the cab driver. Suddenly presented with a lifeline, Felix quickly changed, replacing his formal clothes with a pair of workman's trousers, a merchant's coat, and rubber boots. He stuffed the note in his pocket, gave the prime ministers one final look and then stepped out onto Old Pye Street with a renewed sense of purpose.

Having flagged down a cab on Victoria Street and instructed the driver to take him to the Docklands, Felix used the journey to reacquaint himself with his cover story, determined to master the details and avoid another tragedy like the one he'd created at Houlston and Sons.

Arriving at Limehouse under cover of night, Felix stepped out of the cab and approached the run-down pub. He knocked loudly on the faded door sending a series of thuds echoing into the surrounding streets. He stepped back and waited anxiously. Concerned that he'd arrived too late to catch the landlord at home again, Felix suddenly heard the faint sound of footsteps coming from inside.

'Who is it?' called a voice from behind the door.

'I'm here to see Tom Fellows,' replied Felix.

'I asked who you were?' repeated the agitated voice.

'My name is John Bishop. I'm an importer of foreign goods. I was hoping to conduct a little business with Mr Fellows.'

'What kind of goods?'

'The kind I'm not comfortable speaking about on an East London Street, full of listening ears.'

Felix waited, worried he might have scared the landlord off, when he heard metal bolts being drawn, and the door finally swung open to reveal Tom Fellows.

'Quickly then,' said Fellows, ushering Felix inside.

Felix was surprised by the landlord's meek appearance and nervous disposition. He had been expecting a hardened sailor with a weathered face and battle scars. Instead, Fellows was a small, frail-looking man with blotchy skin, a red nose, and a pitiful frame. His eyes looked like he should have been in his middle years, but his body told a different story, one of alcohol consumption and opium abuse.

'You can never be too careful,' said Fellows, leading Felix through the forlorn inn towards a narrow staircase. 'Especially around here. There are crooks and villains everywhere.'

Fellows lit a bright lamp and led the way down the stairs to the inn's dark cellar. Felix followed, covering his eyes from the glare of the flame. He opened them at the bottom of the staircase to find himself in a dank room surrounded by barrels.

'Now, what's this business you wanted to discuss?' asked Fellows.

'I have a shipment of goods coming into the Docklands. I need a crew I can trust and someone who knows how to get them past the authorities undetected,' replied Felix.

'Why me?'

'Because you have a reputation for smuggling,' said Felix, looking around the cellar, 'and needing the money.'

'How much are you offering, exactly?' called a rasping voice from the darkness.

Felix spun around to see a tall figure standing in the shadows. 'Who's asking?'

Ezra stepped forward, revealing his menacing frame and

prominent red eyepatch. He crossed the room and unbolted the cellar door, allowing a group of rugged-looking men to pour into the cellar. Felix's heart skipped a beat. He recognised the two sailors he had questioned at the Prospect of Whitby the previous evening amongst the rabble.

'Is this him?' asked Ezra, addressing the sailors.

'That's the man,' said the younger of the two.

Ezra turned and approached Felix, his intimidating size casting a shadow over the cellar walls.

'So, tell me about your shipment yours?'

'It's arriving in a fortnight from Iberia,' said Felix, trying to maintain an air of confidence, 'full to the rafters with sherry and port. Enough to flood the London market and push out the competition.'

'I haven't heard about any shipments.' said Ezra, 'And I make it my business to hear about everything coming in and out of these docks, especially if there's a tax due.'

'It's been kept secret. You never know who you can trust these days,' replied Felix, shooting Fellows a stern look.

'A fine story, I'll give you that.' said Ezra, signalling to his men.

They rushed forward and took hold of Felix in a flash, forcing him to the ground.

'What is the meaning of this?' protested Felix.

He tried to fight them off, but with so many, the men didn't take long to subdue him, wrapping a heavy sailor's rope around Felix's chest and arms and tying him to one of the barrels.

'You're making a big mistake,' he called out, 'there's enough money in this deal to make us all rich.'

'Now, why would I want to be rich?' chortled Ezra. 'Where's the fun in that?'

'If it's not money you're after, then what is it?' asked Felix.

'I want to know why you're here. I've got informants all over these docks, and none has ever heard of you or any shipment.'

Felix tried to think of a convincing answer, but his mind was blank. He'd never been in a situation where his life was genuinely in danger. This was an entirely new experience, and one Felix lacked the tools to navigate. He could feel the blood draining from his face and a cold sweat taking over his body. The more he tried to concentrate, the more his thoughts scattered.

'Well?' pressed Ezra, beginning to lose his patience.

Felix took a few deep breaths, trying to regulate his racing heart. It was a method he'd been taught by the family doctor, who'd learnt the technique on a visit to India, tending to an ailing Himalayan prince. Fortunately, the breathing was enough to calm Felix down and restore clarity to his thoughts. It was pointless trying to carry on with his current pretence. His merchant story had been figured out from the start. The only thing it had accomplished was to lead him here, to this point, strapped to a barrel and fighting for his life. He had to think quickly and devise another character that might resonate enough to get him out of his precarious situation.

'I'm a detective at Scotland Yard,' he blurted out.

Felix felt the mood in the cellar change immediately. They were criminals, lawbreakers to the core, but none of them wanted the abduction of a high-profile police officer hanging over their heads.

'The Commissioner has assigned me to gather information on a case,' he continued. 'I just want to ask a few questions.'

The men anxiously turned to Ezra, hoping he might see sense and untie their prisoner. But instead, he spun around to face Tom Fellows.

'If you have anything of value upstairs, now is the time to fetch it.' he warned the landlord.

'What do you mean?' asked Fellows.

Ezra approached one of the barrels. He removed a cudgel from inside his long coat and struck the wooden frame until a crack appeared, and a stream of fine black powder began to pour out.

Fellows looked at Ezra in disbelief.

'This pub is all I have left,' he pleaded.

'All YOU have left?' scoffed Ezra. 'The last I checked, the pub was under new ownership.'

'Yes, for now. But I was going to raise the money and buy it back…'

'Enough!' Bellowed Ezra. 'The George has been compromised. God knows how many more blue boys will show up. It's time to go.'

Ezra grabbed the barrel in his large hands and spun it around, dragging it across the cellar floor, creating a gunpowder trail back to the other barrels.

'What about the copper?' asked the young sailor.

'One less nark to worry about.'

Felix felt his heart sink. They meant to kill him. To blow him up, along with the downtrodden inn. 'Let me go!' he shouted in desperation. 'You can't do this!'

Ezra's men turned to leave.

'Let me go! Please! You can't. I'm the…'

Felix's words were drowned out by the cellar doors closing. Within moments the men had cleared out, covering the room in darkness. He continued shouting his pleas into the void, but it was no good; they weren't coming back.

Felix sat back against the barrel. He could hear their muffled voices outside, followed by the sound of car engines and then vehicles driving away. After a few moments, all that remained was silence. He suddenly felt a wave of hope engulf him. Maybe they'd forgotten about him or had decided to spare the pub after all. Either way, it was good news. He breathed a sigh of relief when he suddenly heard the faint sound of a match striking and the crackling noise of the gunpowder catching alight. He watched the cellar door as a tiny spark appeared, entering beneath its warped wooden frame. It moved across the floor at speed, gathering pace as it ate through the meandering black line, drawing closer to him and the surrounding pile of barrels.

Felix tried to stretch out his leg, hoping to reach the gunpowder and break the line, but it was agonisingly just out of reach. Ezra was far too wise to make a mistake like that. He'd laid the gunpowder close enough to give Felix hope but far enough away to make it unreachable.

Felix watched as the spark darted past his outstretched legs towards its destination. He had often read about the emotions people were supposed to feel when faced with their own death, but he did not feel anything besides regret. He closed his eyes, concentrating on the depth and rhythm of his breath, hoping the end would somehow be easier to bear by remaining calm. He began a countdown in his head, another trick to take his mind off the spark and the barrels, when he heard a noise outside the cellar door. Someone was pulling at the lock, trying to get in.

'Help! Help! I'm in here!' he shouted. 'Quickly, there's gunpowder. You don't have long!'

The door finally burst open, and to Felix's surprise, Mr Houston's young apprentice Alfred rushed in. He froze for a second, taking in the scene.

'Quickly!' shouted Felix, motioning towards the spark

hurrying along the line of gunpowder.

Alfred rushed over and stamped on it before sweeping the line of gunpowder away with his foot and breaking its connection to the barrels.

Felix opened his mouth to thank the young man, then turned to his side and vomited.

'Sorry, it's the shock.' he apologised.

Alfred nodded, unsure where to look. He leant down and untied Felix.

'What were you doing outside?' asked Felix, wiping his mouth.

'I've been here for the past few days, ever since the fire and…'

Alfred stopped, unable to finish his sentence. Felix looked at the struggling young man.

'Thank you,' he said warmly.

Alfred helped Felix to his feet.

'I take it you know I'm not a tax clerk?' asked Felix.

'I was listening at the door.'

'Why were you there?'

Alfred hesitated. 'It sounds a bit foolish now that I think about it.'

'Try me.'

Alfred took a breath. 'I was watching the place, waiting for the landlord to return so I could take him to the police.'

'That's admirable, but not a job for a boy your age. These people are dangerous.'

'I know,' agreed Alfred. 'But after what they did to the shop and Mr Houlston… It's just not right!'

'What do you mean?' asked Felix.

'It's all my fault,' replied Alfred, welling up. 'If I hadn't told them, you'd been in the shop asking questions. Me and my big mouth!'

'I can help you, Alfred.' said Felix, comforting the young man. 'But I need to know what happened once you left the shop.'

Alfred nodded, taking a few more breaths to hold back the tears.

'After Mr Houlston sent me out, I came here. We always picked up our scotch from the George. It's the cheapest place around, and the landlord would send us business from time to time. He'd always ask me how things were going at the shop, and sometimes, if there was anything of interest, he'd give me a nip of something warm to drink in exchange. The other day, when he asked about the shop, you'd come in looking to see our books and asking questions about our orders. I thought he might find that interesting, so I told him. Only, he got all nervous and said he needed to leave. He even gave me the scotch for free. When I returned, you'd gone, and Mr Houlston was closing everything down. One of the printers was kicking up, so I fixed that before turning it in for the night. You see, I ain't got a home, so Mr Houlston let me stay in the back of the shop. It'd been a long day, and I fell straight off. I woke up to some noise coming from the shop floor. I came out to see the walls all covered in flames and Mr Houlston... tied to the printer. I tried to free him but couldn't cut through the rope in time. I tried my best, I swear!'

'It's okay, Alfred,' said Felix, placing a hand on his shoulder. 'It's not your fault.'

'The smoke got so thick, so quickly, I just couldn't see him. But I could hear him. He begged me to leave, to save myself. I didn't know what to do, so I just ran. I knew the shop floor like the back of my hand and found my way out. When I got outside, that's when I saw him, the landlord, just standing there, watching.

Making sure it all burnt to the ground. He didn't see me though. His eyes were fixed on the flames.'

Alfred stopped to take a breath.

'I came to the inn a few nights later to find him. That's when I saw you standing outside, knocking on the door.'

'That was you?'

Alfred nodded. 'I was waiting for him.'

Felix took a moment to process the information. Alfred's revelations had left a bittersweet taste in his mouth. He was relieved not to have been directly responsible for the fire and the old printer's death, but his presence at the shop had set a series of fatal events in motion. Suddenly, it all began to make sense. Once Mr Houlston was discovered, he had hoped to charm Felix into turning a blind eye to the illegal work he'd conducted for Tom Fellows. He'd known that the card job was crooked, but he needed the money to keep the shop afloat. Felix remembered the old printer's fatal words, *at any cost.*

Felix turned his attention back to the young apprentice. He had lost a little weight since they first met, and his clothes looked a bit tired and ragged. Having had a home and a trade with a considerate mentor, he was now jobless and destitute, the victim of a political game far above his station or comprehension.

Felix considered giving him some money and sending him to a hostel. But how long would that last? How long until he was out on the streets again, another lost soul sleeping rough with the rest of London's homeless. If he was going to make any meaningful change to the lives of the poor and needy, it would have to start now.

'Do you have anywhere to go?' he asked.

Alfred shook his head, embarrassed.

'Well, I may know of a place,' said Felix, leading the young apprentice out of the cellar and back onto London's cobbled streets.

It was close to midnight when Felix and Alfred arrived at Old Pye Street. Felix watched his young companion examine his surroundings. He had probably assumed that travelling with a gentleman like Felix would mean heading for an upmarket part of town rather than one of London's run-down and forgotten back streets.

They approached a thin terraced house. Felix opened the door and ushered Alfred inside. They made their way along the narrow hallway towards the sizeable oval office. Felix turned on the generator, casting a dim light over the secret room and bringing it to life. Alfred looked around in awe. He had never seen anything like it; the large oak desk, the telephone switchboard, the hanging portraits, the full-scale model of London. It was like being dropped into an adventure story, not real life.

Felix observed the young man struggling to make sense of it all. He'd thought long and hard in the cab about how best to explain it to Alfred, but nothing he could say would prepare the young apprentice for such a moment. He simply had to see Old Pye Street for himself.

'You're probably wondering what this is all about?' asked Felix.

'You could say that' mumbled Alfred.

'The truth is, I'm not a tax clerk, a police officer, or even a detective,' said Felix. 'I'm the Prime Minister.'

'Give over,' laughed Alfred, 'you can't be the Prime Minister.'

'I realise it's a lot to take in, and there'll be plenty of time for explanations tomorrow. But, for now, we could probably both use some rest. I'll be back in the morning with food and clean clothes,' said Felix, patting the mesmerised youngster on the back.

Alfred looked up at Felix, a hint of belief suddenly visible in his glazed eyes.

'Sleep well, Alfred,' smiled Felix before turning towards the hallway and the tunnel back to Number 10.

The Gambler

The kitchen was alive with activity when Felix entered the following morning. The staff were busy preparing the household breakfast while Mrs Hughes tended to a large basket, packed to the brim with some of her favourite homemade delights. Felix had told Humphrey the previous evening that he would be travelling for the day and needed a sizeable basket of food prepared for the journey. As usual, the wily old steward had questioned him on the nature of his mysterious trip, and unsure how to explain the past few days' events to his faithful friend, Felix was forced to concoct an elaborate cover story.

'There's freshly baked bread, scones and biscuits in there, along with some smoked meat, apples from the garden, and my famous homemade jam,' explained Mrs Hughes, proudly folding a towel over the basket.

'What's in the homemade jam?' asked Felix.

'I'll agree to share my secrets when you agree to a month's paid leave.'

'A month!?' chortled Felix.

A ripple of laughter spread among the listening kitchen staff.

'You don't get owt for nowt in this world, Prime Minister.' said Mrs Hughes, handing Felix the basket. 'We learn that lesson quickly up north.'

Felix thanked the head cook and returned to his office with the basket. Waiting on his desk was a pile of freshly cleaned uniforms he'd requested from the laundry room, alongside some basic grooming apparatus. He took the supplies and returned through the fireplace towards Old Pye Street.

To his amazement, the secret office had come to life. The previously dull bulbs shone brightly, and the lifeless telephone switchboard had miraculously awakened, with small lights flicking on and off as calls were being made or hung up on the exchange. Felix looked around the room in disbelief, finally locating Alfred sitting by the buzzing generator covered in wires and old machine parts.

'I thought you might like to see it all up and running,' said Alfred, trying to twist himself out of the mess. 'Would be a shame to waste a machine like this.'

'But how did you manage it?' asked Felix.

'I don't know. Just good at fixing things, I s'ppose. D'you wanna give it a try?'

Alfred held out the telephone mouthpiece and receiver. Felix took them in his hands and sat down at the switchboard. He considered who to call and connected one of the cords to a socket.

'Professor Amelia Woodruff. Corpus Christi. Oxford,' he announced into the mouthpiece, waiting to be connected. He looked around the newly lit room, suddenly vibrant and ready for service, and smiled warmly at the young apprentice.

'Thank you.'

'For what, exactly?' came a voice through the receiver. 'My unrelenting charm and intellect?'

'Amelia, it's me,' said Felix, lifting the mouthpiece.

'Yes, I know. I could tell from the heartfelt tone and, frankly, saccharine sincerity. You made it out of the printers alive, then?'

'You haven't heard the news?' asked Felix, surprised.

'News?' repeated Amelia, enthused by the promise of misadventure.

Felix explained the past few days' events, starting with his visit to Houlston and Sons before moving on to the motion of no confidence and Alfred's timely intervention at the George Inn. Unsurprisingly, Amelia was sour to have missed out on the fun but was pleased to hear that Felix had escaped unscathed. To Felix, however, the past few days had been anything but fun, and he certainly didn't feel unscathed. Over the past twenty-four hours, his position in government had become untenable, and he'd managed to put his life in danger, only surviving by the smallest of coincidences.

There was, however, one saving grace. Having repeatedly played out his ordeal at the George, Felix had hit upon something he thought might be helpful to the case. While tied to the barrel, he had witnessed a brief exchange between Tom Fellows and the one-eyed man, suggesting that ownership of the pub had recently changed hands. There were many ways to control a person, but as the old printer had proven, chief among them was money. Whoever's name was on those deeds would almost certainly have a connection to the case.

'I need you to do some digging, Amelia.' said Felix. 'Can you find out whose name is on the title deeds for the George Inn at Limehouse?'

'I can have one of my students look into it. She's like a dog with a bone once she gets going.'

Felix thanked Amelia before putting the receiver down. He stood up to face Alfred, who was looking around the room anxiously, pretending not to have listened to his conversation.

'There you have it,' said Felix. 'Now that you know the whole truth, I would understand if you wished to leave. We can find you an apprenticeship somewhere, with food and board, and good prospects.'

'No. I would like to stay.' said Alfred.

'It will be dangerous. I don't want you to feel obliged.'

'Mr Houlston was good to me. He took me in, even when he knew I didn't have a proper education. I want to help. I need to.'

Felix considered Alfred for a moment. There was a burning intensity in his usually timid eyes. After what happened, how could he deny the young man the chance to see things put right?

'Things will undoubtedly get worse before they get better,' he said, giving Alfred one last chance to change his mind.

'I'd still like to stay.'

'Understood. But you must promise to keep our work here a secret. No one must ever know about my involvement in the case or the location of this office. Not while I'm in government. However long that may be.'

'Cross my heart and hope to die,' promised Alfred.

'And, when this is all over, you will take up my offer of an apprenticeship and never look back. Not for a moment.'

Alfred nodded his acceptance of the terms.

Feeling reassured, Felix lifted the basket onto the oak desk and removed the towel, revealing the delicious array of food Mrs Hughes had prepared. Alfred had never seen such a magnificent spread. He waited patiently for Felix to take the first piece before launching himself head-first into the basket. As Alfred gorged himself on scones and jam, Felix took the opportunity to enquire about his family and background, mindful not to push the young man too much.

Between bites, Alfred explained that his mother had been a seamstress for a wealthy family and had been given temporary lodgings in their basement. The family had paid her to stay with them three nights a week to be on hand for the lady of the house and her two daughters. After some years, the damp walls began to take their toll on her breathing, ending her life prematurely. His father was a tradesman. He took great pride in the quality of his work and in passing down his knowledge to Alfred, his only son. But the loss of his wife was crushing, and after her death, he quickly descended into a depression, turning to alcohol and opium for comfort. Unable to cope with his father's addictions and determined to carve out his own path, Alfred left home at thirteen only to quickly find himself on the streets, where Mr Houlston eventually discovered him. He'd been sleeping rough outside a union building when Mr Houlston arrived to enquire about an apprentice to help maintain his printing presses. Fortunately for Alfred, the union had one apprentice left and was reluctant to let him go. Having overheard the conversation and witnessed Mr Houlston's disappointment, Alfred approached the old printer and offered his services. Naturally, Mr Houlston was reluctant, to begin with, but when Alfred explained his situation, the old printer agreed to give him a trial, which Alfred passed with flying colours.

Alfred's story reminded Felix of just how unforgiving society could be. It only took one ill-fated moment to turn a person's life upside down. Particularly someone so young. Fortunately for Alfred, he'd met a good man willing to offer him a second chance. Countless others hadn't been so lucky. It was the type of issue that had attracted Felix to politics in the first place; the desire to help those less well-off or in desperate need of benevolence. Unfortunately, he'd allowed himself to be distracted from the country's growing social issues by the constant political point-scoring in the Commons. However, having seen the plight of so many over the past few days, it had become abundantly clear just how out of touch Felix was with the lives of ordinary people. He would need to speak to the union man who confronted him at Downing Street and listen openly to his grievances if he genuinely wanted to make the changes that had stirred him into becoming a politician in the first place.

'Is everything alright?' spluttered Alfred, chomping on some cheese. He had noticed a sudden change in Felix's mood and a far-off look in his eyes.

'Yes, I was just thinking you'll need some sheets and a pillow if you're to be comfortable here.'

Felix rose from his chair and set off for the corridor back towards Downing Street. Once in his study, he checked his drawers, searching for the petition the union man had handed him on the evening of his parliamentary dinner. He found the scroll hidden beneath some heavy books alongside Thompson's note informing him of Lord Cecil's abduction.

Felix took a moment to study the long petition. There were thousands of signatures, some with accompanying comments; workers venting their anger and frustration at their working conditions and the government's lack of action. Each name Felix read reminded him of Arthur Jenkins, the unfortunate young man who had died at Birchwood. How many more Arthur Jenkins were on this list, he thought to himself. How many more lives are at risk?

Felix reached for some paper and began to compose a letter. He responded to the union's concerns about working conditions and the lack of investment in new machinery, then followed that up with a passionate response to the workers' comments, empathising with their worries and fears and promising to make far-reaching changes if he retained the power to do so. He finished by inviting the union leaders to meet him at their chosen time and place before folding his letter in half and placing it inside an envelope. He found the name of the union man and his organisation at the top of the petition document, it read:

To be presented to the Prime Minister by the hand of William Foster on behalf of the Industrial Workers Union.

Felix had barely finished sealing the envelope when there was a knock at the door, and Humphrey entered.

'Will you need me to light the fire,' he asked, 'or will you be off on another of your escapades this evening?'

'The fire can wait. I need you to send a letter for me. And have the staff bring up some fresh sheets and a pillow.'

'Are you intending to sleep in your study now?'

'They are for someone else. A rough sleeper in need of some comfort.'

'Then they should use the staff's old sheets.'

'Nonsense,' said Felix, brushing Humphrey's pompous protestations aside. 'Some of mine will do fine.'

Humphrey didn't take long to return with the sheets and pillow. He reluctantly handed them to Felix before taking the letter. Felix waited for his steward to leave the study before turning the marble corbel on the fireplace and activating the secret passage. He had hoped to tell Humphrey all about Old Pye Street and Alfred, but there had been little time to explain, and he was sure his steward would disapprove. There had barely been a secret between them since he was a boy, but Felix knew he could only reveal the truth once he could prove their benefit to the case.

Felix found Alfred back at work on the other side of the tunnel. Having devoured Mrs Hughes's feast, the young man had turned his attention to fixing the holes in the walls, hoping to block out the draft that occasionally engulfed Old Pye Street.

'Do you ever rest?' asked Felix.

'I like to keep busy. Stop's me thinking about… things too much.'

'I can understand that' said Felix, laying out the sheets to make Alfred's bed. 'This must be my first time preparing a bed. I've always had someone else do it for me. Pathetic, when you think about it.'

'It's not your fault. You didn't choose the life you was born into.'

'Neither did you,' replied Felix, finishing the bed, and turning to help Alfred.

It was close to ten o'clock when they finally finished working. In that time, they covered all the drafts, fixed the doors firmly onto their hinges, straightened out the bowed wooden shelves and organised the library of encyclopaedias into neatly aligned rows, indexed in alphabetic order.

Felix looked at the clock, unsure where the day had gone. He was about to retire for the evening when a light began to blink on the telephone switchboard. Curious, he reached for the receiver, switched the cord jack, and spoke into the mouthpiece.

'Hello...?'

'It's me...' came the muffled sound of Amelia's voice.

'Amelia? Can you speak up,' said Felix, barely able to hear.

'I have... come to... quick as you can,' she replied, her voice cutting in and out.

'Amelia? I can't hear you. Speak up.'

'Meet... the lobby.'

'Where are you, Amelia? I missed the location.'

'... Club.'

Felix caught the last word before the phone cut out.

'She's gone,' he said, turning to face Alfred. 'She said something about a club, but I didn't catch which one.'

Alfred approached the switchboard. He looked down at the connecting cords. 'The call came from an exchange in London. Area code 470.'

Felix quickly scanned the area codes on a list pinned to the side of the machine. 'Blast it! I told her to stay in Oxford and not to do anything rash!'

He quickly placed the receiver back on the switchboard and grabbed his jacket.

'Do you know where she is?' asked Alfred.

'The call came from Mayfair. She's at the East India Club!'

'Can I come with you?'

'I don't think that's a good idea.'

'I can keep an eye out. Watch the doors in case anyone tries to slip in or out.'

Felix considered the young man for a moment. He was adept at hiding in the shadows, as he had proven while staking out the George Inn, and with the events of the past few days, it couldn't hurt to have an extra pair of eyes keeping watch.

'On one condition,' he replied. 'If you see even the slightest hint of trouble, I want you to return and send word to the police. I don't want you putting yourself in harm's way regardless of what happens to Amelia or me. Understood?'

Alfred nodded his acceptance of the terms. He followed Felix to the full-scale model of London in the centre of the room, where they plotted his journey from Old Pye Street through the backroads and cobblestones to Mayfair. Given the dangerous nature of their trip, Felix did not want Alfred seen arriving with him, potentially endangering his life, so he sent the young man out on foot, then waited thirty minutes before leaving to give him a head start.

On arrival in Mayfair, Felix checked the shadows for any signs of Alfred before approaching the steps to the East India Club. To his relief, the young man was nowhere to be seen, meaning he had listened and stayed out of sight. Felix stepped into the club lobby, where he was met by the elegant hostess, Seema Sharma.

'This way, Prime Minister,' she said, leading Felix through reception towards a long corridor with doors on both sides. 'Your American colleague has taken some private rooms and is anxious to see you.'

They approached a thin door with a small carving of the Hindu monkey god, Hanuman. Seema Sharma pushed the door open and led Felix into a small cluster of rooms beautifully decorated in authentic Indian designs. Felix noted the rich array of ivory and terracotta ornaments and the vibrant silk curtains hanging from the ceiling to the floor. He stepped through the main suite into a small tearoom covered in green and gold cushions where Amelia sat, drinking sweet tea from an emerald teacup and looking very pleased with herself.

'I see you made it then,' she said, sipping from her cup, 'you really must try this tea. It's simply delicious.'

'Christ, Amelia,' sighed Felix. 'I rushed here as fast as I could. I thought you were in danger.'

'In danger? Whatever gave you that idea?'

'Your message…'

'What about my message?'

'It was all garbled and fuzzy before it dramatically cut out. You sounded like you were in distress.'

'Me, in distress? How strange,' chortled Amelia.

'Apologies,' interjected Seema Sharma, 'we are having some minor issues with our new telephone line.'

'You see,' said Amelia, jumping up from her seat, 'they're having some minor issues with their new line.'

'Then why did you ask me to come? I've got…' Felix stopped, suddenly aware of Seema Sharma's presence, 'things that require my immediate attention.'

Amelia looked over at the watching hostess. 'Would you mind,' she said apologetically, 'sensitive information about to be disclosed, I fear.'

'Of course,' whispered Seema Sharma departing and closing the door behind her.

Amelia listened to the hostess's footsteps fading before turning to face Felix. 'My student followed up on your lead, and it appears your instincts were correct. The George Inn has recently changed hands to a Mr G Pulleyn. Have you heard of him?'

Felix shook his head.

'Nor I, or any of my associates, which I find odd, seeing as they make it their business to know anyone of note in London. So, having taken up the challenge of uncovering more information about this Mr G Pulleyn, I decided to dig into his affairs, only to reach more dead ends. It appears someone has gone to great lengths to keep his business dealings out of the public eye.'

'A cover-up?'

'Possibly. The few financial records there were led to Filcher & Co, a small legal firm in York. Naturally, they were reluctant to speak about their client in any way.'

'Naturally.'

'And they decided to cut off communication entirely when we pushed them on the matter. But just as we were about to give up on our search, one of my more tenacious students uncovered an interesting piece of information. The same week that Mr G Pulleyn took ownership of the George Inn, his name also appeared on another set of property deeds. This time for a far more significant holding: the Burbage estates in India and London.'

'Burbage?' replied Felix. He knew the name but couldn't recall how or why.

'Jonathan Burbage,' said Amelia, motioning around the room. 'Think about where we are.'

'Monteagle's associate?' remembered Felix.

'Burbage was here on the night of the abduction. He invited Monteagle to the club to play poker with a group of his business associates. And now we know why.'

'Astonishing,' said Felix. 'Why are we not out looking for Burbage?'

'It's all in hand, Prime Minister,' winked Amelia.

'What do you mean, it's all in hand?'

'Burbage is currently upstairs on one of the club's poker tables. He's been there for some hours now and is a little drunk and heavily in debt.'

'Amelia...'

'His opponent is a gentleman named Phillip Masters, a noted academic and mathematician and a close colleague of mine at the university. He is well known in Oxford circles for his love of games and strategies, and importantly for us, his ability to count cards.'

'I asked you to do some digging, not to put yourself and your colleagues in danger,' said Felix, agitated not to be consulted on the plan.

'What's life without a little risk?'

Felix opened his mouth to respond when they were disturbed by a knock at the main door. Amelia finished the last of her tea and straightened out her clothes. 'It's probably best if you stay in here. We wouldn't want to spook them now, would we?'

Felix reluctantly sat on one of the tearoom stools, out of sight but close enough to hear, while Amelia entered the main room and opened the door. Phillip Masters, a tall, bookish man, entered accompanied by a drunk and crestfallen Jonathan Burbage.

Please, take a seat,' said Amelia, motioning towards the sofa. 'Sweet tea?'

'Just get on with it,' replied Burbage coldly.

'Very well,' said Amelia, turning towards Masters. 'How much is Mr Burbage into you for?'

'Fifty pounds,' replied Masters.

'Fifty pounds,' repeated Amelia theatrically, 'that's quite a sum. And can you pay it?' she asked, facing Burbage.

'You know I can't.'

'What a pity. My father always said that the safest way to double your money was to fold it over and put it back in your pocket. But I suppose it's a little late for old Texan sayings; the damage has already been done. However, fortunately for you, there may still be a way to avoid this debt and save your reputation.'

Burbage looked up at Amelia, confused but hopeful.

'I would like to buy Mr Burbage's debt if you'll agree to sell it?' said Amelia, offering her hand to Masters. 'I doubt you'll see a penny otherwise.'

Masters hesitated, pretending to consider the offer to avoid Burbage realising he'd been set up. Having deliberated for just the right amount of time, he finally stepped forward and shook Amelia's hand, securing the deal. With the debt passed over, Masters wished them a good day and turned, leaving the office and Amelia to question Burbage.

'How about that tea?' said Amelia, pouring two cups from an ornate amber teapot.

'What do you want from me?' asked Burbage.

'I just want to ask a few simple questions,' she replied, handing Burbage a cup. 'And, depending on the sincerity of your answers, I may see fit to wipe your debt. What do you think about that?'

Burbage took a moment to consider Amelia's offer. He was torn between the need to manage the situation and the risk of disclosing sensitive information. But with a substantial debt hanging over his head and his reputation hanging in the balance, he had no choice but to agree to Amelia's terms. After all, what was the point of being financially secure if your reputation was in tatters?

'How long have you known Lord Monteagle?' asked Amelia, sitting opposite the stricken man.

'Over twenty years. We set up our businesses in India together.'

'Are you friendly?'

'As friendly as one can be with a lord, they're not known for their congeniality.'

'Yet you invited him to your club to play cards?'

'It's common for gentlemen to discuss business over a poker game.'

'Is it also common for them to be drugged and abducted from one of your games?'

'I had nothing to do with that horrid business!'

Amelia gave her guest a moment to settle down. She had learnt over the years, lecturing students, that a well-timed silence could be just as effective as any flurry of words.

'I know about the financial issues you've had with your estates,' she said, breaking the silence. 'I also know about your involvement with a Mr G Pulleyn.'

Burbage looked up, his eyes full of worry. It was clear that Amelia had struck a chord.

'Tell me,' she continued, 'was it this Pulleyn's idea to arrange your poker game and invite Lord Monteagle?'

Burbage hesitated. 'He was having trouble expanding his interests in India. He was new money, you see. And the old families, well, they refused to deal with him. Typical establishment. When he found out I'd worked with Monteagle in India, he demanded I set up the meeting and introduce some of his associates. A game of poker seemed like the ideal opportunity.'

'What do you mean some of his associates?' asked Amelia.

'The plantation brothers and the insurer,' replied Burbage.

'You mean to tell me you didn't know them beforehand?'

'It was the first time I'd met any of them. He... Mr Pulleyn, was adamant that I pretended to be in business with them. He said it would keep Monteagle attentive and make the meeting seem more legitimate.'

'And you agreed to all of this?'

Burbage's eyes filled with shame. 'I realise it seems ill-considered to you, but he offered me a way out. A healthy commission if I could just facilitate the meeting. I had no idea that they were going to take him. I swear it!'

Amelia took a moment to absorb this new information. She'd been sure of Burbage's involvement from the moment her student found the amendments to the Burbage deeds, but she hadn't counted on Burbage having been hoodwinked.

'Where is he now?' she asked.

'I have no idea. I've never met the man.'

'What?' replied Amelia, shocked.

'He did all his communicating via a runner. A drunk publican from the Docklands.'

'You handed over half of your assets to a man you've never met?'

'He offered me a way to save my family estate. I had no choice.'

'There is always a choice,' said Amelia. 'And now, you are faced with another. I will clear your gambling debt and preserve your reputation, and in return, you will tell no one of this meeting, not a soul. And should this Mr G Pulleyn try to contact you again, you will feed that information directly to me. Is that understood?'

Burbage nodded his acceptance of the terms.

'Then, you are free to go,' said Amelia, dismissing him.

She waited for Burbage to leave before turning to face Felix, who, having heard the shamed gambler depart, had entered from the tearoom.

'Well, there you have it. Is there anything you British won't do to protect your precious reputations?'

'Did you believe him?' asked Felix.

'People often do the unthinkable when they are desperate.

He seemed sincere enough.'

'See what else your students can dig up about, Mr G Pulleyn.'

'What will you do?' asked Amelia.

'Speak to these associates of his. Now that we know they were hand-picked for the poker game, they won't be able to hide behind their false statements or Burbage's protection any longer. If they haven't already gone to ground, that is.'

Armed with nothing more than an obscure name, Felix thanked Amelia and slipped out of the East India Club into a waiting car. He directed the driver through the backroads from Mayfair to Westminster, keeping an eye out for Alfred along the way. Back at Number 10, he hurried to his study and made his way through the secret passage towards Old Pye Street, where he waited for over an hour, checking his watch anxiously before Alfred finally returned.

Relieved to see his young ward back safely, Felix explained the night's revelations and Jonathan Burbage's involvement with the mysterious Mr G Pulleyn. His words, however, lacked their usual pluck. He could not hide his disappointment with how the evening had played out. Having exposed Burbage's role in Monteagle's abduction, Felix had been hopeful of finally solving the case, only to have left the club no closer to finding the missing lords or their abductors.

It was a reoccurring pattern. Every time they'd unearthed a meaningful lead, it either evaporated into thin air or ended in tragedy. Maybe it was finally time to speak to Commissioner Thompson, thought Felix. He had already focused too much energy on the case when he should have been focusing on his role as the British prime minister and protecting his position in government. His enemies were circling, and the impending vote was an opportunity to put the final nail in his coffin. He needed to strike back and prove to his cabinet and the parliamentary members that he still had enough fight to do the job.

If there was one thing that Burbage's situation had proven, it was that a person needed to maintain a strong position in life to avoid compromising themselves or their principles.

Game of Trust

Felix spent the evening impatiently working through his parliamentary admin. Having been preoccupied with the case, he'd allowed his paperwork to pile up and was still paying the price for his absent-mindedness in the early morning hours when he finally slipped into bed.

Although tired, he rose with a sense of purpose the following day, having decided to pass the case on to the police and focus on the parliamentary vote instead. He jumped out of bed and set straight to work writing a detailed account of the recent events and revelations, ready to hand over to Commissioner Thompson and relieve himself of the burden. He documented his exploits at Houlston and Sons and the George Inn before writing a comprehensive account of Amelia's meeting with Jonathan Burbage and his links to the mysterious Mr G Pulleyn.

It wasn't until later that morning when Humphrey entered with a tray of tea and the day's newspapers, that Felix finally looked up from his work.

'Is the bed on fire?' asked Humphrey.

'Not quite,' replied Felix, clearing space for the tray, 'there is lots to be done if we still hope to turn our fortunes around.'

'Oh, you're back to being Prime Minister today. Do excuse me; it is rather hard to keep up.'

'Enjoy the moment, old man,' said Felix, ignoring Humphrey's priggish grin. 'However, I do admit, your advice may have been, a touch merited.'

'Just a touch?'

'No one likes a know-it-all. Besides, from now on, we shall be concentrating our efforts on governing and governing alone. Send word to Percy. It's time to start planning our campaign strategy.'

'It would be my pleasure,' replied Humphrey bounding off to conduct affairs.

With the letter for Thompson finally completed and his steward departed, Felix turned his attention to the day's newspapers. He unfolded one of the large broadsheets, peeling the pages away to reveal a startling headline: *The worst industrial disaster since the Albion Colliery.*

Felix scanned the article, shocked to discover that there had been a series of explosions at factories on the outskirts of London. They had happened in the early morning hours, first in Morden, then Worcester Park and finally at a converted mill in Surbiton. Three different disasters, with devastating effects on the factory buildings and the workers inside, many of whom were reported missing or feared dead.

Inferno-like fires had engulfed the factory buildings in Morden and Worcester Park, ripping through them in minutes, whilst a massive explosion at the converted mill in Surbiton had torn the front of the old brick building clean off.

There was little known about the cause of the disasters, but what was evident from the article was its unforgiving tone. Aside from the strongly worded attacks on the factory owners and the government, who the newspaper blamed for this current spate of catastrophes, there were also several accusatory questions: *Why were the factories still running in the early morning hours? Why were staff being made to work such unrelenting shifts? Why were exhausted workers operating faulty machinery?*

For each question, the answer was soberingly obvious, the pursuit of profit. And who was reaping the rewards of these profits? The factory owners and the government.

Felix thought about the poor souls caught up in the fires and their family's receiving the news of their loss. He thought too about Arthur Jenkins and Mr Houlston and, to his shame, about the impact this news would have on the impending confidence vote. With his position in government looking ever more precarious, these factory disasters couldn't have come at a worse time. He hated himself for considering it, but was it possible that the unfortunate timing of these atrocities was more than just a coincidence? Were his opponents ruthless enough to coordinate such destruction and loss of life simply to oust him from government and wrestle power for themselves?

Felix was finally distracted from his thoughts by Humphrey returning with news that Commissioner Thompson had arrived at Downing Street seeking an audience. Having dressed and sealed the letter, Felix entered the study to find Thompson standing in the same spot he had occupied on his previous visit, clearly a creature of habit. However, to Felix's surprise, the commissioner looked unusually drawn and dishevelled, with a few locks of his pristine grey and black peppered hair out of place, and his trousers, although still perfectly creased, stained and scuffed like his usually polished shoes.

'Do excuse my appearance, Prime Minister,' began Thompson, 'I am yet to return home. I've been all over the city visiting the factory sites, you see.'

It was the first time Felix had witnessed the commissioner looking anything but immaculate. It made him seem more human and reassured Felix of Thompson's honesty and dedication to the job.

'Please, don't apologise. I have just been catching up with the news myself.'

'A terrible, terrible business, sir.'

'Do we have an estimate on the casualties?'

'Unfortunately, not. The factories in Morden and New Malden are still on fire, and our heroic firefighters are struggling to control them, despite their best efforts. There's been no opportunity to enter the buildings and assess the full extent of the destruction, but I'm sure the human cost will be... extensive.'

'Do we have any idea who might be responsible?'

'We'll know more once the fires are out, and we can start our investigations. Assuming there was any foul play, that is, of course.'

'Surely you don't believe this is simply a coincidence, three factories all at once?'

'It's not about what I believe. It's about the evidence. I'll wait for some more meaningful information before jumping to conclusions.'

Felix nodded his acceptance of the point. 'Is there anything we can do to help?'

'We'll need men and machinery to help clear the debris.'

'I'll speak with the Home Secretary.'

'And I would consider deploying the army.'

'The army?' said Felix, a little taken aback. 'Why would we need the military?'

'Rioting has already begun, Prime Minister. They started this morning in London and have already reached as far as Yorkshire. God only knows how bad things will get by this afternoon.'

Felix considered the Commissioner's words. He could sense Thompson's anxiety at containing widespread riots, having already asked so much of his officers. However, deploying the army was not something any prime minister wanted on their record, particularly not a liberally minded one like Felix. But he was caught between two equally damaging options. No matter how he manoeuvred, Felix knew that his colleagues in the Commons would view his actions as a failure. If he engaged the army, he would be called a tyrant, and if he chose not to, it would be seen as yet another sign of weakness by his enemies.

'I have a better idea,' said Felix, thinking aloud, 'I will speak with the trade unions. Let's see if they can't appease their workers before we take any drastic measures.'

'The unions!' scoffed Thompson. 'They probably started these riots in the first place. Opportunists, the lot of them.'

'Perhaps,' agreed Felix, eyeing the Commissioner's fire-stained clothes, 'but they have good reason in light of recent events.'

'Perhaps... in light of recent events,' conceded Thompson.

'That's settled then,' said Felix, closing the meeting. 'In the meantime, I'll ensure you have every available resource.'

The Commissioner nodded his thanks and turned for the door.

'Sorry, one last thing, Commissioner,' remembered Felix, stopping Thompson mid-stride.

He reached into his pocket and took out the letter he'd prepared earlier that morning, containing the case details. He stepped towards Thompson, ready to hand it over when he suddenly found himself reluctant. Perhaps it was inappropriate, he thought, given the circumstances and the need to concentrate on the factory fires, or maybe he'd just become too close to the case. Whatever the reason, something in Felix's gut was holding him back, preventing him from cutting ties.

Rather than deliver the letter, Felix gave Thompson a brief account of Burbage's debts and his financial arrangement with Mr G Pulleyn. He also recommended that the other players from the poker match be re-interviewed and questioned on their dealings with Burbage's mysterious benefactor now that a motive had been established.

'And how did you come about this information?' asked Thompson, amazed by Felix's revelations.

'You know what these gentlemen's clubs are like, Commissioner. No one's financial affairs are their own. I simply heard a rumour that Burbage's estates were in trouble and had someone investigate the deeds for me. I'm surprised you hadn't heard about it yourself.'

'As am I,' said Thompson, embarrassed to receive this information from the Prime Minister and not one of his investigating officers.

Thompson agreed to have his team investigate the identity of Mr G Pulleyn and to bring the other poker players in for further questioning before departing. Felix took a moment to reflect on their meeting. He scolded himself for holding back. He may have doubted the police, but it was not for a prime minister to deceive or mislead those trying to assist him. It was just another reason, in a growing list, as to why he doubted his eligibility for the role. The Iron Duke would never have acted in such a way, scrambling to concoct a false story, and telling half-truths to cover his tracks.

Fortunately for Felix, he only had a little time to analyse his growing list of failures before Percy arrived. The Home Secretary had been hard on the campaign trail over the past twenty-four hours, petitioning members and giving rousing speeches to galvanise the party's support. Unfortunately, the factory disasters had gone a long way to undoing his excellent work, and he looked like a spent force by the time he bounded into Felix's study.

'I take it you've seen the news?' he said, slumping into one of the study chairs.

'Unfortunately,' replied Felix.

'It may very well have put an end to our chances, old boy,' lamented Percy, reaching for the plate of biscuits on Felix's desk. 'And just when I was getting some traction with the members.'

'Maybe it's a sign, Thomas?'

'Well, if it is, it's a particularly brutal one,' replied Percy, munching on a shortbread.

'Or, perhaps it's a sign that we're concentrating our efforts in the wrong places.' said Felix, thinking aloud.

'What on earth do you mean?'

Felix to a moment to organise his thoughts. 'We have been so focused on trying to convince the members of our suitability to lead that we've stopped leading.'

He moved around the desk to face Percy, a hint of optimism shining in his eyes. 'Rather than being judged by our words, let them judge us by our actions. We'll show them what effective leadership looks like by responding to these disasters with everything we've got. We can start by sending all the resources we can muster to help our emergency services do their jobs. I want the police force, the fire service and our wonderful medics given every possible assistance. I want to put them at the centre of everything we do from this point on. And I want the people and the newspapers to see us doing it.'

'Sounds dangerously like socialism to me, Felix.'

'Call it what you will, Thomas. I want our great British servicemen and women to emerge as the heroes of these disasters. Their support will hold the key to our success.'

With lunch concluded and Percy departed, Felix set off for Old Pye Street to relay the day's revelations to Alfred. Having witnessed the fire at the printers and the death of Mr Houlston first-hand, he wasn't sure how Alfred would react to the news. He wanted to be the one to tell him and be on hand to help the young man through any unnecessary feelings of guilt.

Felix passed through the fireplace and down the secret passage, arriving at the office to find Alfred sitting at the telephone switchboard, engrossed in a flurry of flashing lights.

'What going on?' he asked, alerting Alfred to his presence.

'The network's gone crazy,' said Alfred, pointing at the brightly lit panel. 'Something big's happened.'

'Ah, yes. Something big indeed,' replied Felix. 'I've just had the Police Commissioner and the Home Secretary pay me a visit.'

Alfred stepped away from the switchboard.

'There have been some incidents at several factories around London.

'Fires?' asked Alfred.

'I'm afraid so.'

Felix could sense the anger building in the young man. 'We're still waiting on the information...'

'What for?' snapped Alfred. 'We know who did it.'

'No, we don't. Well, not for sure, anyway. It's possible that these factories may have suffered from faulty machinery.'

'All at the same time?'

'We were warned in parliament that something like this could happen, given the age of some of our...'

'It was no accident. It was him! That landlord.'

'Even if dark forces were at play here, I could name several people who'd benefit from seeing our factories burn to the ground, not just Tom Fellows. At this point, it does no good jumping to conclusions. The best we can do is wait a few days and see what the police find.'

'I can't wait.' replied Alfred grabbing his coat and a few leftovers from Mrs Hughes' food basket. 'I need to do something now.'

'You can't just leave,' said Felix. 'We have an arrangement.'

'I haven't forgotten my promise,' said Alfred, turning for the door. 'I'll be back once I've found Tom Fellows.'

Trades Union Congress

Although he'd only known Alfred a short time, Felix couldn't help but feel responsible for the young man and anxious about his sudden departure. Having seen his life turned upside down by the death of his mother and father's depression and his chances of learning a trade with a caring master disappear in flames at Houlston and Sons, he was now back on the streets, where Mr Houlston had found him. It seemed selfish and improper that Felix hadn't taken the opportunity to correct the trajectory of his short life by insisting he take up an apprenticeship rather than keep him at Old Pye Street to assist with the case. Now, all Felix could do was wait and hope for Alfred's safe return and a chance to put things right. In the meantime, he would set his mind to doing whatever he could to stop the riots sweeping across the country.

Having arranged a meeting with the head of the Trade Union Congress, Humphrey prepared the state car, a new 12 horsepower Daimler, for Felix's journey along the Thames to Farringdon Street and the Congregational Memorial Hall, where the trade unions hosted their meetings. While it had been of the utmost importance to remain anonymous when investigating the case, visiting the TUC required a very different approach. The tenacious spirit of the union representatives was legendary, and Felix was determined to show the full might of his ministerial authority and influence before negotiating with them.

It was late afternoon by the time Felix's car pulled to a halt outside the Congregational Memorial Hall. He exited the vehicle and approached the imposing building taking in its large steeple and Gothic architecture. It had been erected on the old Fleet Street prison site and had become home to many left-wing groups and trade union bodies. They had gathered there four years earlier to create the Labour Party, a political arm to represent them and their workers in Parliament. A dogged group of MPs well known in the Commons for their brash manners and hardened politics.

Felix took a deep breath and stepped into the building's reception hall. It was surprisingly grand for a socialist headquarters, with high ceilings and a vast lobby filled with light pouring in through its enormous windows. He watched in awe at the buzz of workers ferrying documents and tea trays around, barely avoiding knocking into one another.

'I have an appointment with Mr Ernest Booth?' He said,

approaching the lobby desk.

'He'll be ready shortly,' replied the receptionist casually, without looking up from her book.

Surprised by her dismissive tone, Felix stepped closer to her desk. 'Do you not require my name or the nature of my business?' He asked.

'That won't be necessary, Prime Minister,' she replied, turning the page.

Felix was about to respond when it suddenly dawned on him that the receptionist's disregard for his presence was likely a ploy to unsettle him before his meeting. The unions were well known for engaging in such psychological tactics. They believed that by putting their opponents on the back foot from the start, they could significantly improve their hand at the negotiating table. Instead, Felix smiled at the receptionist and took a seat. After some time observing the organised chaos, he was finally greeted by a thin, older man in an oversized suit.

'I'm to take you up,' he said, extending his hand. 'Tim's my name.'

Felix observed Tim's black-stained palm before shaking it.

'A life spent down the pits,' said Tim, following Felix's eyes. 'I've tried everything; soap, alcohol, sand, but it won't come out. S'ppose you can't hide what you are, no matter how many fancy suits they put you in, eh?'

There was an unfortunate truth to the old man's words that resonated with Felix, yet his tone felt forced, almost rehearsed. Having negotiated the dismissive receptionist, Felix realised that he was now faced with the second character in the union's pre-meeting pantomime: the veteran miner.

'No more digging for me now though,' continued Tim, 'not since the union found me this job, on account of my age and troublesome back.'

'That's very decent of them,' agreed Felix, playing along.

'I'd say so. God knows where I'd be now, probably six feet under. I'm just thankful to still be in work.'

'Well, let's hope we can stop this rioting and get more people back to work,' replied Felix.

'Right you are,' nodded the old miner, leading Felix through the melee towards an old service lift. He opened the gates and invited Felix to step inside.

'Fourth floor, please, Errol.' He said, instructing the equally decrepit lift operator.

Errol shut the gates and pulled the lever, bringing the rickety old lift to life. As it stuttered upwards, Felix watched Tim disappear beneath him, wondering what other surprises the TUC had in store for him.

'Errol is it?' he asked, facing the lift operator. 'Let me guess, you've been here for under a year, probably transferred from one of the collieries, because of your age and physical condition, and you couldn't be more thankful for the opportunity?'

'Spot on,' exclaimed Errol, 'but how'd you…'

'Call it intuition,' answered Felix before Errol could finish his question.

The fourth floor was less chaotic than the bustling reception hall, with portraits of influential union men lining the corridor walls on both sides. Felix stepped out of the lift to find William Foster, the union man he'd encountered at his parliamentary dinner, waiting eagerly for him.

'We meet again, Prime Minister.' said Foster in his thick Yorkshire accent. 'Only this time, you're in my house.'

'It would appear so,' replied Felix.

'I did warn you, didn't I? I did say we'd strike all over the country, but you'd not listen, would yeh? Not to the likes of me, anyway.'

'You were intruding.'

'Yeah, I was, and with good reason. You needed to understand the severity of the situation.'

'There's never a good reason to break into another man's home.'

'That's where we differ, us lowly folk and you privileged lot. We don't give a monkeys for your gentlemanly dos and don'ts. All we care about is survival, and we go about that any way we can.'

Felix took a moment to consider Foster's words. He understood the cause more than most in Parliament but disagreed with the union's tactics. Regardless, there was little point in arguing with the miner, not when he'd come to ask the TUC for help. Instead, Felix nodded his way through Foster's justifications with reticence before finally being led down the corridor towards the meeting room.

'Don't think they'll be impressed by you in there,' said Foster, stopping outside the door. 'There are no prime ministers here, or kings or queens. Only men and women.'

Foster pushed the door open, and Felix entered. His eyes were immediately hit by a bright light. He lifted his hands to block out the glare, suddenly realising that he was facing two huge windows, one looking out onto St. Milton's Hospital on the east and the other Fleet Street on the west.

'The two contrasting sides of this great city, eh?' called out another broad Yorkshire accent.

Felix swung around to see two figures sitting at an oval table. Nearest was the voice's owner, Ernest Booth, a lump of a man dressed in a simple suit and union tie. Alongside him was Agnes Lock, a much older lady dressed in a faded frock with her hair hidden under a scraggy boater hat.

'On the one side, you've got St Bart's', continued Ernest, 'a haven for the poor and destitute in our society, and on t'other side, the epicentre of the civilised world. And sat bang smack in the middle of it all is us, fighting to bridge the gap between the rich and the poor. The question is, Prime Minister, who are you here representing?'

'Everyone,' replied Felix, taking a seat. 'That's the nature of the job.'

'Sounds like a thankless task to me.'

'It can be,' nodded Felix, 'that's why I need your help. I want to bring this rioting to an end.'

'Is that right,' chuckled Ernest, amused. 'You want us to help you? I'm not sure that would be very popular with our members. You see, you've got blood on your hands, Prime Minister.'

'No more than you.'

'What are you talking about?'

'I wonder how your members would react if they knew you were making deals with the likes of Milton Cavendish?'

'Divide and rule, the establishment's oldest and most effective weapon.' muttered Agnes.

'Fortunately, no amount of propaganda would have our members believe anything of the sort,' added Ernest.

'So, you deny it then?' asked Felix.

'Wholeheartedly,' replied Ernest. 'Although, we've heard about your little popularity vote int'Commons. Perhaps it might suit us to back the winning horse for a change.'

'If I lose that vote, we all lose, including the unions.'

'That's a touch dramatic, isn't it, Prime Minister?'

'Think about it for a moment,' said Felix. 'These riots are opening the door to the opposition, most of whom have vested interests in these businesses you are striking against. How do you think they'll respond once they're in power?'

'You're all part of the same club. It matters little to us which of you is in power.'

'You couldn't be more wrong,' said Felix. 'And believe it or not, after everything your workers have been through, you, their union representatives, are currently the biggest threat to their cause.'

'He's scaremongering,' observed Agnes quietly.

'Now, now Prime Minister, play nice,' said Ernest, wagging his finger at Felix.

'There's no time for games, Sir. I'm one of the few politicians in the Commons with both the influence and the desire to see things radically changed. But with the workers rioting and the country in chaos, there is little chance of me winning this vote and staying in office. Should that be the case, Parliament will be dissolved, and there will be a snap general election. Unfortunately for you, that will mean losing your current momentum and returning fairly quickly to the status quo.'

'You don't know that for sure.'

'No, I don't,' replied Felix, rising from his seat. 'But what I do know is that it takes weeks, even months, to form a new government, which could leave your members out of work and waiting with little to sustain them aside from boredom and regret. And then what? Even if by some miracle they don't turn on you in those weeks, what do you think will happen once the opposition is in power? Do you really think Cavendish will simply cave to your demands? Or, more likely, that he'll take as hard a line as possible with you to show the voters that his is a strong and steady administration? Like I said, if I lose, we all lose.'

'What are you offering?' asked Agnes.

'The chance to make a real difference.'

'That's hardly a tangible offer, Prime Minister. We're going to need something more than emotional rhetoric.'

Felix considered Agnes for a moment, then stood up tall and determined. 'I will take your demands to the Commons and fight for them with everything I have. And if my efforts should fall on deaf ears, I will resign from my post and stand aside. You have my word on it.'

Shocked, Ernest looked from Felix to Agnes and back again.

'We'll need time to think it through,' he said.

Felix nodded his acceptance, then stepped away from the table to leave when a thought suddenly struck him.

'One last thing,' he said, facing his hosts. 'If not by Cavendish, how did your man break into Number 10?'

'Oh no, Sir,' replied Ernest, the bounce returning to his voice. 'We can't possibly divulge that kind of information. Not unless you have something more to offer in return. You don't get owt for nowt in this world, Prime Minister.'

Felix took a moment to consider Ernest's words. There was something oddly familiar about his last comment. He was sure he'd heard it somewhere before. He racked his brains, trying to recall where and when he may have come across the saying when suddenly it hit him. It was a phrase Mrs Hughes used on occasion, one of the few remaining traces of a childhood spent in East Riding, Yorkshire. A thought began to materialise in Felix's mind; William Foster, Ernest Booth and even Mr G Pulleyn's lawyers, Filcher & Co, were all from Yorkshire, just like Mrs Hughes. Even the young miner, Arthur Jenkins, who died so needlessly at the Birchwood Colliery, was from the county. This series of unfortunate events began with his accidental death at the Rotherham coal site. Surely it was more than just a geographical coincidence.

The journey back to Downing Street was bittersweet. Although satisfied with the outcome of the meeting, Felix could not help thinking about Mrs Hughes and her potential part in the miner's appearance inside Number 10 at his parliamentary dinner. Of all his staff, she was one of the last he'd have ever suspected. Like Humphrey, Mrs Hughes had been with the Grey family most of his life and had always been a trusted and dependable figure. Was it something he'd done to offend her? Or perhaps something he'd forgotten to do? He tried to think back on all her years of loyal service. She'd always seemed happy enough, content in her role. It had become customary in the Grey household to reward the staff every Easter and Christmas, and Mrs Hughes had often commented on the family's excessive generosity. Why, then, would she choose to betray him in this way?

Death's Own Carriage

Having returned to Number 10 with few answers, Felix marched through the house, towards the kitchens, to question his head cook in person. He had barely passed through the main hallway when Humphrey intercepted him.

'Prime Minister, the staff are engaged in a minor hysteria over a scotch stain on the study floor. Did you happen to drop…'

'Not now, Humphrey,' barked Felix without stopping.

'Is everything alright?' asked Humphrey, following him.

'Everything is fine. Do you not have chores or some errand to see to?'

'Nothing that can't wait,' replied Humphrey, struggling to keep up.

'In that case, allow yourself some personal time.'

'No, I'd prefer to stay with you, actually.'

'And why is that?' asked Felix.

'Because I've seen that face on more than a few occasions over the years, and it has always preceded trouble in one form or another, particularly when you were a young boy.'

Felix stopped and looked back at his faithful steward. How well he knew him. He felt a surge of gratitude rush through his body, accompanied by one of guilt at his recent dishonesties.

'Now, will you tell me what has got the Prime Minister marching through his own house like a man possessed?' asked Humphrey.

Felix hesitated, unsure how much to divulge. Although convinced of Mrs Hughes' connection to the miner and the TUC, a part of him still hoped she might be innocent or at least have a valid explanation for her actions.

'Would you mind following me to the kitchens?' he asked.

'Is that what this is about, your stomach?' huffed Humphrey. 'If so, I can have something brought up to your study. Like I do most evenings.'

'It's not my stomach. I just need someone with a calm and wise head on their shoulders.'

Humphrey nodded, and the men turned and continued towards the kitchen. Inside, the staff were preparing the evening meal. Several pots and pans were bubbling on the stoves, and the kitchen hands were busy chopping their way through a mountain of vegetables. Felix scanned the large room, looking for Mrs Hughes. Shocked by his unusually surly presence, the staff stopped what they were doing and stood to attention.

'Mrs Hughes?' asked Felix firmly.

After a short silence, one of the kitchen maids nervously pointed towards a door at the room's far end. 'She's in her office, Sir.'

Felix crossed the kitchen, watched by the curious staff.

'As you were,' said Humphrey, beckoning them back to work.

Felix stopped outside Mrs Hughes' office. He took hold of the door handle and then hesitated.

'Are you going to tell me what all this is about?' asked Humphrey, concerned by Felix's erratic behaviour.

'Do you remember the union man who decided to attend our parliamentary dinner uninvited?' asked Felix.

'How could I forget? He ruined a perfectly executed evening.'

'Well, it appears he may have had an accomplice.'

Humphrey looked at the door. 'Mrs Hughes? Don't be ridiculous! I don't believe it, not for one second.'

'I sincerely hope you're right,' replied Felix, finally turning the handle and opening the door.

The office was a small, uneven room with a low ceiling and crooked walls. It had once been the house larder before a newer and more modern kitchen was installed, freeing up space for the head cook to occupy and conduct her affairs. Mrs Hughes was sitting at her lopsided desk, finishing her monthly supplies list, when the men suddenly entered unannounced.

'Prime Minister?' she squeaked, surprised to see Felix. 'Is everything alright?'

'Do you have a moment?' he asked, eyeing the paperwork on her desk.

'Now, if it's about your food, I can assure you that everything is as locally sourced as we can manage, just like you requested.'

'I've not come to discuss the food. Unfortunately, I am here about a far more serious matter.'

'Really? Whatever is the problem?' asked Mrs Hughes.

'I've just returned from a meeting with the TUC. Where something that was said got me thinking back to the evening of the parliamentary dinner and the appearance of our unexpected union guest.'

'Something that was said?' repeated Mrs Hughes anxiously.

'An old Yorkshire saying, actually. The kind you like to use on occasion.'

'Well, those sayings are very popular with folk these days,' said Mrs Hughes, wriggling in her seat.

'As it appears are secrets,' replied Felix.

'I don't follow you, Prime Minister.'

'It only really occurred to me today, after hearing that old saying, that Yorkshire is the common connection in all of this. The miner, the trade union hierarchy, Arthur Jenkins, and perhaps, even someone in my own household?' But surely not someone close to me. Not someone I have come to know and trust.'

Mrs Hughes's eyes filled with tears. There was a momentary silence as she struggled to gather herself and speak.

'If you don't mind,' she stuttered, 'I should like to leave my post quietly and without fuss.'

'I don't understand,' said Humphrey, shocked. 'Eleanor, this can't be true, not after all your years of loyal service?'

'I had no choice. They were going to take our family home.'

'Who were? The TUC?' asked Felix, confused.

'No, the banks,' replied Mrs Hughes. 'My brother lost his job and couldn't keep up the payments. They threatened to take the house unless I covered the shortfall. The home my father built.'

'Who gave you the money?' asked Felix.

'I wouldn't, not for any sum of money.' replied Mrs Hughes, hurt by the implication.

'Then why?' asked Humphrey.

'They gave my brother a job and an advance to help cover the debt. He worked hard for it, with lots of long hours and late nights to repay their kindness. Then one day, they pulled him into the office to meet some well-to-do politician. He said that working conditions in the plants were at an all-time low and that the government was ignoring the workers' pleas. That somebody could die. He implored my brother to help for the sake of his colleagues and their families. They wanted to get their message to the government, and someone had heard about my role here. They said that if I could get a man into the house to present their petition directly, it would make a huge difference. My brother didn't feel like he could say no, what with how they'd helped him, well us. They told him he'd be a hero among the workers.'

'Do you know the name of the politician?' asked Felix.

'He didn't give a name, and my brother was too respectful to ask.'

'What about the company your brother works for?'

'They're called the Holgate Road Carriage Works. They're a local York firm.'

Felix turned to Humphrey' Contact Amelia. Explain what has happened here and ask her to have her students look into the board of directors at the Holgate Road Carriage Works and their political affiliations.'

'The vote is only a matter of days away...'

'More reason to act quickly,' replied Felix, cutting across Humphrey's concerns. Humphrey nodded his consent and reluctantly departed to carry out his orders.

'I should like to pack my belongings, if I may?' asked Mrs Hughes.

'That won't be necessary,' said Felix, facing his downcast cook. 'You won't be leaving our services today, Mrs Hughes.'

'I won't?'

'You've been the victim of a rather sinister plot against me, for which I can only apologise. However, you should've come to me the moment they approached you.'

'If I could go back to that day, that is precisely what I would do.'

Felix took a moment to observe his long-serving cook. Although hard to watch, her heartbreak had reassured him of her sincerity.

'Let us leave this in the past,' he said. 'If you wish to help me now, carry on with your duties as usual. I don't want our enemies to think anything has changed or that we are on to them.'

Mrs Hughes smiled warmly through her teary eyes. 'Thank you, Felix.'

Felix's head was swimming by the time he returned to his study. He poured himself a glass of scotch, the first he'd allowed himself since his embarrassing fall, and watched the sun setting outside his window.

Even though disappointed, he could not blame Mrs Hughes for her actions. She, like Alfred, was a victim of circumstance. A target for those looking to undermine Felix and the British government. It was a valuable lesson for Felix, who had naively believed his staff's loyalty was unfaltering. Unfortunately, everybody was vulnerable in some way, and on this occasion, Felix's enemies had managed to uncover a chink in his head cook's armour and use it to their advantage. Was that the case with Monteagle and Cecil? Had these dark forces infiltrated their homes and inner circles, clearing the way for their swift and professional abductions?

Having resolved things with Mrs Hughes, Felix focused his mind back on the vote and the job of governing. He set about writing a letter for publication in the national newspapers, addressing the families of those presumed missing in the factory disasters, praying for their safe return, and promising all the help and support the government could muster. Over the past few weeks, he'd become all too familiar with writing these types of letters. It had both deepened his resolve and made him feel deeply inadequate about his suitability to lead. He poured himself a second scotch, preparing to settle in for the evening, when the study telephone rang. He picked up the receiver and pulled it to his ear, only to hear the metronome-like voice of Commissioner Thompson on the other end.

'Hello. Prime Minister.' began Thompson as though dictating a telegram, clearly unused to the workings of a telephone. 'Body found. Shad Thames. On route now. Meet at the scene.'

Having delivered his message, the Commissioner hung up immediately. Felix's heart began to race. Could it be one of the abducted lords? They'd been missing for some time, long enough for the gases to build in a dead body and help it rise to the water's surface if not weighed down properly. But why only one body? Why not two? Felix felt his stomach lurch. Could it be Alfred? He'd feared for the boy's safety the moment he'd left Old Pye Street to pursue Tom Fellows. He'd been gone for nearly twenty-four hours without a word on his whereabouts or condition. What if he'd stumbled upon the crooked innkeeper and his cronies while plotting their next atrocity? Or worse, the man with the red eye patch? Felix had witnessed his disregard for human life first-hand. He wouldn't have thought twice about murdering Alfred and throwing his body into the Thames.

In some ways, tossing the body of a working-class boy into the river was the perfect distraction. It would throw the police off their scent entirely. Tom Fellows would have known all about Alfred's time on the streets and Mr Houlston's charitable intervention. He would most likely presume that Alfred had no one looking out for him or interested in making enquiries should he suddenly disappear. It would take the police weeks to identify the body of an ex-street urchin, and in that time, any traces of their involvement would have vanished along with Alfred's future.

Felix reached for his coat and hurried out of the study. He ran down the stairs, whizzing past his shocked staff and exited Number 10, stepping onto Downing Street. He continued down the cobbled walkway, weaving through groups of onlookers, agog to see the Prime Minister suddenly emerge from the famous address and hail down a cab like an ordinary member of the public. But public perception was the last thing on Felix's mind. All he could think about was the dead body and Alfred.

Felix directed his driver to Shad Thames, guiding him through several small roads and backstreets that even he, a professional driver, had never heard of; such was the level of knowledge Felix had acquired about London's roads from the full-scale model at Old Pye Street. Having crossed the river at Westminster Bridge, they proceeded through Lambeth and Southwark before finally joining the main road at Tooley Street and turning onto Shad Thames, where a police blockade greeted them. Felix paid the driver and exited the cab, stepping through the police barriers towards the crime scene.

'Prime Minister,' called Thompson from a small gathering

of officers.

Felix approached the men, only to find them huddled around two figures splayed out on the riverbank.

'We've just fished a second one out,' said Thompson.

Felix could barely bring himself to look. To his great relief, neither of the bodies belonged to Alfred or the missing lords. However, it didn't take long for Felix to recognise the men. They were the sailors he had encountered in Sailortown and then again at the George Inn.

'Sailors?' he asked, pointing at the tattoos on their arms and necks. 'Probably got into a skirmish and copped it,' said one of the officers. 'You know what these sea dogs are like; they don't half love to drink and fight.'

'That will be all chaps,' said Thompson. 'Have their bodies taken to the mortuary for identification.'

The officers placed the bodies on wooden stretchers before transferring them to a waiting carriage. Felix watched as the dead men were loaded into the tall gothic vehicle and pulled into the night by huge, black horses. It was the type of otherworldly scene one would expect to read about in a penny dreadful, not witness on the banks of the Thames; death's own carriage delivering two more black souls to his dark gates. But why had the sailors been murdered and dumped? Had they seen too much? Surely the man with the red eye patch would have heard about Felix's escape from the George Inn by now. If he believed Felix's cover story, he would undoubtedly assume that the entire police force was searching for him. It would then stand to reason that, if on the run, he might feel the need to dispose of anyone who might be a liability or, even worse, lead the police to his whereabouts. Like the officer said, sailors liked to drink, and when they drank, they often got into trouble.

'Prime Minister,' said Thompson, distracting Felix from his thoughts. 'Walk with me for a moment, if you will.'

Thompson led Felix away from the crime scene to a quiet spot along the river, out of the way of any listening ears.

'I know the identity of one of the corpses,' he said, looking over his shoulder to ensure they weren't being listened to. 'His name is John Williams. He was one of my undercover officers working in the Docklands area. Well, before he turned, that is.'

'You mean he switched sides?' asked Felix.

'He stopped communicating with us over three months ago. We don't know why. Generally, it's either down to money or fear. Or, perhaps, he just preferred the life of a criminal. Either way, he became a huge liability to Scotland Yard.'

'Are you implying that someone inside the police might be responsible for these murders?'

'It's a possibility. They may have got wind of his identity and decided to profit from the information. I'm loathed to admit it, but there are still officers among our ranks who are easily corrupted.'

'And the alternative?' asked Felix.

'The alternative is that perhaps he got too close to the organisation's secrets and paid the price. These criminals like to cut some fat from time to time. It helps to weed out any informants in their ranks. Particularly if they felt we were getting close to them. It tends to happen before they go underground.'

'And then what?' asked Felix.

'London is like a great warren of rat holes,' replied Thompson. 'Perfect for society's vermin to disappear into. If they have gone underground, then there's little chance of us flushing them out anytime soon.'

'Then why did you ask me to meet you here,

Commissioner?' asked Felix, suddenly confused.

Thompson took a moment to consider Felix's words. 'Because, Prime Minister, I need you to see and understand what we're up against. And, I need to know if there's anything more you may have heard in your gentlemen's clubs that you're not telling me?'

Felix observed Thompson a little taken aback by the boldness of his words. 'Are you implying that I'm keeping secrets from the police?' he asked.

'Not secrets,' replied Thompson. 'Information, perhaps.'

'And why would I do that?'

'I asked around the East India Club, as you suggested, and it appears that Burbage's financial woes are far from common knowledge. In fact, there was no knowledge of them at all. Which made me think, how did the Prime Minister come across such valuable information?'

'It's not what you know, Commissioner; it is who.'

'And who do you know with such access to a person's private financial affairs?'

Felix hesitated. He couldn't name Amelia or explain her students' efforts without divulging the ploy to trap Burbage on the poker table and giving away the rest of his work on the case.

'I'm the Prime Minister, Commissioner. I know many people in high places.'

'And there's nothing more these *people* have expressed to you that I, as the head of the police, should know?'

'If there were anything more to be said, you would have heard it,' replied Felix turning abruptly and departing.

Lost to his thoughts, Felix barely registered the journey back from Shad Thames. It was almost as if he'd stepped into the cab, passed through the vehicle and out the other side already at

Downing Street. He returned to his study to document the day's revelations. He wrote a detailed account of everything he'd witnessed at Shad Thames and the content of his private conversation with Thompson. Usually, committing his thoughts to paper calmed Felix, but on this occasion, it simply magnified his anxiety. Surprisingly, it wasn't observing the two dead bodies on the riverbank playing on Felix's mind, but the sudden sense that the case was slipping through his fingers and, with it, any chance of ever finding the missing lords. It had been close to a week since their disappearance, and without Tom Fellows or the one-eyed man, there was little else to go on.

Felix examined his notes, trying to piece together all that had happened over the past few days, but the case was still as vague and disjointed as it had been every day since the news of Monteagle's disappearance. The only line of enquiry appeared to revolve around Mr G Pulleyn and his connection to the gamblers at Burbage's poker table. But whoever Burbage's mysterious benefactor was, he had gone to great lengths to protect his identity. There was also a tenuous link to Yorkshire. But could it be merely a coincidence that Mr G Pulleyn's lawyers, William Foster, and the politician who callously plotted his entry into Number 10 were1 from the county? Either way, Felix would have to wait for news from Amelia about the Holgate Road Carriage Works and the Commissioner's investigation into the poker players before he could even hope to start piecing it all together.

Carlton Club

Felix awoke the following day to a tray of messages. Humphrey had left him to catch up on some much-needed sleep, placing a light breakfast of smoked fish and bread on his desk beside the neatly folded newspapers and a cluster of envelopes.

The first message Felix opened was from Amelia. Her students had discovered some interesting information on the Holgate Road Carriage Works, and, sick of being cooped up at the university, she had purchased a ticket on the afternoon train to London to present her findings to Felix in person. It would be good to have the Professor's presence and energy around the place, thought Felix. Having spent another night tossing and turning, he desperately needed an injection of optimism, and

Amelia administered those in abundance.

The second note was from Commissioner Thompson. It was characteristically blunt and to the point, informing Felix that the factory fires had finally been put out and the smoke cleared, paving the way for the police to enter and carry out their investigation.

The third note, however, took Felix entirely by surprise. It had come from the leader of the opposition, Milton Cavendish.

Prime Minister.

With the confidence vote looming, the investigation into the lords bearing no fruits, and the country in the grip of widespread rioting, I feel it only fitting that we, the leaders of the two major parties, meet to discuss a meaningful solution to mending our broken country. Therefore, I invite you to meet me at the Carlton Club this afternoon to discuss these most extraordinary times and make the necessary arrangements before the state re-opening.

Milton Cavendish

Felix placed the note to one side, unsure how to feel about his opponent's invitation. It was unlike Cavendish to offer an olive branch when there was an opportunity to use the stick. But these were *extraordinary times*, as Cavendish had noted, and perhaps he was prepared to put his duty for his country above his ambitions for the time being. Curious to uncover the truth, Felix prepared himself for the journey to Pall Mall and an audience with his great nemesis.

The Carlton Club was an elegant-looking building that stood imperiously on the corner of Pall Mall and Carlton Gardens, curiously close to the Reform Club, the famous Liberal Party equivalent. It was another great oddity of the British political establishment that, not fully satisfied with crossing each other's paths in the great halls of Westminster, these political foes had chosen to set up their members' clubs a mere stone's throw away from each other in Mayfair.

'Prime Minister?' called a crisp voice, garnering Felix's attention as he entered the lobby.

Felix turned to see the club's host approaching. He was an older man, immaculately dressed in a tailored suit with a member's pin on the collar of his double-breasted jacket next to his regimental Dragoon Guards badge. He limped slightly as he walked and used a stick with a silver horse's head in recognition of his time in the British Cavalry.

'Mr Cavendish is awaiting your presence,' he said formally, 'if you could follow me.'

Felix followed the host through the hall and up the ornate staircase. The older man's laboured pace gave the watching members time to study Felix as he passed, much to his annoyance. He had hoped to make a quiet and unobserved entrance into the Conservative stronghold rather than have his presence ballyhooed around the club within moments of entering. If it had been planned this way, it was a masterstroke from Cavendish, another point in their game of cat and mouse. Alerting the political establishment to Felix's arrival at the club would only add more buzz to the speculation surrounding his future, creating further uncertainty for Felix's few remaining supporters.

At the top of the stairs, the host finally came to a stop by a stained oak door. He knocked twice, then opened it, ushering Felix inside.

The room was surprisingly dark, with heavy brocade curtains covering the tall windows. In the dull light, Felix could make out sets of Chesterfields, separated by elegant mahogany tables, and portraits of prominent Conservative leaders lining the walls between rows of bookshelves and ornately framed mirrors. His eyes were suddenly drawn to a cloud of smoke drifting above a trolley laden with scotch and crystal glasses.

'I wouldn't usually indulge at this time of the day,' said Cavendish, stepping into the light, puffing on a cigar, 'however, with no one here to entertain me, I found myself getting rather bored. Does that ever happen to you, Felix? Does your mind require something to fill the silence?'

'I rarely receive the gift of silence,' replied Felix. 'There is always so much to think about in this job.'

'Then consider yourself fortunate. My father used to say, a busy man is a content man.'

'Or a sleep-deprived one.'

'Scotch?' proposed Cavendish. 'Parliament is in recess after all.'

'Not for me, thank you.' replied Felix.

'Suit yourself,' said Cavendish, pouring himself a small measure. 'My father also liked to say that, at times, a man can take on more than he can endure, and although unintentional, will cause more harm than good.'

'And by *a man*, am I to assume you're referring to me?' deduced Felix.

'Well, naturally,' replied Cavendish, raising his glass with a smile.

'You invited me, and I'm here,' said Felix, trying to hide his irritation. 'So, how would you have us save this great country of ours?'

'I would've thought that was obvious?' replied Cavendish scornfully. 'Oh, come now, Felix, surely you never really expected to stay the full term? The tide of popularism that sailed you into power was always likely to drag you back out, kicking and screaming. That, unfortunately, is how tides work.'

'I'm aware of the mechanics of tides.'

'You see, old boy, trivial fancies may last a few years, but true leaders,' declared Cavendish waving his cigar at the figures on the walls, 'well, they last for generations.'

Felix took a moment to look around the elegant room. He studied the large portraits, the towering bookshelves, and the beautifully crafted furniture. It oozed wealth and privilege from every corner and, undeniably, success. He turned back to Cavendish, supping on scotch and smoking his cigar, when it suddenly dawned on him that this wasn't a meeting at all but a victory parade. A chance for his adversary to lord it over him before delivering the decisive blow in the Commons. Cavendish was not merely content with winning; he wanted to savour the moment in front of the great Conservatives of the past.

'Perhaps I will have that scotch after all,' said Felix.

'That's the spirit, old boy,' clapped Cavendish, pouring Felix a glass.

'What with the riots, the missing lords, and not to mention the tenuous support in my own cabinet, what would be the point in continuing?'

'I couldn't agree more.' said Cavendish. 'I suggest we inform his Majesty of your desire to step down immediately and spare your reputation the unnecessary embarrassment of a vote.'

'Although, this rather irritating voice in the back of my mind keeps telling me that there is much more at stake here than just you or I.'

'What could be more important than being the British Prime Minister?' scoffed Cavendish.

'Does it not seem odd to you that all of these events are happening simultaneously? The abductions, the disasters, the riots? You said it yourself in your message, *these most extraordinary times.*'

'When it rains, it simply pours...'

'Until it stops entirely,' replied Felix. 'I don't suspect I'll be visiting his Majesty any time soon. Not while there's still a chance.'

'A chance!? There is no chance,' barked Cavendish. 'You will lose this vote and, with it, your government and any last semblance of a reputation.'

'Perhaps,' replied Felix. 'But not without a fight.'

Cavendish opened his mouth to respond when he was halted by a commotion coming from outside in the hallway. Agitated, he marched across the room and swung the door open.

'What's all the racket about?' he bellowed. 'I am trying to conduct a meeting in here!'

'The riots have stopped, Milton,' came a voice from out in the hall. 'All up and down the country, they've called it off.'

'What!?' exclaimed Cavendish, turning to face Felix.

'And just like that, the sun pokes its head through the clouds,' said Felix, placing his untouched drink on the table. 'See you in the Commons, Milton.'

Felix felt a surge of euphoria engulf him as he stepped out of the Carlton Club and onto Pall Mall. It had been a small victory in the grand scheme of things, but rather than sealing his fate, the meeting had ushered in the first shoots of recovery. Instead of returning to Parliament defeated, he could now return to his cabinet with his head held high, having not only brought an end to the riots but also faced down the opposition leader in his own gentlemen's club. It was the kind of tabloid fodder that had made prime ministers, not broken them. His euphoria, however, was short-lived when a convoy of police wagons galloped past him at full tilt before turning onto St James's Square. Concerned, Felix followed, turning the corner a few moments later to find the carriages parked outside the East India Club.

Felix entered the members club to find the main hall cordoned off and the police preventing anyone from leaving. The primary focus of their investigation seemed to be a room at the far end of the hallway. Felix stepped forward to look at the door, recognising it immediately from the small carving of the Hindu monkey god, Hanuman, on the outside. It was the same room Amelia had questioned Jonathan Burbage in a few days earlier. He made his way down the hall towards the thin doorway and stepped inside only to find the once gloriously decorated cluster of rooms ransacked and plundered. The beautifully crafted ivory and terracotta ornaments that had caught Felix's eye were now missing, and the bright silk curtains had been torn and ripped from their hooks.

'When was she last seen?' asked a familiar voice from the adjoining room.

Felix turned the corner to see Commissioner Thompson and a handful of officers deep in discussion.

'Commissioner?' he said, alerting Thompson to his presence.

'That will be all, chaps,' said Thompson, quickly clearing the room. 'How did you know we were here?' he asked, facing Felix.

'I stepped out of a meeting at the Carlton Club when I saw your carriages hurtling down the Mall.'

'Rather convenient, wouldn't you say?' replied Thompson.

'If you don't believe me, have your men look into it. I'm sure half of Westminster could verify my whereabouts by now. I was in a meeting with the leader of the opposition.'

'I see,' mumbled Thompson. 'Apologies, it's been a trying

few days.'

'No apologies required,' said Felix, looking around the small emerald room with its ornate tea sets and handmade sculptures twisted and strewn everywhere. 'Who do you suspect did this?'

'We know who did it, the question is, why?' said Thompson, closing the door to give the men some privacy. 'We received a message from the club reporting a burglary. One of the staff had walked in on the Indian hostess looting the room of all its valuable antiquities. When he tried to stop her, he was struck with a club, leaving him unconscious.'

'And where is the hostess now?' asked Felix.

'Gone,' replied Thompson. 'And I don't have much hope of finding her, either.'

'That's a little pessimistic, even by your standards, Commissioner,' said Felix.

'Everything you see here has been staged, Prime Minister,' replied Thompson, motioning around the room. 'The robbery, the vandalism, even the eyewitness. It's all been carefully crafted to make us believe that the hostess fled, having carried out a callous robbery.'

'But why?'

'After our meeting at Downing Street, I had my officers bring in the poker players who'd shared the table with Lord Monteagle. It soon became apparent under questioning that neither James nor Henry Coleridge, or that slimy insurance man they associate with, Clement Morris, had ever heard or done any business with anyone named Mr G Pulleyn.'

'And you believe they were telling the truth?'

'I do,' replied Thompson. 'They did, however, furnish us with some fascinating information. It wasn't Jonathan Burbage who invited them to the East India Club to play cards on the evening of Monteagle's abduction. Neither was it, Mr G Pulleyn. Each of the guests received a hand-delivered invitation from...'

'The hostess,' answered Felix.

'Precisely,' said Thompson. 'Once word got out that a connection had been made to Burbage's estate debts, she knew it was only a matter of time until we uncovered her part in Monteagle's abduction. Having realised the game was up, it appears she staged this robbery, hoping to throw us off the scent and make her escape in the meantime.

'Disappearing underground,' concluded Felix.

'I'm afraid so,' replied Thompson gravely. 'I have deployed some of my best men to find her, but I suspect she is very far from reach by now.'

Felix took a moment to consider Thompson's explanation of events. He knew that Burbage hadn't been familiar with his guests before the night of the poker match but had assumed that by being hand-picked to attend, each man would've had a personal connection to Burbage's mysterious benefactor. The police would only have to question them and find the link. He hadn't considered that the hostess might have organised their attendance on Pulleyn's behalf, no matter how obvious it seemed now.

How quickly one's fortunes changed in this world, thought Felix. He'd barely stepped out of the Carlton Club, enthused for the first time in weeks when his attention had turned to the East India Club and another loose end. There was also the continued absence of Alfred. Barely had a moment passed when he had not been in Felix's thoughts. With the vote looming and much to document, Felix made the journey back to Downing Street, determined to complete his work and begin his search for the young man, when he was greeted in the hallway by a disgruntled-looking Humphrey.

'Is everything alright?' he asked, surprised to see his steward so flustered.

'The gunslinger is in the Cabinet Room,' bristled Humphrey, taking Felix's coat. 'She's regaling the footmen with stories of her time lassoing cattle in the Wild West.'

'I see,' said Felix, trying to mask his amusement. 'Leave it with me. I'll see to it that she stops distracting the staff.'

'If you could, Prime Minister,' replied Humphrey.

The Cabinet Room was long and rectangular, with high ceilings supported by Corinthian columns. Midway along the south-facing wall stood a colossal marble fireplace with a portrait of Sir Robert Walpole sitting imperiously above it, flanked on either side by two bookcases housing the prime minister's library. The cabinet table sat in the middle of the room as the central feature, and sitting in the prime minister's seat, holding court with a handful of Downing Street staff was Amelia Woodruff.

Amelia was dressed in a curious outfit, a collision of American and British fashion, consisting of a cravat and braces alongside the type of full-length leather hide overcoat one would typically associate with a rancher.

'... and that's why I never accept a drink from anyone carrying a rope or spitting tobacco!' she concluded, accentuating her Texan, much to the amusement of the watching staff.

'Not the most orthodox Cabinet meeting I've ever witnessed,' said Felix, entering the room. 'Nor is it the worst.'

'Apologies, Prime Minister.' bowed one of the young footmen, quickly hurrying out of the room, followed closely by his colleagues.

'Am I in trouble?' quipped Amelia, watching them depart.

'They'll be treading on eggshells around me for months now.' replied Felix.

'Perhaps Humphrey can reassure them. It will help him develop his more-sensitive side. Come to mention it, where is the great man? He was here one minute and gone the next. You don't think he dabbles in black magic, do you?'

'If he did, I'm sure you'd be the first target on his list. Now, have you come to cause havoc with my staff or assist me?' asked Felix. 'You mentioned some information about the Holgate Road Carriage Works in your note?'

'To business then, if we must,' replied Amelia, sitting up straighter. 'The Holgate Road Carriage Works is a large manufacturer of train engines and carriages, as the name so cunningly suggests. They've been established in the area for nearly twenty years and employ many local men and women. As you can imagine, they wield great influence in the area and are connected to several local politicians, all looking to garner support for their campaigns. However!' exclaimed Amelia, pausing for effect, 'there is a person of particular interest who sits on their board and recently helped them raise a large sum of money to extend their premises.'

'Well?' pressed Felix after another of Amelia's exaggerated silences.

'None other than the Honourable Member for Scarborough and Whitby, Mr Barnaby Shaw.'

'The Shadow Chancellor?'

'Precisely,' replied Amelia, sitting back in Felix's chair.

'He would know how a factory works...' mused Felix.

'I should hope so,' joked Amelia. 'Or he'd be a pretty substandard choice to run one.'

'That's not what I meant. To orchestrate these disasters, a person would need to know how an industrial plant operates.

'Agreed,' nodded Amelia.

'They would also need the financial and political means to influence people and conceal their involvement?'

'That too.'

'Now consider the profile of Shaw. He is from a wealthy Yorkshire family with the financial and political influence required. He has a vested interest in toppling the government, and given his relationship with the Holgate Road Carriage Works, he also knows the workings of a factory. He could have planned these disasters and made them look like accidents to stir up unrest among the workers.'

'The theory has merit.'

'He would even have the luxury of watching the political fallout from each event in the Commons,' continued Felix, on a roll, 'simply instructing his cronies in the unions to strike as and when required.'

'Yes, but why then, in that case, would the TUC decide to call off the riots?' asked Amelia, questioning the theory.

'Perhaps they were unaware of his plan and believed the disasters to be genuine accidents, like the rest of us.'

'Or perhaps they decided to switch sides,' suggested Amelia. 'You know what you Brits are like; you'll do anything to back the winning horse.'

'I'm hardly winning, as Cavendish was so quick to point out during our meeting. But you're right; the union connection doesn't make sense. There's still a missing link.'

As Felix pondered the information, Humphrey entered to inform them that Percy had arrived. However, before the old steward could finish his announcement, the Home Secretary marched past him, looking red-faced.

'Now, Felix, I realise it has been an extremely testing time, and on the surface of it all, things may seem a tad hopeless,' he blurted out without taking a breath, 'but I must insist that you refrain from agreeing on any deals with that snake Cavendish and face this vote head-on. The riots have stopped, and we are on the up!'

'It's fine, Thomas,' said Felix, concerned by his colleague's pulsating chest. 'There will be no deals,' he continued, lowering Percy into one of the chairs to catch his breath.

'But I heard you were at the Carlton Club?'

'Cavendish requested a meeting. He wanted me to step down and gently rub my nose in it. But I refused.'

'Thank God,' puffed Percy, finally relaxing. 'The arrogance of the man, to think we would step aside for him and his cronies without a fight!

'Yes, well, the fight is far from won, but with the riots ended, we may have just given ourselves a puncher's chance.'

'Then there is no time to waste!' exclaimed Percy, springing back out of his chair. 'We need to maximise our every advantage. I'll rally our members and have the whips whipping up a storm,' he said, bounding out of the Cabinet Room with a renewed vigour, much to Felix's and Amelia's amazement.

Old Kent Road

Back in his study, Felix jotted down a record of his meeting with Cavendish, followed by the events at the East India Club and Amelia's findings on the Holgate Road Carriage Works. As he committed the details to paper, Felix's mind drifted back to his previous meetings with Thompson, the appearance of William Foster at Number 10, and even his time at Houlston and Sons, searching for a link that might complete the chain and unlock the entire mystery.

He flicked back through the journal, reading past accounts, trying to find a connection. The most obvious link was the Shadow Chancellor. Shaw was from a wealthy Yorkshire family and had the money and power to influence people and keep his business affairs out of the public eye, much like Pulleyn's affairs had been. A thought suddenly struck Felix. What if Shaw was Pulleyn? He had unparalleled access to Parliament and the missing lords' schedules. He would only have to follow them briefly to learn their routines and plan the ideal moment to strike. Once the abductions were committed, he could simply sit back and conduct his affairs from Westminster, keeping informed of the police's progress and manoeuvring his cronies as required. It all added up, except for the most important detail; why?

Felix could understand the need for the factory disasters. They provided the opportunity to cause large-scale unrest, weakening his position in government and leading to a vote of no confidence. But why the lords? Why would he go to the trouble of abducting such highly regarded men? It was a gaping hole in his reasoning, alongside his uncertainty over any connection to the TUC. In reality, Shaw's only crimes were his connection to the Holgate Road Carriage Works, a local company in his constituency with a loose connection to William Foster and being from Yorkshire. Felix could name several parliamentarians with affiliations to local businesses in their voting area. It was common practice and certainly not evidence enough to convince Thompson of any wrongdoing. He would need something more concrete before daring to accuse a fellow member of Parliament of anything so heinous.

Felix closed his journal and reached for the crystal decanter housing his scotch. He barely removed the stopper when he heard a scratching sound coming from the fireplace. He crossed the room, looking curiously at the marble mantelpiece, when a soft voice echoed from behind the coal-stained panel.

'Prime Minister,' it called softly. 'It's me.'

Felix quickly turned the marble corbel, opening the secret

passage, and Alfred stepped through the fireplace into the study. He looked scruffy, with wild hair and puffy eyes, like he hadn't slept or washed in weeks.

'Welcome back,' said Felix gently. 'You have been missed.'

Alfred's face turned red. He'd rarely received such warmth from his own father, let alone from the British Prime Minister.

'I've found him, Tom Fellows,' he blurted out, bursting with nervous energy. 'He's holed up on the Old Kent Road. If we go now, we'll be able to catch him before he…'

'Slow down,' said Felix. 'Tell me how you came about finding him.'

Alfred nodded, taking a few deep breaths. 'When I left,' he began, 'I went straight to the Docklands, but no one had seen him in days. He'd gone on the missing list. I thought about coming back, seeing as how cold it was on the street and all, but every time I thought about it, I could see Mr Houlston's face tied to that old printer staring back at me. So, I went to the George Inn and waited there, hoping he'd show his face. And he did. Only for a moment, mind. He came back to pick something up and was in and out before you knew it. I didn't recognise him at first. He looked smaller, and he'd let his beard grow out. He didn't look right in the eyes, either.'

'What was he picking up?'

'Money. I saw him counting it through the window before he left. There was a bit. Enough to keep him going for a while anyway.'

'Then what?'

'I followed him to Old Kent Road. He walked all the way. It took forever. He kept stopping to look over his shoulder. Nervous he was being followed.'

'Are you sure he didn't see you?'

'I'm sure,' said Alfred. 'Anyway, I don't think he was looking for the likes of me. He looked scared out of his wits.'

'Where is he now?'

'He's taken a room in a pub.'

Having listened to Alfred's account and desperate not to let another lead slip through his fingers and disappear underground, Felix decided to journey to Old Kent Road to confront the villainous innkeeper himself. He led the way back through the study fireplace and down the secret passage towards Old Pye Street, where he replaced his tailored suit jacket and Oxford shoes with a tradesman's coat, hat and boots from the collection.

'I'll flag us a cab,' said Alfred eagerly.

'That won't be necessary,' said Felix, stopping him in his tracks. 'I want you to stay here.'

'I don't understand?' replied Alfred. 'I found him. I waited all those hours in the cold for him to come back. I need to…'

'Rest,' said Felix, cutting in. 'You need to rest. You've done what you set out to do, Alfred. You found him. Now let me do what I must, while you regain your strength.'

'But…'

'I insist,' said Felix, interrupting him. 'You can't do it alone, and nor should you have to. Not when you have friends in your corner.'

Alfred reluctantly nodded, turning even redder than before. He gave Felix details of the pub where Tom Fellows was staying and a brief description of the landlord's dramatic change in appearance so that he would recognise him, then collapsed on his makeshift bed to rest.

Outside, Felix could smell the moisture in the air. He hurried through Old Pye Street and onto Victoria Street, where he hailed a Hansom cab before the heavens finally opened, covering

London in another of its famous downpours. Felix instructed the driver, and they set off eastwards towards Old Kent Road. He hadn't realised he'd fallen asleep until the driver banged on the carriage box to wake him.

'Here we go then!' he called out. 'The Bricklayer's Arms, Old Kent Road.'

Felix quickly rose and stepped out of the carriage. He paid the driver, who, having pocketed the money, quickly pulled on the reins and ordered his horses away, reluctant to hover in the area any longer than necessary. Old Kent Road was one of London's notorious thoroughfares. Part of an ancient trackway built by the Romans linking London to the coast, it had been repeatedly shortened over the years, housing groups of industrial workers and blossoming into a haven for organised crime.

Felix took a moment to study his surroundings. The area was a hub of commercial activity, with narrow streets of stall owners and barrow boys selling all manner of unusual and exotic trinkets. The carriage had barely departed when Felix was offered the first of his many *deals of a century* on goods ranging from Spanish ivory to elegant silks from India.

Having navigated the energetic merchants with his wallet still intact, Felix crossed the dirty cobbled street towards the Bricklayers Arms. The pub was a large building set over four floors at the end of a row of terraced cottages. Green and maroon tiles covered the outer walls, and a vast red-and-white sign advertising the pub's stout adorned the upper level. Felix took a deep breath and entered.

The pub was overflowing with industrial workers washing off the dust from a long day on the job. Felix slowly walked through the crowd, carefully observing each face as he passed, looking for Tom Fellows. He could see why the errant landlord had chosen

Old Kent Road as his hiding place. With such a massive volume of people passing through every day and the constant influx of industrial workers, it was the perfect place for a person to disappear. Even the locals would struggle to bump into a familiar face from one day to the next.

Having walked the length of the pub with no sign of Fellows, Felix was about to circle back when a man in an ill-fitting suit and flat cap stepped in front of him, holding an expensive-looking leather suitcase with two brass locks and a briefcase of the same style.

'You look like a man of taste,' he said, flashing the items in Felix's face. 'How would you like to be the proud owner of one of these fine cases?'

'I'm not interested,' said Felix, trying to step past the man.

'Hold your horses,' protested the salesman blocking Felix's path. 'You haven't even looked at them yet.' He held up the leather suitcase. 'This one 'ere is what the gentlemen in Mayfair call, 'and luggage. You could go a long way being seen with one of these in your 'ands.'

'I said I'm not interested,' repeated Felix.

'On the other 'and, this one,' continued the salesman, raising his other arm to showcase the briefcase, 'is more your City of London style item. All the bankers carry these. Make you look like you're from proper stock. And you can't put a price on that now, can you?'

Irritated by the intrusion, Felix stepped to the side to leave when he spotted a shadowy figure weaving through the crowds towards the exit. Out of the window, he saw a thinner, more bearded Tom Fellows depart the Bricklayer's Arms and step into the hubbub outside. Felix looked back at the salesman, suddenly realising what was happening. Having spotted him enter the pub,

Fellows had paid the salesman to keep Felix occupied long enough for him to escape. Felix quickly pushed past the decoy and fought his way back through the crowds, exiting the pub, only to find that Fellows had disappeared. Evaporated into the chaos of Old Kent Road.

Felix berated himself. How could he have failed so soon and so spectacularly? How could he have been so foolish? Clearly, the streetwise landlord would have been on high alert, looking closely for enemies trying to find him. He would always have eyes and ears on the pub door, just waiting for the moment to flee. Simply strolling in, undisguised, was always destined to fail, like setting a bear trap to catch a mouse.

He scanned the street in both directions, as far as his eyes could see, but with so much life around him, it was like looking for a black cat in a coal cellar. He was about to turn and leave when he heard a loud yelp from one of the adjoining streets. He turned and sprinted towards the alleyway, only to find Fellows knelt on the cobbled floor, cradling his arm in agony. Stood over the landlord, gripping a length of scrap piping, was Alfred.

'He was trying to get away,' he said apologetically.

'You were supposed to stay away,' said Felix, unable to hide his disappointment.

'I tried to. But I kept seeing his face every time I closed my eyes. I was worried the same might happen to…'

Alfred stopped, realising that Fellows was watching.

'I was just going to keep an eye out; in case you needed me. Honest. Until I saw him run like the rat he is.'

Alfred pointed the pipe at Fellows.

'Don't hit me,' cried Fellows, curling his thin frame into a ball on the floor.

Felix took a moment to study Fellows. He suddenly looked

pathetic, a far cry from the man he'd met just a few days ago at the George Inn.

'We aren't going to hurt you,' said Felix.

'You're not?' said Fellows, cautiously looking up.

'No, we're going to take you back inside that pub, and you're going to tell us everything you know. Or, I'll have you arrested right now and put behind bars. Understood?'

'Understood,' replied Fellows.

Felix secured a table in a quiet corner of the pub and ordered a jug of stout to help settle Fellow's nerves before commencing with his questions.

'Where are the missing lords?' he asked in a low voice, mindful of any listening ears.

'What are you talking about?' sneered Fellows. 'I don't know anything about any missing lords.'

Felix studied Fellows. He seemed genuinely perplexed by the mention of the lords. Was it possible that he didn't know what the cards he printed were for?

'You expect us to believe you?' bristled Alfred, finding it hard to contain his anger now that he was faced with Mr Houlston's killer.

'Believe what you want, young'un,' said Fellows. 'It doesn't matter to me either way.'

Fellows took a long swig of stout, wiping the foam off his beard with his sleeve.

'Well, this might matter to you,' said Felix, 'Two lords have been abducted, and those cards you had printed at Houlston and Sons were left at each of the crime scenes.'

'I didn't know what they were using them for! You can't pin that on me! I'm just another one of their lackeys. They tell me what to pick up and drop off, and I do it. I don't ask any questions.

That's how you end up dead.'

'Like Mr Houlston?' asked Felix.

'I had nothing to do with that!' replied Fellows.

'Or your two sailor friends?' added Felix.

Fellow's eyes dropped to the table.

'We fished them out of Shad Thames last night,' continued Felix.

'I had nothing to do with that either,' said Fellows, taking another gulp of his drink. 'I may be many things, a crook, a thief, an alcoholic. But I'm not a murderer.'

'That seems hard to believe, given the circumstances,' said Felix.

'It's the truth!' barked Fellows.

'Then tell us what happened?' pressed Felix. 'We might be able to help.'

'I'm beyond helping,' replied Fellows, holding his head in his hands. 'I didn't know what he was planning. I can still hear them now, clawing at the door to get out,' he continued, gulping down the rest of his drink. 'More stout!' he shouted across the bar.

'Who can you hear?' asked Felix.

'Them poor workers in those factories,' replied Fellows, looking up sorrowfully. 'It was just like at the printers. We were only supposed to damage the building. You know, make it look like an accident. The old printer even stood to make a pretty penny on the insurance. But that wasn't enough for him. No, he needed to destroy it all, even the old man. He tied him to that machine and just stood there, watching him burn. It was the same at the factory. He had us bolt the doors, trapping everyone inside. We couldn't do anything about it. No one would dare question him.'

'Who?' asked Alfred, shocked.

'The one-eyed man,' replied Felix, putting it all together.

'Ezra Fox is his name,' whispered Fellows looking over his shoulder nervously. 'He's the devil.'

'Where is he now?' asked Felix.

'I don't know. I fled as soon as I got the chance. After what happened to the others, I figured I was next on his list.'

'What is his connection to all of this?'

'I don't know, but it must be someone high up. Let's just say Ezra's the one usually giving the orders.'

'Who?'

'You're not listening to me! I don't know! I'm just a lackey. Someone he could kick around and use, like a stray dog.'

'Listen to me,' said Felix, trying to pull Fellows out of the melancholy rapidly consuming him, along with the stout. 'If everything you say is true, then you still have a chance. But you need to help us find him before he causes any more destruction. Is there anything else you can remember, anything at all? It could make all the difference. It could save lives.'

Fellows looked up at Felix, struggling to hold back his tears. It was clear that the past few days' events had weighed heavily on his shoulders and that he believed any hope of redemption had turned to ash, along with the factories.

'I did overhear them speaking about something,' he said, trying to recall the conversation. 'One last job, somewhere in East London. *A place with a significant workforce* is what Ezra said. *The kind of job no one would ever forget.*'

'Do you have any idea where?' asked Felix.

'That's all I heard.'

'Think!' pressed Felix. 'Is there anything else? Anything you did or spoke about, however small, or out of the ordinary?'

'He did say something about the flames,' replied Fellows.

'What flames?' asked Felix.

'I can't remember fully!' said Fellows. 'Something about the wood and chemicals, and the flames…'

'Wood and chemicals?' repeated Felix, frustrated. 'That could be any factory in the country! What else?'

'I don't know!' bellowed Fellows, starting to shake. 'I can't think. I just kept my head down and obeyed orders,' he mumbled, tears streaming down his face. 'I was scared. I was so scared.'

Alfred stood up, unsure where to look. It was hard to witness Fellows breaking down in front of him. He'd spent such a long time blaming this man for Mr Houlston's death that he suddenly felt a tug of remorse hearing his explanation and seeing his grief.

Having spotted Alfred's discomfort, Felix rose from his seat. 'It's okay,' he said, placing a hand on the young man's shoulder. 'We're finished here.'

'You're going?' asked Fellows. 'What am I supposed to do now?' he asked, the panic returning to his voice.

'Leave and go straight to Scotland Yard,' said Felix. 'When you get there, ask for Commissioner Thompson and tell him everything you have just told me.'

'Hand myself in?' questioned Fellows. 'That'll be the day.'

'You could stay here and take your chances,' said Felix. 'Although, if we managed to find you, I'm sure it won't be long until your enemies do the same. The police are your only hope.'

'Hope?' sniggered Fellows. 'All my hope died with them poor folk in those factories.'

Fellows gulped down the remainder of his stout and pulled the large jug towards him, ready to lose himself for the night.

With little left to say, Felix turned and led the way back through the rowdy punters and out of the Bricklayers Arms, followed closely by Alfred.

Match Makers of Bryant and May

Dismayed by the news of another impending disaster, Felix and Alfred returned to Old Pye Street, determined to uncover the location of the new factory target before Ezra Fox and his men could cause any more death or destruction. Based on the account Fellows gave of a conversation he'd overheard while in Ezra's employment, they were looking for a site in East London with a *significant* workforce. It would have to be a large manufacturer with an enormous staff if the plan was to match or exceed the significance of the previous disasters. But even shrinking the field down to large enterprises didn't help narrow the search a great deal. Over the past few years, East London's population had boomed, and large commercial sites had popped up all over the East End. Felix had even patronised two earlier in the year, the new Hartley's Jam Factory in Bermondsey, and the Truman Brewery, which showed no signs of slowing down its expansion in Brick Lane.

However, there was one distinguishing detail from the case that could help narrow the search down. Each of the previous disasters had occurred at a long-established factory with seemingly old or malfunctioning machinery. Ezra Fox and his cronies had capitalised on the worker's anxiety around their outdated equipment to plan the disasters and conceal their involvement, making each tragedy appear the consequence of political penny-pinching rather than foul play. If they were to locate the target, Felix and Alfred would have to find a site with both the appropriate size and age.

Before turning his attention to the Old Pye Street encyclopaedias, Felix drafted a letter to the Chief Record Keeper at the Public Record Office asking for lists of all the large-scale factories operating in the East London area over the past twenty years. Alfred watched the telephone switchboard, hoping to spot any call patterns that might help narrow the search even further. Neither looked up from their work for hours until a ray of light broke through the crooked window frame, bouncing off Felix's desk. Felix checked his pocket watch; it was almost six in the morning. He stepped away from his desk and approached the telephone switchboard.

'Alfred, the sun is rising; we've worked through the night,' he said, placing a hand on the young man's shoulder.

To his amazement, exhausted, Alfred had fallen fast asleep upright in his chair. Felix carefully lowered him onto the makeshift bed he'd set up on the floor and covered him with a sheet before quietly gathering his papers and leaving.

Having passed through the secret passage back to his study at Downing Street, Felix placed his papers on the desk with a note requesting that Humphrey deliver his letter to the Public Record Office, then went to his bedroom to change clothes and prepare for the day.

Felix entered the dining room to find Amelia sitting at the long table with her head buried in a letter. She was dressed in a green and red tartan jacket with a matching shirt and wore a Texan rancher's hat with its brim edges rolled up, exposing her face. It had been a while since Felix had seen Amelia so quiet or the environment around her so tranquil. It was a troubling feeling that gave the immediate impression that something terrible had happened.

'What is it, Amelia?' he asked, approaching the professor.

'A message from my students. They've been looking into the name Pulleyn, hoping to shed some light on its etymology.'

'And?'.

'And it appears that the name was quite active in mainland Europe... until the early 17th century when it suddenly died out. Well, until now, that is, of course,' smiled Amelia.

'Then why are you smiling?'

'Because it means, Prime Minister, that this Mr G Pulleyn isn't real. It's a spurious name.'

'You mean we've been searching for someone who doesn't exist?'

'Yes! Wonderful, isn't it?' beamed Amelia.

'No, it's not wonderful, Amelia,' said Felix. 'I don't see how chasing after shadows this whole time can be a good thing. Not when people are being murdered.'

'Whomever Pulleyn really is,' said Amelia, placing the note on the table, 'he would've known about the name and its obsolescence; otherwise, it seems hugely coincidental that he would've opted to use it and not simply concoct some meaningless entity instead. You see, there must be some connection to the name, some method to it. A reason for him to want to retain it.'

'What kind of connection?'

'I'm not sure, but if we can uncover why it disappeared as it did, it may give us a clue as to who has resurrected it and why.'

'How do we find out why the name disappeared?' asked Felix.

Amelia toyed with the brim of her hat, considering the question. 'Why does a name die out?' she asked.

'By natural process?' suggested Felix. 'Perhaps the remaining Pulleyns were incapable of conceiving any children?'

'It's possible, as is the prospect of financial ruin, social exclusion, and disease. My knowledge of historical epidemics is a little hazy, but I believe there were several outbreaks of the plague during the mid-17th century. That would have done away with whole towns of people and generations of family names.'

Felix had barely had the chance to consider Amelia's words when Humphrey entered, looking a little flustered.

'Commissioner Thompson is here to see you,' he said, glancing from Felix to Amelia and then back again.

'Is that your not-so-subtle way of asking me to leave?' questioned Amelia.

'You really are picking up on our customs marvellously,' replied Humphrey.

'You know something, Humphrey,' said Amelia, standing up and straightening her hat, 'if it doesn't work out for you here, you could always start a career in hospitality. I could see you as the front of house at some swanky gentlemen's club or even as a pub landlord, with that delicate touch of yours.'

'Pubs are for commoners and babble-mouths,' replied Humphrey. 'Perhaps you might find one while the Prime Minister conducts his business with the Commissioner?'

Amelia smiled and stepped away from the table.

'It's taken some time, but you're finally starting to warm to me!' she declared.

'Like cattle to a lasso,' replied Humphrey.

'I knew it! I knew you couldn't resist listening to my little narrations.'

'I may have overheard a word or two. It's my job to be the eyes and ears of this house. Likewise, if I were looking for a name that had mysteriously died out but had since been resurrected by a criminal, I would first investigate any historical references to its criminal past. Criminality breeds criminality, you see.'

'Of course!' said Amelia. 'Had the name passed into infamy, then there would have been an execution or a long imprisonment, which would have been documented.'

'And which may have left a lingering sense of injustice and the need for retribution.' added Humphrey.

Excited, Amelia reached for her overcoat.

'Where are you going?' asked Felix.

'To visit an old friend,' replied Amelia, hurrying for the door.

With the calm restored, Humphrey led Commissioner Thompson into the dining room.

'Tea?' offered Felix, pouring himself a cup from a freshly brewed pot.

'Not for me, thank you,' replied Thompson. 'I don't plan on taking up too much of your time. I've come to disclose some recent information.'

Felix looked up from the tea tray, intrigued.

'This morning, a rather peculiar incident occurred at the station. A shabby and destitute-looking man named Tom Fellows walked into Scotland Yard and asked for me directly. He said he was involved in the disasters at Birchwood, Morden, New Malden and Surbiton, all of which had been planned and executed by a group of criminals from the London Docklands led by a local ruffian named Ezra Fox. He also said that he had been persuaded by one of my investigating officers to hand himself in. Yet, having questioned my men, it appears that none of them has ever heard of this Tom Fellows, let alone advised him to come forward.'

'That does sound peculiar,' agreed Felix, trying to look surprised.

'He did, however, describe this investigating officer,' Thompson continued, reaching into his pocket, and taking out a folded piece of paper. 'I had my best man sketch a rough version of his face.'

Thompson unfolded the paper and handed it to Felix.

Felix studied the drawing. The likeness was unquestionable. It was as though he was looking at himself in a mirror. He felt his stomach lurch. He knew how damaging this could be to the case and the impending vote should news of his involvement get out. It was almost unthinkable for the Prime Minister to engage in such low behaviour. Felix turned his attention back to Thompson. Over the past week, he had begun to respect the Commissioner's diligent work ethic and commitment to the job, but there was still a question mark in his mind over which side he was working for. If the past week's events had taught Felix anything, it was that nobody was ever quite what they seemed. It had been the case with Mr Houlston, Jonathan Burbage, Mrs Hughes and, even more recently, Tom Fellows.

'This is absurd,' he said, returning the paper to Thompson. 'He has clearly given a description of me to deflect from your investigation.'

'But why would he,' asked Thompson, 'when he has handed himself in and willingly given over valuable information?'

'Perhaps he wanted to derive some merriment at your expense?'

'So, you've never met with this Tom Fellows?' asked Thompson.

'And where exactly was I supposed to have encountered this criminal? Here? In the Commons? At Buckingham Palace?'

'The Old Kent Road…' said Thompson, suddenly aware of how absurd his accusation sounded when said out loud.

'Let me see if I understand what you're suggesting, Commissioner,' said Felix. 'You believe that the Prime Minister, already busy with a spate of industrial disasters, national riots and with a vote of confidence in a mere two days, has had the time – let alone the inclination – to have been carrying out erroneous meetings with criminals on the Old Kent Road?'

'Well, when you say it like that…'

'Interesting theory,' continued Felix, cutting across Thompson. 'Let's try some alternative theories, shall we? You said that this man, this Fellows, had been prompted to hand himself in by one of your investigating officers. Is that correct?'

'Yes,' replied Thompson.

'You also said that none of your men had come forward to claim their involvement in his sudden appearance at Scotland Yard?'

'That's correct.'

'Had it not occurred to you then that perhaps this

investigating officer of yours, keen to protect his identity, given that one of your other undercover officers was recently fished out of the Thames, had sworn Fellows to secrecy? Or perhaps, this Fellows chap, having realised the game was up and decided to hand himself in, has concocted this story to help his cause?'

'There is merit in both possibilities.'

'Either way,' continued Felix, on a roll, 'when asked to describe the investigating officer, and keen to not disappoint, he probably recalled a face he was familiar with that he'd seen in a newspaper or pamphlet. It could just as easily have been the King's face or Captain Scott's. I suppose I should be flattered. It's not often I get preferential treatment from the public.'

'Yes, well, I think I've taken up quite enough of your time, Prime Minister,' said Thompson sheepishly. 'I should probably be making my way back to the Yard. We have reason to believe that these criminals may be planning another disaster somewhere in London.'

'Do you have any promising information or leads?' asked Felix, pretending to be surprised.

'Nothing of any substance. We believe the target to be closer to the East of London than the previous attacks and larger in scale. We have men scouring the area, assessing as many sites as possible, but we simply don't have the manpower to watch them all.'

'Of course not,' sympathised Felix. 'Let me know if I can help in any way,' he added, ending the meeting cordially.

'Thank you, Prime Minister,' said Thompson, taking his leave.

Although the meeting had been trying, news that the police were also looking for the next factory target filled Felix with the hope that they may still find Ezra Fox and his men before it was too late. By informing the police of the impending disaster, Tom Fellows had taken the first step on a long road to redemption and, in the process, ensured that hundreds of bobbies would be out on the streets, monitoring industrial sites all over East London. If Felix and Alfred could find a way to uncover the target, they would have every resource needed to apprehend these criminals.

Felix returned to Old Pye Street to continue his search. He entered the oval-shaped office to find Alfred back at the telephone switchboard, hard at work. He watched the young man for a few seconds, impressed by his perseverance. If only half the politicians in Westminster had the same sense of purpose or enviable moral compass.

'Morning, Alfred,' he said, alerting the young man to his presence.

Alfred turned to face Felix. 'Sorry about last night. I, erm, must've nodded off,' he stuttered.

'That's quite alright. You must have been exhausted. Anything of any note?' asked Felix, pointing at the telephone switchboard.

'Not yet,' replied Alfred.

Felix approached the large, full-scale model of London in the centre of the room, scanning its flawless detail, looking for anything that might assist their search.

'Why East London?' he mused. 'There are police on every street. Eyes everywhere.'

'Maybe on every street, but not the river,' said Alfred.

'There are no police on the river?' questioned Felix, surprised.

'Some,' replied Alfred, stepping away from the telephone switchboard, 'near Westminster and the city, where the rich folks are. But once you get a bit further down the river,' he said, pointing at the area around London Bridge and leading out east, 'there's not a bobby in sight. That's how we smuggled materials into the city from the docks.'

Alfred stopped, suddenly realising what he was admitting and to whom 'We, erm... only did it to keep the business afloat.'

'At times, we do what we must to survive,' said Felix reassuringly before returning to the model. 'So, they could use the river to avoid the police.'

'That's their best bet,' replied Alfred.

After hours spent scouring the encyclopaedias at Old Pye Street and learning everything there is to know about the quays and wharves of East London, Felix returned to Downing Street to fetch supper for himself and Alfred. He had barely stepped out of the secret passage and sealed the entrance when the study door opened, and Humphrey entered.

'Dinner will be served at seven o'clock sharp?' he said, stalking across the room to place a handful of letters on Felix's desk. 'It will be roasted chicken with a black truffle sauce and vegetables.'

'Could you have it sent up. I plan to continue working this evening. And have Mrs Hughes fill the plate. I'm feeling surprisingly hungry today.'

'One chicken or two?' mocked Humphrey.

'One will suffice,' replied Felix, approaching his desk to check the newly delivered post.

At the top of the pile was a large envelope with an official government stamp emblazoned on it. Felix quickly opened it. As he had hoped, the letter was from the Chief Record Keeper at the Public Record Office, returning a list of all the major factories operating in the East London area over the last twenty years. The list was endless. Felix could feel his heart sinking further with every page he turned.

'Fire?' asked Humphrey.

'I'm not thirsty,' replied Felix, focused on the letter.

'I said, fire.' repeated Humphrey, rattling a box of matches to get Felix's attention.

Felix looked up. He stared at the large box of matches in Humphrey's hand. On the front, in bold letters, were the words *Bryant & May's Special Safety Match*. His mind immediately jumped back to his journey to Oxford just over a week ago and the article about the Bryant and May matchmaking factory in the East End, with its impressive site and the large-scale employment of women and young girls. He thought back to his recent conversation with Tom Fellows in the Bricklayers Arms the day before, recalling the broken man's words, *something about the wood and chemicals and the flames, a place with a significant workforce*.

Suddenly it all started to make sense. It wasn't merely the size of the factory that would make the disaster more significant in scale or meaningful in people's minds. It was also the target of their attack. A large and famous factory along the river at Bow, with a workforce made up of mothers, sisters, daughters and wives.

'I asked about the fire?' repeated Humphrey, getting irritated.

'Not for now, thank you,' said Felix, 'just the food.'

He waited patiently for Humphrey to leave, inwardly counting every second, then sprung from his seat and hurried to the fireplace, activating the secret passage. He sprinted through the long tunnel, arriving at Old Pye Street sweaty and out of breath.

'Patch me into Scotland Yard!' he called to Alfred, bursting into the room.

Alfred lifted the cord and placed it in the appropriate jack, making the connection. He handed the receiver to Felix.

'Commissioner Thompson,' bellowed Felix down the mouthpiece. 'I don't care if he's busy. You tell him it's the Prime Minister on the line.'

Within moments Felix heard the regimented voice of Commissioner Thompson on the other end of the call.

'Prime Minister?'

'Commissioner. I have reason to believe the next attack will be at the Bryant and May matchmaking factory in Bow. They have nearly two thousand staff there, mainly women and young girls. I cannot disclose how I came about this information, but rest assured, it has come from a credible source. I need you to immediately divert your men to the site. Time is of the essence.'

Felix placed the telephone receiver back on the switchboard and hurriedly exited the building via the Old Pye Street entrance, followed closely by Alfred. He hailed a cab and instructed the driver to follow the river east towards Bow and the Bryant and May matchmaking factory.

A calm silence welcomed Felix and Alfred as their cab approached the factory gates. Felix studied the industrial site, appraising the state of play before stepping out of the vehicle. He had learnt his lessons the hard way at Houlston and Sons and the George Inn and was determined not to rush in and potentially plunge himself into another compromising situation.

The factory was a cluster of huge red brick buildings with sprawling walls covering many acres of land and encasing two large courtyards. Each courtyard had an impressive tower that burst into the sky and could be seen for miles. Historically, the site was used to manufacture candles, crinoline and rope before Bryant and May moved in and regenerated the dilapidated buildings to manufacture their matches. The high roadside walls and the director's cottage were set in front of the imposing site, and a second-floor bay window overlooked the tall factory gates, with the brand's emblem, an image of Noah's Ark and the word security emblazoned on it.

On the surface of things, nothing seemed to be out of the ordinary. There were groups of workers, predominantly women, moving in and out of the cluster of buildings and going about their daily routines. Some even had time to gather outside for a chat, a well-earned cigarette, and a cup of tea. It seemed like just another ordinary day at the factory.

Felix approached the open gates confused; he felt a sudden anxiety building in his chest. What if he had got it wrong? What if he'd just diverted the police's attention away from the actual site to a fictitious threat at the matchmaking factory? After all, it was entirely possible that he may have read too deeply into Tom Fellows' words and the Bryant and May article in the newspaper.

'What now?' asked Alfred, staring up at Felix.

'I'm not sure,' he replied, 'maybe we should look around?'

Felix led the way through the gates, across the grass bank and into the first courtyard, where he was greeted by one of the site foremen.

'Can I help?' he asked, looking Felix and Alfred up and down.

'We were hoping to look around your site,' replied Felix casually.

'You'll have to get approval from the directors, I'm afraid.' coughed the Foreman, suffering from years of overexposure to the white phosphorous found in the matches.

'It's nothing formal. We're simply visiting out of whimsical curiosity. Surely, you can allow a few minutes for an interested party?' pressed Felix.

'It's not down to me.' replied the Foreman. 'It's company policy. You never know who's trying to steal your ideas.'

Felix was about to protest when a loud explosion shook the opposite courtyard lifting Felix, Alfred and the Foreman off their feet and sending them hurtling onto the grass bank. It took Felix a few breaths to regain his senses. He could hear a cacophony of shouting and screaming and saw a large plume of smoke reaching into the sky above one of the factory buildings. He looked to his side, relieved to see Alfred and the Foreman slowly rising to their feet.

Felix climbed off the floor and sprinted towards the burning building, followed by Alfred and the Foreman. A group of women were trying to prize open the large factory doors but with little success.

'It's locked.' shouted the Foreman through a gap in the door. 'You need to remove the wooden plank!'

But his voice was drowned out by the cries of fear and panic from those trapped inside. With the flames rising and their hope fading, the Foreman tried using brute force, charging at the doors with all his might. But the thick oak panels hardly moved under his weight.

'Stay here,' said Felix to Alfred.

He followed the line of the factory wall, looking for another way into the building, finding a small, boarded-up shaft hole for passing buckets in and out of the site to clear the waste. He stepped back and used the heel of his shoe to break its wooden frame, revealing a small gap hardly big enough to fit an adult. Determined, Felix removed his jacket and emptied his pockets of anything that might catch before leaning down and wriggling his body through the small opening.

Black smoke engulfed the factory, making it hard for Felix to see. He felt his way back along the wall towards the entrance. As he got closer to the front, Felix ran into the panic-stricken workers trying to get to the exit and escape. They were coughing heavily, screaming, and crying. Felix used all his strength to force his way through the crowd. He could feel his energy draining with every exertion and the heavy smoke beginning to clog his lungs. He finally reached the front and felt around in the darkness until his hands landed on the large wooden plank secured across both doors, trapping everyone inside. He tried to lift it, but the plank would not move; it was far too heavy for one person to shift. He could hear the muffled voices of the Foreman and Alfred outside shouting at the trapped workers to lift the wooden plank together, but trying to organise them was futile.

Felix began to cough, finding it difficult to breathe. He needed to act quickly if he was going to save the lives of the people trapped inside, including himself. There was no going back now. He felt around, reaching for the people on either side of him. He placed a calming hand on theirs, trying to get their attention, then guided their hands onto the wooden plank. There was confusion at first amidst the panic, but slowly and surely, they began to understand. Each person he directed did the same to the person next to them and then the ones next to them until there was a line of people with two hands on the vast wooden plank.

After a few seconds, the group began to lift, exerting all their remaining energy to finally shift the heavy object and unlock the large factory doors.

Workers began to burst out of the building in their droves as the doors were finally flung open. Having spent their remaining energy releasing the plank, Felix and the rest of the front row collapsed under their weight, gasping for air. It was like a stampede as the frantic workers poured out over the top of them, bolting for the light and gasping for oxygen.

Those who had witnessed the incident from outside hurried to help those colleagues who had either passed out or could not move under the rush. Alfred spotted Felix sprawled out on the floor. He fought his way through the crowd, pushing past the workers and grabbed Felix by his limp arm, pulling him out of the chaos, much to the surprise of the watching women. They'd never seen or heard of a gentleman risking his life for common workers before.

In the background, Alfred could hear the police arriving, along with the fire service. It was pandemonium, with people from all corners of the site attempting to extinguish the fire and assist the stricken workers. He mustered everything he had to pull Felix away to safety, but struggling with the weight of his limp body, Alfred was forced to stop.

'Help!' he shouted desperately over his tears. 'I need help!'

But his words were lost in the chaos. It was like a war zone, with the colossal factory fire raging and people groaning everywhere he looked.

Alfred carefully placed Felix on the floor. He looked down at his unresponsive face, unsure if Felix was alive or if he was cradling the Prime Minister's dead body in his hands. He leant over, placing his ear by Felix's mouth, anxiously listening for his breath. It was a trick he'd learnt as a young boy when his booze-stricken father wouldn't wake up. But there was nothing, just the stillness of Felix's chest.

Alfred slumped to the floor, exhausted, when he heard a faint whisper.

'Old… Pye… Street,' murmured Felix.

'You're alive!' exclaimed Alfred, overcome with relief.

He felt a surge of adrenaline rush through his body. He wrapped Felix's limp arms around his neck and spoke into his ear.

'I need help to get you up. I need you to pull on my neck as hard as you can. Are you ready? Now... PULL!'

Alfred felt Felix tug on his neck. He planted his heels into the hard ground and pushed with everything he had, slowly lifting Felix off the floor and onto his feet. He placed his arms around Felix's waist, and together they slowly staggered out of Bryant and May.

Tower of London

The Thames was busy for the time of year, with tugboats carrying timber from Russia, tea from India and sugar from the Americas to processing plants and warehouses along its riverbanks. The few remaining passenger steamboats that still ferried people up and down the river's meandering waterway were less frequent than in previous years as the steamboat industry continued shrinking under the London underground's growing expansion. With little sign of a steamer approaching, Amelia hailed a longboat and paid the ageing boatman a few coins to carry her east down the river towards Tower Hill.

'Yankee are you?' he asked crudely, dipping his oars into the water.

'Do you know the United States?' asked Amelia.

'Can't say that I do. I could tell from that hat and your accent. We get a lot of your kind looking to visit the Tower.'

'I'm not a tourist,' protested Amelia, 'I live here, and I'm conducting research at the Tower, not sightseeing.'

'Research, you say. You're not looking into the ghosts, are you?' asked the boatman.

'A ghost of sorts.'

'You know that Anne Boleyn still haunts the place? If you look up from the river at night, you can sometimes see her spectre on the ramparts of the Bloody Tower.'

'Is that so?' asked Amelia. 'Sounds a little far-fetched to me.'

'That's 'cause you're an American, see.' replied the boatman. 'You ain't got enough history to have proper ghosts.'

'Nonsense! There were natives in America for thousands of years before we landed. Next, you'll tell me that you can see Guy Fawkes' head floating around on a spike if you look closely enough.'

'It wouldn't surprise me.' replied the boatman.

'Well, have you seen any of these phantoms?' asked Amelia.

'No, not personally. But there have been plenty of others working these waters that have. I've heard about similar sightings from lots of them.'

'And it didn't strike you as odd that they all told the same story?'

'It just proves that it's true.' said the boatman. 'Why?' he asked, suddenly curious.

'Because, my good man, repetition is how fiction to the superstitious mind morphs into fact.'

The boatman opened his mouth to respond, then stopped, perplexed by Amelia's words. Unsure what she meant and too proud to ask, he turned his attention back to rowing, mumbling about ghosts under his breath, much to Amelia's amusement. He steered the boat through the Embankment and past Temple towards Blackfriars. Amelia took the opportunity to absorb the many incredible sights along the riverbank. As an enthusiastic anglophile, she loved being surrounded by the city's historical treasures, and Somerset House, The Inns of Court, and St Paul's Cathedral were among her favourites.

Having passed through Southwark, it wasn't long before they reached London Bridge. It was the busiest crossing in the city, with thousands of pedestrians and vehicles passing over it every hour. Two years earlier, the bridge had been widened to help with traffic flow when they'd discovered it had been sinking half a centimetre a year.

The boatman guided the longboat under the bridge's dark arch, emerging on the other side. Amelia rose from her seat to take in the commanding sight of Tower Bridge in the distance. Tower Bridge had taken nearly a decade to build and was a feat of architectural and engineering mastery. It had become a symbol of London's greatness, with one newspaper claiming that *earth hath nothing to show more fair* and a sight that Amelia never tired of.

After what had felt like an eternity to the boatman, but only a brief turn on this majestic river to Amelia, the vessel finally arrived at the Tower of London, docking between the Byward Tower and Traitors' Gate. Amelia thanked the boatman in her usual theatrical way, much to the old seadog's displeasure, and then disembarked.

The Tower of London was a mishmash of buildings, towers, and grounds, all set within two concentric rings of defensive walls and a moat. It was best known for its use as a notorious medieval prison and torture chamber but also served as a grand palace, a royal residence, an armoury, a treasury, a menagerie, and the home of the Crown Jewels of England. But it was the Tower's historical use as a public record office that Amelia was interested in. Its records were rumoured to go back as far as William the Conqueror and held every state secret since the Norman Conquest.

Publicly, the last Keeper of the Records at the Tower had left his position in the mid-19th century when the records were sent to the new Public Record Office in Chancery Lane. However, Amelia knew that not to be entirely accurate and that a particular collection of documents had secretly remained. Having been given access to the site for a research project some years earlier, she had decided to explore the infamous and highly off-limits White Tower. Having evaded the yeoman warders, Amelia made her way to the basement discovering a small room, unchanged since medieval times, with rows of withered shelves housing several historical documents, ledgers, and rolls. As she settled down to read one of the old manuscripts, she was disturbed by the Tower's senior curator. Aghast to find Amelia in the secret chamber, he reluctantly explained the room's history and significance if she agreed to leave.

The thin archive was all that remained of the infamous Black Hall, the Tower's original record office, which had been supposedly consigned to history some centuries earlier. Although many of the Tower's records had moved, they had mostly been copies or less controversial documents like land registry deeds, birth certificates, and marriage decrees. Unbeknown to the public, who associated the Tower with the missing Plantagenet princes and, more recently, the Crown Jewels, the original records were still kept there, secretly hidden in the remains of the Black Hall, too valuable and murky to risk moving.

It was the same senior curator that Amelia sought out as she approached two of the Tower's yeoman warders at the Henry III Watergate.

'I'm here to see Mr Francis Banks,' she said, appearing from the riverside walkway.

'The tourist entrance is at the Byward Tower,' replied one of the beefeaters.

'I'm not a tourist,' bristled Amelia. 'I'm a professor.'

'Course you are!' scoffed the other warder, taking in Amelia's odd attire and mild American accent.

Amelia reached into her pocket and took out her university identification, waving it in the air.

'I am Amelia Woodruff, Dean of Corpus Christi, Oxford University. Ever heard of it? It's a little seat of learning just northwest of here. Now, if you would just let Mr Banks know that I am here, I'm sure we can get this matter cleared up quicker than you can say, South Texan Longhorn.'

'Of course, Professor,' said one of the beefeaters, quickly scampering off to enquire.

After a few moments, he returned with a smartly dressed, academic-looking man.

'I was under the impression we had an agreement, Professor Woodruff?' said Francis Banks frostily. 'I enlighten you about our little room, and you never return unless in line with the other tourists?'

'That was our agreement, and it was done so in good faith when it was struck. However, something unforeseen has occurred, a matter of national security, which unfortunately necessitates me further examining some of the contents of our little room.'

'Remind me, what was your excuse for being down there last time?' asked Francis. 'Ah, yes. You were in search of Turrim

Vespertilio, the notorious…'

'Tower bat,' interjected Amelia, glancing at the amused warders. 'Yes, that was a touch fanciful. But you must believe me; this is of the utmost importance.'

'Do you have the story of the boy who cried wolf in America, Professor?'

'Indeed, we do. If we could just go inside and talk, I would be happy to explain the situation, and if you are not entirely convinced, I promise I'll leave without a fuss. You have my word. And a Texan's word is stronger than oak.'

Francis took a long, unconvinced look at Amelia, then turned and marched back towards the large wooden doors.

'Err, Mr Banks?' called Amelia, confused.

'You've got five minutes,' he replied, pushing the doors open. 'Make them count.'

Amelia quickly scampered after Francis as he marched into the castle's innermost ward, cutting a path through the tourists and across the large grass bank towards the White Tower. Amelia tried to keep in step but found herself constantly slowed by the incredible displays, including the magnificent tournament armour of Henry VIII.

'You do realise this is eating into your time?' warned Francis, turning to see her gazing in awe at the gilded armours of Charles I and James II.

'Yes, of course, apologies!' replied Amelia, hurrying after him.

Having passed through the Tower's main exhibition chamber, they entered a quiet staff room with a small table, chairs, and a series of notes nailed to the beautiful Portland and Kentish ragstone walls.

'So,' began Francis, facing Amelia, 'I'm listening.'

'Not even a cup of tea first?' quipped Amelia, trying to thaw the frost. 'This is most un-British.'

'Three minutes to go,' replied Francis, checking his watch. 'I really would get a move on if I were you.'

'Straight to it then,' said Amelia, sitting on one of the chairs and crossing her legs as though about to read a bedtime story. 'I will tell you what I can, but there are certain details and persons that, for security reasons, must remain a secret.'

Francis nodded his acceptance of the terms, and Amelia began. First, she explained the abductions of the lords, the cards left at the crime scenes and their odd symbols. Then, with the curator engrossed, she quickly and theatrically moved on to the Masons, Houlston and Sons, the poker match at the East India Club and her questioning of the gambler, Jonathan Burbage. Like any great detective, having laid out the setting, the crime and the mystery, Amelia then concluded by listing the suspects and the sequence of events that had led her to the Tower of London.

'How utterly fascinating,' said Francis, pulling up a seat beside Amelia. 'It certainly beats explaining the difference between tournament and battle armour to a gaggle of Neanderthal tourists. So, you think the last Pulleyn died here in the Tower?'

'I can't be sure, but it would certainly explain the name's sudden extinction.'

'You do realise how many criminals have passed through these gates over the past nine hundred years? It would take an army of researchers to get through all those ledgers.'

'It's the best chance we have,' conceded Amelia.

'That's why I'm going to help you,' declared Francis, suddenly alive with adventure. 'I know these archives better than anyone. If the answer is down there, I will help you find it.'

Having guided the way back out of the staff room, through numerous corridors and down several flights of stairs, Francis finally led Amelia into White Tower's basement and the forgotten Black Hall.

'Where do we start?' puffed Amelia, scanning the medieval room, out of breath.

'The old keeper had a unique archiving system,' replied Francis, pulling over a small wooden ladder. 'He used a combination of registers, indexes and other finding aids he'd created over the years to keep a tab on everything. Early 17th century, you said?'

'Yes, that's right,' nodded Amelia.

Francis positioned the ladder under a dusty old shelf full of parchment scrolls. He climbed up and read the tags on each, passing a selection down to Amelia, who carefully placed them on a long table in the centre of the Black Hall. He continued along the shelves, removing other scrolls and faded leather-bound journals passing each into Amelia's waiting hands.

'That should see us through the night,' he said, looking down at a sizeable collection safely assembled on the table.

Amelia smiled at Francis in admiration. She'd never met a man who could match her enthusiasm for research before.

'Thank you,' she said, uncharacteristically self-aware.

'What for?' Asked Francis.

'For believing me and for helping.'

'You can thank me once we've found our man,' replied Francis, sitting at the table and handing Amelia a scroll. 'Now, if you will, Professor.'

Together, they unrolled their parchments and buried their heads in their work.

Despite reviewing hundreds of pages and thousands of lines

of text, many hours passed without the slightest hint of a breakthrough. Feeling their energies begin to sap, Amelia suggested a different approach.

'Perhaps we should narrow our criteria?'

'In what way?' asked Francis.

'Rather than search through all the criminal cases in the period, we should focus on the more extreme cases first. The hangings and beheadings, even the tortures, then work our way back?'

Francis sorted through the journals on the table, removing a dozen or so from the pile.

'These are the lists of the most notorious prisoners,' he said, dividing them between himself and Amelia.

Together they scanned every word, line and paragraph, working through the evening with little progress. Beginning to doubt that the answer was even in the Black Hall, Amelia stepped away from the table.

'What if the name died out under different circumstances or in another country?' she said, 'Or if we've somehow missed it, scanning past the entry without realising?'

'You're tired and worried,' said Francis gently. 'Trust yourself, Amelia. Answers are like mountain peaks. It takes time and effort to reach them.'

'And discipline,' added Amelia, returning to her seat a little embarrassed.

'If the answers are here, we will find them,' said Francis reassuringly, adding to Amelia's admiration.

With the night drawing in, they separated the task into shifts, each taking a turn to sleep while the other continued the search. Amelia took the first shift, searching through a pile of records before restocking the table with journals for Francis to continue with once her time was up. They continued this way until the early hours of the morning, when Amelia, having all but given up, pulled a bulging journal off one of the remaining shelves and flicked through its pages, only to find it contained the names of all the infamous prisoners' visitors to the tower from 1500-1700. It listed the family members of Anne Boleyn, Catherine Howard, and Elizabeth Throckmorton – the maid of honour to Queen Elizabeth I, who secretly married Sir Walter Raleigh behind her monarch's back, leading to his imprisonment in the Bloody Tower.

Intrigued, Amelia scanned the long rows of names, flicking through page after page until she finally placed her shaking finger on the name she'd been searching for all this time. Listed below her, alongside the date December 12, 1605, was the name Maria Pulleyn.

'Francis,' whispered Amelia, gently waking the curator, 'I found it.'

'Found what?' asked the groggy curator, slowly sitting up.

'The name.' said Amelia showing Francis the listing. 'We were searching for a woman all this time. Her name was Maria Pulleyn. She made a single visit to the Tower in December 1605.'

'That's when Guy Fawkes was imprisoned,' said Francis, amazed. 'You mentioned a connection to this politician in York. Guy Fawkes was born and educated in York! If I remember correctly, a member of his family even held the title of Lord Mayor of York some decades before.'

'Do you have a list of marriage certificates here in the Tower?' asked Amelia, thinking aloud. 'Preferably in the York area?'

'No, never for the North. But I know someone who does.'

Francis placed the records on their shelves and led Amelia

back through the corridors towards the White Tower's main office. He picked up the telephone receiver and spoke into the mouthpiece,

'Public Record Office. Chancery Lane.'

After a few moments, he heard a voice on the other end of the line.

'Richard. It's Francis from the Tower. I need a favour. Would you be able to investigate something for me? I was hoping you could check your records for a woman named Maria Pulleyn, 1590 to 1605, concentrated in the towns and parishes of the city of York.'

Amelia looked out the window, surprised to see daylight shining on the Tower grounds and lines of tourists beginning to form outside again. They had worked solidly through the night and into the morning. It was a strange sensation. She felt tired but also full of energy. She was so close to figuring out an essential part of the jigsaw that she could hardly contain herself, let alone service the need for sleep.

She suddenly heard a faint buzz from the telephone receiver and a voice speak on the other end of the line. She looked at Francis, who anxiously raised the telephone, placing the receiver close to his ear.

'Hello, Richard,' he said, full of anxious excitement. 'Did you find anything?'

Amelia hurried over and placed her ear alongside Francis's, touching her cheek to his.

'It appears Maria Pulleyn was descended from the Pulleyns of Scotton Hall, a small town outside of York.' said Richard, 'She was born in 1573, the second of two girls, and attended the local parish school until age fifteen. That's when the records start to get a little hazy. Aside from references to her baptism and the premature death of her older sister, there is very little information about Maria. No records of how, where or when she died. She simply vanished off the face of the earth from around 1588 onwards. There is, however, a rather curious document in the records that is barely even legible, which suggests…'

Richard paused for a moment.

'Yes?' pressed Amelia impatiently. 'I mean, carry on,' she said softly, trying to mimic Francis's voice.

'Well, I cannot verify its provenance or indeed its truthfulness,' continued Richard, 'and it feels rather odd to say this out loud, but the document seems to suggest that she was married to Guy Fawkes.'

Amelia and Francis looked at each other in bewilderment. They could hardly believe what they'd just heard.

'Thank you, Richard. That's been most helpful.' said Francis, quickly replacing the receiver and finishing the call. 'Remind me of those lord's names again?' he asked, turning to Amelia.

'Monteagle and Cecil.'

'Of course!' exclaimed Francis, kicking himself. 'How could I not make the connection! The old Lord Cecil is widely believed to have masterminded the entire gunpowder plot and the arrests to position himself as the King's saviour. And it was Lord Monteagle who exposed the plot after the conspirators sent him a letter warning him not to attend Parliament. It all adds up!'

'Francis, I need you to do something for me,' said Amelia, suddenly panicked.

She reached for a piece of paper and a pen and scribbled something down.

'Take this to Downing Street as quickly as you can. Ask for a man named Humphrey and tell him I've sent you. Place this note in his hand, no one else.'

Francis nodded, somewhat confused. Before he could ask why or even say goodbye, Amelia turned on her heels and hurried out, leaving the Tower of London quicker than you can say South Texan Longhorn.

Magic of Misdirection

Felix was still feeling the effects of his exposure to the smoke at Bryant and May when he finally came around. His head was pounding, and there was a burning sensation in his chest and throat. He looked around, trying to gather his bearings, only to discover that he was lying in Alfred's makeshift bed on the floor at Old Pye Street.

'You've been out for ages,' said a concerned voice. 'I didn't know if I should call for a doctor.'

Felix looked up to see Alfred sitting close by. It was clear from his drawn face and tired eyes that he'd been by Felix's side the whole time, keeping a close eye on him.

'I'm okay, thank you, Alfred,' said Felix, slowly sitting up.

'What happened?'

'You saved them,' replied Alfred, 'I thought they were all goners. But you got them out. You're a hero.'

Felix nodded, acknowledging the compliment. He appreciated the young man's sentiment but did not see himself as a hero or someone to be revered. Yes, he had managed to save the lives of those workers at Bryant and May, having placed himself in great danger, but he was merely balancing the books, making up for past failures of which there were many.

'What time is it?' he asked.

'Early morning, you slept through a whole day and night.'

'Early morning! I need to get to Parliament,' said Felix, springing up from the bed.

'Are you sure you're up to it?' asked Alfred, concerned.

'I don't have a choice,' croaked Felix. 'The vote is today. I must address the Commons and state my case to the members.'

Felix hurried out of the oval office and down the long tunnel to his study at Downing Street. Humphrey had left the morning newspapers on his desk along with a rather sour note, questioning whether Felix intended to bother with the parliamentary vote, given his recent habit of disappearing without a trace.

Felix picked up the newspapers and scanned the headlines. The events at the Bryant and May matchmaking factory dominated the front pages. He read some of the worker's accounts, detailing the explosions, the fiery infernos, and their miraculous escapes. Fortunately for Felix, there was no mention of him personally, only references to a strange but courageous gentleman entering the building and saving those trapped inside.

There was, however, something else of concern for Felix, given the impending vote. Some of the newspapers had interviewed union representatives who, up until this point, had agreed to call off their protests, but in light of the recent disaster and believing it to be the result of more faulty machinery, had expressed a renewed anger with the government, even calling for their fellow workers to march on Parliament.

Felix's deal with the TUC had only just come into effect, pushing him a few rungs back up the political ladder, but now he could feel himself tumbling back down it again. Although successfully thwarted, the events at Bryant and May had been enough to re-ignite the social unrest among the workers and, in all probability, ensure the loss of the impending vote and an end to Felix's time in power.

Felix placed the newspapers back on his desk and reached for his journal. He flicked through the leather-bound book, observing the long paragraphs of information, commentary, and conversation he'd jotted down over the past few weeks. The jigsaw parts to this mystery were buried somewhere inside these pages, but they felt almost impossible to piece together with so much happening and so many moving parts.

Felix approached the study window, gazing out onto the street. He watched the people pass by, blissfully unaware of the events that had consumed his life over the past fortnight. Perhaps the adage was true; ignorance was bliss. He took a moment to look around the famous Downing Street study, his home and refuge over the past few years, where he had spent many a long night trying to make a meaningful difference. How little the voters knew about the actual work that went on inside this historic house. How fortunate they were.

Felix's eyes fell back upon the journal in his hand, but this time, not in some vain hope of solving the case, but with a sinking realisation that his fixation with this investigation had cost him his time in office. He should never have allowed himself to get caught up in it in the first place. If he had just left it to the proper authorities, as Percy had urged, he wouldn't have been so distracted from his role as prime minister. An honour that was now slipping through his fingers. Frustrated, Felix tossed the journal aside and left the study to prepare for Parliament and the vote.

Having decided to walk to Westminster, much to Humphrey's consternation, Felix took his favoured route via the park, with its tall canopy of trees, wildlife, and beautiful lakes. It was the first time he'd found the picturesque walk lonely since becoming prime minister. He tried to enjoy it, to make the most of each step, aware that it could be his last along this famous route once he was removed from power and his residence at Number 10. However, as usual, his mind was firing in all directions, still trying to find solutions to his problems, even though it all felt hopeless.

As Felix turned into Great George Street, approaching Parliament Square, he heard the raucous sound of shouting and chanting. A large group of protestors had massed outside the Great Palace at Westminster. They had turned out in force, just as they'd threatened, and were continuing to arrive in great numbers. Some voiced their frustrations, while others carried signs calling for an end to slave labour and the sub-standard working conditions they were forced to endure under his government.

Although Felix knew the disasters were criminal acts plotted and carried out by Ezra Fox and his men, it didn't change the fact that his government had failed to improve the lives of ordinary workers. Their inability to reform and modernise these factories had allowed their enemies to capitalise on the growing ill-feeling and stir up anarchy. Rather than becoming the great liberal reformer he aspired to be, Felix had become a largely ineffective prime minister. It was a bitter pill to swallow. Especially having presided over some of the worst industrial failings in the country's history, not to mention the deaths of several decent, hard-working people.

Rather than divert his path and take the back entrance into Parliament to avoid the protestors, Felix floated towards the growing mob like a moth drawn to a flame. He couldn't explain why he'd chosen that route with its apparent dangers. Maybe it was habit, routine, or perhaps something more profound, a need to show himself and make amends for everything that had happened. He entered the crowd, passing through unnoticed amidst the cacophony of noise and animated gestures, until one of the protestors, distracted by his smart suit, realised a gentleman was walking among them.

'It's the Prime Minister! It's Felix Grey!' he shouted, garnering the attention of those who could hear his voice over the melee.

One by one, the protestors began to turn, nudging the person next to them and pointing at Felix until the entire crowd had been alerted to his presence. Felix continued to walk forward as the shocked protestors began to step aside, creating a narrow pathway for him. They watched his every step in stunned silence. The hush seemed to last an eternity for Felix, as did the long walk towards Parliament's gates. As he drew closer, Felix heard a wave of whispered insults thrown his way. The *how dare yous* and *you've got a nerves*.

Once a few people in the crowd had gathered enough courage to speak their minds, it didn't take long for the rest of the group to turn their angst on Felix. Even the most silent whispers quickly escalated into angry shouts, and Felix felt a surge of movement at his back as the crowd began to swarm forward, closing off his pathway. They barged and jostled to get within earshot and deliver their furious tirades. Felix fought his way through the crowd, pushing forward, trying to get to the safety of the police line as the disgruntled protestors continued to shout and bark in his face.

With the crowd squeezing against him, Felix suddenly felt a strong hand grab his collar and extract him from the melee. He turned to see a colossal policeman being marshalled furiously by an animated Percy.

'Make way for the Prime Minister! Make way, I say!' bellowed Percy at the protestors as the line of policemen stepped forward, pushing them back.

Percy seized Felix by the arm and pulled him away towards the Houses of Parliament. They entered through the small Gothic doorway to shocked glances from the members who had gathered at the windows to watch the scene developing outside.

'What were you thinking, Felix?' asked Percy, bewildered. 'You're lucky they didn't tear you limb from limb!'

'They have every right to feel that way, Thomas,' said Felix, trying to understand what had just happened. 'Something was telling me that I needed to show myself to them.'

'Whatever it was, it was either incredibly brave or downright foolish!'

'Possibly a bit of both,' said Felix, taking in the reactions of the watching faces.

'Well, it was always going to take something out of the ordinary to win this blasted vote.'

'What is the current state of play?' asked Felix.

'As far as I can tell, Cavendish has healthy support across the house,' replied Percy. 'However, our whips have been kicking up dust over the past forty-eight hours. The question is, have they done enough?'

'It will all come down to how convincing we both sound when we address the house,' said Felix, thinking aloud. 'That will be when the members' votes are truly won or lost.'

'The final stand!' snarled Percy, shaking his fist.

As the men continued through St Stephen's Hall towards the House of Commons, the density of members increased, as did the volume of their gossiping. Felix and Percy passed a group of loud parliamentarians nattering away in Central Lobby, followed by an even-louder collection in the Common's Corridor, before finally running into an entire herd in the Commons Lobby. Through their incessant chitchat, Felix heard a familiar voice. He stepped to one side to see Humphrey conversing with one of the members.

'It's a matter of pride rather than good housekeeping,' he said earnestly.

'Humphrey?' called Felix, surprised to see his steward. 'What on earth are you doing here?' he asked, stepping away from Percy.

'You forgot your journal, Prime Minister,' said Humphrey, handing Felix the leather-bound book he had tossed aside in his study some hours earlier. 'Everything you need for today is inside.'

'Thank you,' said Felix, looking curiously from the journal to Humphrey.

'Now, if you don't mind, I have chores to attend to,' said Humphrey. 'Number 10 looks like a *bomb* has hit it.'

Felix was about to question Humphrey on his odd behaviour and choice of language when the doors to the Commons sprung open, and the members began to stream in. Felix stepped into the crowd and felt himself being carried along with the wave of bodies, eager to get inside and get on with the vote. He cut through the human traffic towards the front bench, sat and opened his journal, finding a note wedged into the middle pages close to the spine. He took the paper out, carefully unfolded it and read the message inside. It was from Amelia, it read:

Felix,

The name Pulleyn is descended from Guy Fawkes and his secret wife, Maria Pulleyn. Monteagle's and Cecil's predecessors betrayed Fawkes and the plotters to the king. The vote of confidence is a set-up. Part of an elaborate plot to blow up Parliament and finish Fawkes' work.

Amelia

Felix read the note in disbelief. He looked around the Commons at his colleagues taking their seats. Every one of their lives was in danger. He wanted to stand on his bench and shout from the top of his lungs. But with the house full of members baying for his blood, Felix knew that any attempt to disrupt the vote would be met with scepticism on both sides of the chamber, slowing down any possibility of an evacuation. It was a delicate balance. He wanted to keep his colleagues safe and prevent the destruction of Parliament but could not afford to arouse suspicion, not while the plotters were potentially watching and waiting to detonate their explosives.

Felix felt a terrible twisting in his stomach. He took several deep breaths, trying to calm his nerves and clear his mind, just as he had done at the George Inn. He needed to think fast if he was going to avoid the most catastrophic event of them all. He studied Amelia's note again. She had provided the missing link, the connection to the name, the place, the ancestry and the abductions, Guy Fawkes. Humphrey had even warned him about the gunpowder sitting in the parliamentary undercrofts, waiting to be detonated. All he had to do was piece it together and uncover the culprit.

Felix cast his mind back to the past few weeks' events. It was clear that whoever had orchestrated the abductions and the factory disasters had meticulously planned them to build to this moment. He scanned the chamber, studying his fellow members. He felt confident that the mastermind behind everything was a politician or at least someone with a working knowledge of politics. How else could he have managed to manipulate events to such a degree? He would have to have known the minds of the Commons members, the TUC and the working people to have simultaneously caused national riots and forced a vote of no confidence in the government. Only a person with status and knowledge of the parliamentary system could have wielded that level of power.

Felix looked across the table at Barnaby Shaw, engaged in conversation with his leader, Milton Cavendish. Was Shaw the local politician Mrs Hughes' brother had encountered at the Holgate Road Carriage Works? If so, was he working on behalf of his own interests or his leader's orders? It seemed coincidental that Cavendish's attacks had followed so swiftly after each disaster. First at Felix's parliamentary dinner, then in the House of Commons, and finally at the Carlton Club. But then, could he blame the opposition leader for using every opportunity available to capitalise on his opponent's failings? Wasn't it to be expected in the murky world of politics? A few well-timed political attacks certainly didn't implicate him in any criminal activity nor provide any reason to believe he was Mr G Pulleyn. But if not Cavendish or Shaw, then who?

Felix felt his head beginning to spin. It could be anyone in the chamber. He looked around at the rows of seated politicians and the many others who stood by the chamber doors. They all looked identical in their tailored suits, polished shoes, and top hats. It was like a great magic trick, hiding the guilty man in a room filled with people who all looked alike. As had been the case so often over the past weeks, Felix once again found himself searching for a needle in a haystack. Only on this occasion, with a ticking bomb in his ear.

If he could not solve the mystery, the least he could do was raise the alarm and give the members a fighting chance at evacuating rather than allowing them to die so mercilessly. He stood up, gesturing towards the Speaker of the House, trying to get his attention, but the Speaker was too distracted by the opposition.

Suddenly a thought occurred to Felix. His time in power had always been like this, fighting to be seen and heard. The only constants in his life were the distractions, the meaningless debates and petty quarrels that diverted his attention away from the real work and his promises to the public. It had been the same with the case. It had never felt obvious or clear-cut. There had always been a hidden surprise or some kind of smokescreen. Like the great magicians of the time, whoever had concocted this heinous plan had undoubtedly mastered the use of misdirection.

It had begun with the poker match, made to look like a business meeting between gentlemen when, in reality, it was a collection of strangers brought together to arrange the abduction of Lord Monteagle. Then there were the cards left at both abductions with their strange secret society symbols implying masonic involvement to throw the police off the scent. The factory disasters came next, each made to look like faulty machinery to incite the riots, followed by the burglary at the East India Club to cover the hostess's tracks and the murder of the two sailors at Shad Thames to expose the undercover detective. Finally, a parliamentary confidence vote to divert the gaze away from a plot to blow up the Houses of Parliament and everyone inside. They even went to the trouble of amassing demonstrators outside to distract the police. It all slotted together perfectly.

Felix sat back down on his bench. Fortunately, all the major players were still inside the chamber. All he had to do was think of a way to make the mastermind show his hand. He quickly scribbled down two notes, calling for the house clerk. He placed them in the clerk's hand and whispered some instructions in his ear. The clerk had barely set off on his errand when the Speaker stood up, beckoning the chamber to come to order before proceeding with the day's business.

'Let us begin directly with the no-confidence motion. The leader of the opposition,' he announced, motioning towards Cavendish.

Cavendish rose from his bench to a chorus of cheers.

'I beg to move that this house has no confidence in His Majesty's Government. Although I must say, there isn't much of a government left to have any confidence in.' he joked, much to the amusement of the house.

Felix could feel Percy wriggling in his seat with rage. He placed a reassuring hand on his colleague's shoulder, trying to calm him down.

'Political pressure has been mounting for some weeks now,' continued Cavendish, 'leading to the protests you see outside Parliament today. There is only one plausible solution to these terrible events. The British people must be allowed to have their say. We need a general election!'

Cavendish stepped away from the table to a rapturous round

of applause and waving handkerchiefs.

'The Prime Minister,' called the Speaker to a muted response.

'Mr Speaker,' began Felix, rising to address the chamber. 'It is only right for the opposition to challenge the government of the day. It is also their democratic duty to test the confidence of this house if they believe the circumstances warrant it. I make no complaint about that. Let us proceed with the vote.'

Felix's words were greeted with shock and amazement. Never had the house witnessed such a capitulation from a serving prime minister. It was so spectacularly strange that a rare silence fell over the members. Even Percy, with all his bluster and gusto, turned to face Felix, speechless.

Felix, however, kept his eye on the clerk as he handed one of his notes to the Speaker before passing the other across the opposition bench to Shaw.

'The question is…' began the Speaker, reading Felix's note, 'that this house has no confidence in His Majesty's Government. As many as are of that opinion, say Aye.'

The chamber rang out with the sound of deafening Ayes.

The Speaker waited for their yelps to die down before continuing.

'Those of the contrary, say No,' he called to the whispered sound of a few loyal Nos.'

The members watched and waited for the Speaker to announce the result. Usually, with such an overwhelming and undeniable victory, there would be no need to take the motion to a physical vote. However, to everyone's surprise, the Speaker appeared to be stalling.

Choruses of *Come on!* and *The Ayes have it!* rang out from the benches and the impatient members. After some confusion, the

Speaker finally rose to declare the result.

'Division!' he shouted at the top of his voice to a cacophony of disbelieving boos. 'Clear the lobbies!' he continued, undeterred.

The division bell rang out across the chamber, prompting the members to leave their benches and march towards the lobbies to cast their votes.

As they reluctantly rose from their seats and began to exit the chamber, Felix followed, staying close to the migrating herd and keeping a close eye on the Shadow Chancellor, Barnaby Shaw.

MARIO THEODOROU

The Descendant

Barnaby Shaw left the House of Commons with the other disgruntled members. As his colleagues marched towards the voting lobbies to cast their votes, he quietly broke free from the pack, taking a different route through Central Lobby towards the stone staircase leading to the historic Westminster undercrofts. He glanced over his shoulder, scared of being followed, as he scurried down the stairs towards the infamous dark vaults.

It took a few moments for Shaw's eyes to adjust to the low light. He could make out the undercroft's cracked and uneven floor, worn arches, and long wooden beams and taste the polluted Thames on his lips. He scanned the cavernous rooms, trying to get a sense of their scale, but the dark shadows warped and manipulated their shape, giving the impression they were narrow in some areas and broad in others. Shaw plucked up the courage and moved deeper into the crypt when he heard something moving in the shadows.

'Who's there?' he called out anxiously.

He edged forward, feeling the stone floor turn to grit under his shoes. He took another step only to find his path blocked by something broad and solid. He felt around in the darkness, his hands landing on a large wooden object, oval-shaped with strips of studded metal running along it. He leant forward, trying to focus on the obstruction, when he was overcome by a sharp dank odour that singed his nostrils. It was so strong that it even overpowered the potent stench of the Thames.

Shaw stepped back, gasping for air, when he heard movement again, coming from somewhere in the undercroft.

'What is the meaning of this?' he snapped into the darkness, a tremble of fear in his voice.

He waited, watching nervously, but again there was no response. He quickly turned, determined to leave, but in his haste, slipped on the grit, landing heavily on the floor. He pushed himself up, only to find he was covered in a dark, grainy substance. He tried to dust himself down, but the grit was too sticky to brush off. Suddenly the smell of burnt air was all over him. He hurried towards the Thames, sucking in the dirty river pollution, when he heard a third noise, this time more pronounced and undoubtedly the sound of someone approaching. He stood up tall, bracing himself when to his surprise, the plump frame of Thomas Percy emerged.

'What an earth is going on, Thomas?' barked Shaw, relieved to see a familiar face.

'I might ask you the same question,' replied Percy.

'Excuse me!? You asked to meet here. Although now I see that it was merely for your amusement. A very unsporting reaction to losing your place in government.'

'I did not invite you here!' protested Percy.

'You mean to say you never sent me this message?' asked Shaw, reaching into his pocket and removing a note for Percy to see.

'I did not. Why in heaven's name would I ask you to meet me here of all places?'

'But, if not you, then who?'

'It was me,' called a voice from behind them.

Both men turned to see Felix emerge from the narrow stairwell carrying a small lantern.

'What's all this about, Prime Minister?' demanded Shaw.

'Yes, what on earth is going on, Felix?' asked Percy.

'Life can be a rather strange undertaking, wouldn't you agree?' asked Felix, looking around the dark undercroft. 'I've always had a bizarre curiosity about other people's lives and what drives them to do what they do. Perhaps that's why I chose a life in public service.'

'Have you completely lost your mind?' asked Shaw, beginning to lose his patience.

'Far from it,' replied Felix, holding up his journal. 'You see, I make a note of all my thoughts in this book to ensure against that very thing. It's easy to second guess oneself in this role, to believe things are one way when they are, in fact, another. Although even my journal doesn't guarantee against tying oneself in mental knots. I used it to note all the information about the missing lords in the naive hope of piecing the puzzle together and finding them. But my inexperience in such matters was abundantly obvious throughout, and regardless of my detailed annotations, the perpetrator always managed to keep a step ahead of me. Well, more than just a step, if I'm honest. Until today, that is.'

'What are you suggesting?' asked Shaw.

'That the abductions of the lords and the recent spate of factory disasters were all orchestrated by the same person to destabilise the government and force a vote of no confidence.'

'That sounds a little far-fetched, Felix,' added Percy apologetically.

'It sounds utterly absurd, Thomas.' agreed Felix. 'Hence why it took me such a long time to recognise the threat. And why so many people have suffered as a consequence. A mistake I will regret for the rest of my life.'

'And what threat is that exactly?' asked Shaw.

'That burnt odour wafting off you is gunpowder. And somewhere in this undercroft are barrels of the stuff, ready to be detonated, just as Guy Fawkes had planned three hundred years ago.'

'Guy Fawkes?' chortled Shaw. "You really have lost your mind.'

Felix lifted the lantern to reveal a large wooden cask on the floor in front of the men. He moved his light across the room, exposing several more stacked on top of each other.

'How could you?' said Percy, facing Shaw.

'It wasn't me!' protested Shaw. 'I had nothing to do with any gunpowder!'

Percy brushed Shaw's arm, lifting his fingers to his nose to smell the gunpowder stuck to the Shadow Chancellor's clothes.

'That was an accident!' squealed Shaw. 'I slipped in the darkness. It's all over the floor.'

'Barnaby Shaw,' began Percy, taking the Shadow

Chancellor by the arm, 'I arrest you in the name of His Majesty, King Edward VII, on the charge of high treason!'

'This is preposterous!' bellowed Shaw. 'I've been set up.'

'Lead the way, Felix,' said Percy, ignoring Shaw's pleas.

But Felix didn't move. Instead, he remained rooted to the spot, with a look of deep regret and sadness etched on his face.

'It's not Shaw, Thomas,' he said, the pain clear in his voice. 'It's you.'

'Don't be ridiculous, Felix.' snorted Percy. 'How could you possibly believe I...'

'I didn't,' interrupted Felix. 'I didn't dare to believe it could be you until today. You see, having put it all together, I knew the culprit was likely to be a member of parliament, given his power and influence and his intimate knowledge of the system. All I had to do was draw him out. So, I decided to try some misdirection of my own. I asked the Speaker to call a division and send the members to the voting chambers. It was the only way to separate Shaw from the others and divert him here to the undercroft. I knew that the culprit, whoever he was, and with his senses on full alert, would have noticed even the smallest threat to his plan, let alone the Shadow Chancellor receiving a curious note in the chamber and suspiciously sneaking away. Driven by the fear of having his plot exposed, I assumed the guilty man would follow to prevent him from raising the alarm. I just didn't expect it to be you, Thomas.'

'In the end, it's those who are closest who disappoint us the most,' said Percy, releasing Shaw's arm and quickly pulling a gun out of his pocket. 'Keep your hands where I can see them,' he shouted, pointing the weapon at Felix and Shaw.

'It's over, Thomas. The Speaker will have evacuated the lobbies by now, as I instructed. There is nothing left to gain from this.'

'Oh, there's still plenty left to gain, Prime Minister,' replied Percy. 'I can still raise this house of corruption to the ground in his honour. It's the least I can do.'

'But why?' asked Shaw confused.

'Why?' repeated Percy. 'Because, you pompous cretin, it's people like you, the landed, wealthy, privileged careerists, who have kept the British people from fulfilling their true potential all these centuries. This corrupt establishment that only gratifies a chosen few at the expense of millions and worships a monarch like a god is no longer fit for purpose. He knew that three hundred years ago and was punished for trying to bring about real, meaningful change.'

'So that's why you orchestrated the murder of so many people?' asked Felix. 'To bring about meaningful change?'

'My name is Guy!' shouted Percy. 'Guy Pulleyn!'

'That name does not exist, Thomas. It's nothing more than a shadow. A soiled past trying to lurch its way back up from the cesspit of human indecency.'

'You will soon regret that comment, Prime Minister,' said Percy, hearing a boat approaching.

'The police!' exclaimed Shaw, relieved.

'I think not,' replied Percy as a dark barge appeared from the riverside. 'You see, the Prime Minister has a healthy distrust of the police. I can't say I blame him. Never trust a man you cannot buy or scare, and Commissioner Thompson, well, he's boringly honourable. It's these ex-army types; their incorruptibility is of no use to anyone. Although, he did let slip the name of his undercover officer in the Docklands. That proved very useful in throwing the police off our scent and striking some renewed fear into people. Two birds with one stone, as the expression goes.'

Felix felt his stomach lurch. He had misjudged the commissioner and, in doing so, had kept a valuable ally at arm's length this entire time. Had he trusted Thompson from the start, he may have prevented the factory disasters and saved the lives of those poor victims.

'I did warn you,' Percy continued. 'Do you remember that night, in Downing Street, when Thompson first presented the card to us? I said leave it to the authorities, Felix. Of course, I knew you wouldn't listen. You're the prime minister. You're too high and mighty to listen to your lowly colleagues or the people you are supposed to represent. It's just another example of the entitlement this outdated system confers on a person. Well, not anymore.'

Percy turned to face a group of burly men approaching from the barge. At their head, marshalling the abducted lords, was the intimidating frame of Ezra Fox.

'You're late!' barked Percy.

'We had some trouble on the river,' replied Ezra.

'I thought you owned the river?'

'There were double the blue shirts than normal. That's twice as many hands to bribe.'

'I'm aware of how bribes work,' squawked Percy. 'Your failure could've sabotaged the entire plan. Remember who pulled you out of the gutter as a boy and fixed your eye. You'd be nothing without me!'

'It won't happen again,' seethed Ezra.

'It had better not. Now tie them up!' ordered Percy.

Ezra and his men rushed forward and took hold of Felix and Shaw, strapping them to the gunpowder barrels alongside the two missing lords.

'It's not too late, Thomas,' said Felix, wrestling with his binds.

'You're wrong, Felix.' replied Percy. 'It's nearly three hundred years too late.'

'And what about her? What about Maria Pulleyn? Is this what she would have wanted, too?' asked Felix.

'What do you know about her?' fumed Percy.

'I know that she married Guy Fawkes and that they had a child whose line continues to this day.'

'You know nothing. She had to watch her husband, the father of her child, tortured on the rack, day after day, until it broke him. And even when he could barely lift his arm, he was forced to sign a confession just to end the excruciating brutality. But that was just the beginning for her. Her pain endured. After the execution, she wouldn't dare retain her married name or even her birth name, Pulleyn. Both had become toxic. She had no identity, and neither did her child. She was forced to remarry. Can you imagine the shame? Her new husband agreed to take the boy on if he denied his name. But the boy never forgot his history. No, he passed the dirty family secret on, and it continued to be passed on through the generations until it finally got to me. By then, the family had moved south, adopted a new accent, and become *respectable*. But the injustice never left.'

'Injustice?' questioned Felix. 'Listen to yourself. He attempted to blow up the Houses of Parliament, to murder hundreds of people.'

'How naive you are, Felix. The history books may paint the picture of a heartless monster, but as we know, the victors get to write their narratives, and, as always, they bend the truth to fit their purpose. I think it's high time you all had a little history lesson. But this time, the truth, not that rubbish the establishment feeds our children to keep them complicit in its lies and corruptions.'

Percy clicked his fingers, prompting one of Ezra's men to step forward. The man lifted a thick wooden stick in the air and wrapped a piece of cloth around it before drenching it in kerosene. Ezra lit a match, touching it to the soaked cloth, which burst into flames, instantly filling the undercroft with light. Suddenly the colossal mountain of gunpowder-laden barrels stacked under the dark arch became visible for all to see. Felix stared at the barrels in horror. There was enough to blow up the Houses of Parliament many times over. Having lured his enemy to the undercrofts and instructed the Speaker to clear the Commons, Felix had naively believed that he had averted the danger. He hadn't expected to find himself tied to another barrel facing a similar fate to the one he had survived in the George Inn. Having spent all this time scouring London's underbelly for the lords, not to mention sacrificing his role as prime minister, he was now about to share in their fate.

Ezra's man handed the torch to Percy, who approached Felix and the men tied to the barrels.

'The gunpowder plot is not quite the story you had handed down to you in your knickerbockers, woollen stockings and Eton collars,' he began, crouching down. 'No, it's much more calculated than the history books would have you believe. The lords, Robert Cecil and Monteagle were falling out of favour with King James, so they concocted a most ingenious plan to win him over. First, they found some disgruntled Catholics, active opposers of the Tudor Reformation, and groomed them into believing they'd been chosen to carry out God's work. They then furnished their unwitting recruits with all the resources and religious indoctrination required, even meeting with them secretly to reinforce their grand calling. However, once the plot had been cemented and the wheels were in motion, they betrayed their conspirators, catching them in the unholy act and exposing their treasonous plan. They were made to look like heroes, the King's saviours, while my ancestor was labelled one of history's greatest villains and disposed of like a pawn on a chessboard. They destroyed him and his wife and condemned generations of their descendants, each tainted with the mark his name came to bear. A mark that carries to this day, but no further.'

Percy stood up and backed away. Ezra stepped forward with a small barrel of gunpowder and used it to run a thick line of the black sand from the bound men across the undercroft to the riverside, where the barge was moored.

'It's time,' called Percy, instructing the men to exit. Once they had all cleared the undercroft for the barge, Percy approached the gunpowder trail, hovering his flaming torch over a small pile at the end of the line.

'You don't have to do this, Thomas,' implored Felix.

'I'm afraid I do. Goodbye, Felix,' said Percy, leaning down to ignite the gunpowder.

His torch had almost touched the black grains when Percy was disturbed by the sound of a rifle being cocked somewhere in the shadows.

'Who's there?' he shouted, pointing his torch into the darkness.

'Step away from the gunpowder, Home Secretary,' called a voice in a mock British accent.

'Why don't you come out and show us your face?' said Percy inching forward to get a better look.

Suddenly a gunshot fired out of the darkness, brushing the wall above Percy's head and causing him to duck for cover.

'I said, step away!' the voice repeated, a hint of an American accent breaking through. 'Or I'll shoot you where you stand.'

'Is that you, Professor?' mocked Percy. 'If you shoot me, I'll happily send us all to kingdom come.'

'You're bluffing,' replied Amelia, stepping out of the shadows and pointing a long Winchester at Percy. 'You wouldn't risk hurting yourself. You prefer to murder innocents.'

'This is not the wild west, Professor. We don't bluff here.' replied Percy, throwing his torch onto the line of gunpowder, and setting a spark racing along its thick black trail.

Amelia instinctively pulled the trigger, firing her gun at Percy, who dived to one side, barely avoiding the oncoming bullet. She hurried to reload before Ezra and his men could return fire, but her gun jammed. Suddenly outnumbered and outgunned, she leapt towards the arch for cover but was too late and took a bullet in her chest, falling back into the shadows.

'Amelia!' cried out Felix. But there was no response. Only silence.

Satisfied that the risk had passed, Percy signalled to his men, and they hurried to the barge, setting sail down the Thames, and fleeing the undercrofts.

In the dark silence, Felix watched the spark draw closer. He could feel Lord Monteagle shaking furiously beside him and Shaw reaching his leg out, trying to break the line of gunpowder. But none of it mattered. All he could think about was Amelia.

He suddenly heard the slightest sound coming from the shadows.

'Amelia?' he called out hopefully.

'Yes?' she replied.

'Are you okay?'

'I wouldn't say I'm okay, but I'm alive.'

'Can you make it to the gunpowder?'

'I can try,' she replied, crawling out of the shadows.

Amelia shuffled her body across the cold stone floor, blood seeping from the wound in her shoulder. She slowly inched forward, groaning with every movement, trying to catch up with the flickering light hurrying along the trail. As she pushed through the pain, closing the distance, she reached for the spark only to come up short and watch it race by her hand. Aware that she would not catch it in time and in excruciating pain, Amelia rolled onto her back and closed his eyes.

'Amelia!?' implored Felix as two gagged lords groaned and gesticulated at her not to give up.

But the Professor remained on her back, incapacitated, and bleeding out on the stone floor as the spark hurried along the trail and past their feet towards the waiting barrels. The men closed their eyes, tensed their bodies, mumbled their prayers, and waited, and waited, and waited, when... nothing happened. The spark hit the barrels at speed and immediately fizzled out. They looked at each other in disbelief.

'What happened?' asked Felix.

'They were empty,' groaned Amelia.

'What do you mean, empty?!' asked Shaw, still in shock.

'I mean, we emptied their contents hours ago,' replied Amelia, barely conscious.

'Why didn't you say?' asked Felix angrily. 'And who is *we* exactly?'

'We… is us,' replied a voice as two figures in smart suits approached from the riverside entrance.

'Them,' added Amelia.

The figures stepped into the light. Felix saw that one was wearing a crow mask, the other an eagle. They were followed by a group of younger, more athletic figures wearing monkey masks. The monkeys swarmed the undercroft. They untied Felix, Shaw and the lords and lifted Amelia off the stone floor, taking her to a waiting boat for medical assistance.

'Prime Minister,' bowed the figure in the crow's mask.

'Did you catch them, Percy and his men?' asked Felix.

'No,' replied the woman in the eagle's mask. 'We let them escape.'

'What?' said Felix in disbelief. 'But if you had time to empty the barrels, surely you had time to plan their capture.'

'The Home Secretary and his men are fully exposed now, Prime Minister,' said the man in the crow's mask. 'They have nowhere else to hide, but they do have a further purpose to serve. They've become the bait through which we hope to catch a larger and much more significant fish.'

Felix took a moment to study the figure in the crow's mask. His mannerisms and tone seemed oddly familiar, like he'd met him somewhere before. He looked down at the man's clothes, noticing his freshly polished boots and the precisely pressed creases in his trousers, alluding to his many years in the British army.

King Edward VII

It had been over a fortnight since Felix had foiled the plot to blow up the Houses of Parliament, but he was still finding it difficult to sleep. He blamed himself for not spotting Percy's betrayal earlier or alerting the police to his investigation sooner. Although having noticed similarities between the Commissioner and the masked mason in the parliamentary undercrofts, Felix had begun to wonder if Thompson had known about his investigation this whole time and whether disclosing the information would have made any meaningful difference. Even so, the thought brought Felix little comfort.

After another night of tossing and turning, he was relieved to see the sun finally rise outside and hear the Downing Street staff spring to life. With the vote of confidence lost and a general election looming, Felix had been summoned to Buckingham Palace for an audience with the King. It was like being asked to meet with the hangman in advance of him securing a noose around your neck.

It didn't matter that Felix had exposed his former Home Secretary's plot or that news of his astonishing bravery had dominated the front pages of newspapers worldwide; he was still subject to the democratic laws of the land and a defeat in the House of Commons was still a defeat, regardless of his perceived heroism.

Felix approached the old, cushioned valet stand, where Humphrey had assembled a finely pressed suit, polished shoes, a tie and a perfectly folded handkerchief for his jacket pocket. He took a moment to examine the beautifully tailored clothes hanging off the elegant piece of furniture. How he would miss the traditions of the job, he thought. The dazzling pomp and ceremony that made it so uniquely British. Yet, having listened to Percy's tirade about the *entitlement of the few*, he suddenly felt self-aware, almost unworthy of such treatment, even if prime minister. Perhaps his former friend's words had merit, despite his despicable actions.

'It's not wise to keep His Majesty waiting,' said Humphrey, entering the room with a tea tray.

Felix smiled, taking hold of his clothes.

'It takes more than just a fine suit and some polished shoes to make a man,' he said, reflecting on the past few days.

'Indeed, it does,' agreed Humphrey, placing the tray to one side. 'But this is no ordinary suit. It was given to you by the British people. It is your armour; wear it with pride.'

Felix placed a warm hand on his steward's shoulder. 'Thank

you, Humphrey.'

'I didn't say I liked the suit.' replied Humphrey. 'The colours are a little bold, and the cut is far too modern for my taste.'

Felix rolled his eyes in amusement.

'Now, will you be taking the car, or should I prepare the footmen for the long, wet walk?' asked Humphrey.

'The car will do nicely, thank you.'

Having finished his preparations, Felix descended the long staircase towards the main hallway. To his surprise, his staff had gathered in two lines by the door to form a guard of honour and wish him well. Felix nodded his thanks to each as he passed before stepping through the iconic black door and into his waiting car.

The drive to Buckingham Palace was marked by silence. During his short time in government, Felix had only met with King Edward VII a handful of times, and each had been brief and formal. He could feel a nervous anxiety in his chest and the sweat tingling on his neck. How could he possibly explain the past few weeks' events to his King? He sat back in his seat and closed his eyes, playing everything over in his mind, trying to order his thoughts and prepare his words. Was it better to keep his explanations brief or disclose every detail, regardless of the negative implications on his time as prime minister?

Felix's car drove through St James's Park and onto The Mall, following the long road to Buckingham Palace, the King's lavish London residence. Originally known as Buckingham House until King George III purchased the entire plot from the Duke of Buckingham as a private residence for his wife, Queen Charlotte, it had been through several structural enhancements, the last and most significant of which had been to the east wing and the famous central balcony where Queen Victoria watched her troops depart for the Crimean War, and the landmark Felix now approached.

Having passed through the palace's black iron gates with their royal crests of golden lions, unicorns and cherubs, Felix's car finally stopped in the red gravel courtyard, and a royal footman opened the door.

'This way, Prime Minister,' he said, ushering Felix through a high-arched passageway towards the Grand Entrance and the palace's main hall.

Felix followed his guide up the winding black-and-gold staircase and across the gallery's scarlet carpet towards the King's audience chamber. The footman knocked twice on the door before opening it and stepping inside.

'The Prime Minister, Your Majesty,' Felix heard him say.

Felix waited for the footman to wave him forward before entering the room. The chamber was elaborately decorated and entirely overrun with antique furniture, family portraits and gifts from world leaders. A small ornate lamp lit the area around the King's desk, where thick plumes of smoke spiralled into the air from his cigar.

'Your Highness,' bowed Felix.

King Edward VII was a heavy man with warm eyes and a neatly cropped beard shaped into a rounded ducktail at the front of his chin. To Felix's surprise, he was dressed in a casual tweed jacket and wore a homburg hat rather than the formal suit or naval uniform one would expect for a ceremonial meeting with the prime minister. But then, the King was renowned for his love of fashion.

'Please, take a seat, Prime Minister,' he said, motioning towards one of the chairs in front of his desk.

Felix crossed the room and sat down.

'It is strange to have to tell one's prime minister that having performed such a heroic service for his country, he will now have to relinquish his position and make way for a general election.' said the King.

'Heroic may be a little strong, Your Majesty.'

'Nonsense!' countered the King. 'If anything, it undervalues your efforts.'

'But I…'

'Yes, I know,' interjected the King, swatting Felix's doubts away like an irritating fly. 'You made mistakes, took your time, made bad choices, and didn't sniff it out earlier. Do you think you're the only leader who ever felt guilty about his decisions? Heaven knows being the prime minister is not an enviable job, like being a King. All that is required is to do your best with the time you are given.'

'Thank you, Your Majesty.' replied Felix, suddenly feeling reassured.

'Call me Bertie,' said the King, looking down at the open diary on his desk. 'Now, shall we say November 18th for the general election?' he asked, marking the date. 'Four weeks. That should give you enough time to muster the troops and give the opposition a run for their money.'

'Me?' replied Felix, amazed.

'But of course.' smiled the King. 'Many have walked through the doors of Number 10, but few have been curious, benevolent or adventurous enough to truly understand what it is to be the British prime minister.'

Felix stared at the King in amazement. Did he know about Old Pye Street, or was his choice of words merely a coincidence?

'Some of us are born to this life,' continued the King, 'no matter the cost, regardless of our failures and insecurities, and even though we're quite sure to be unloved and misunderstood.

That's what it means to serve.'

The King stood up and offered Felix his hand. Felix shook it warmly, then turned and departed. He followed the footman through the palace, reflecting on the King's parting words, then stepped out into the large forecourt. He passed back under the arch and across the red gravel square, approaching his waiting car, when something in his periphery caught his attention. Felix quickly spun around to see a figure hurtling towards him at speed. Having evaded the royal footmen, a large man in a ragged suit with greying stubble and wild eyes launched himself at Felix's feet as though begging for money.

It took Felix a few moments to recognise him.

'Thomas?!' he said, taken aback by Percy's appearance.

'They're trying to kill me, Felix!' ranted Percy, looking over his shoulder. 'I have nowhere else to go. Please, help me! Take me in! I want to be arrested! I confess! I confess to it all and more besides. Please arrest me! I can tell you things about your enemies that will make you…'

Percy was about to deliver the next word when a small wooden dart struck him in the side of his neck, rendering him instantly unconscious. The footmen quickly formed a protective circle around Felix, scanning the gates for any sign of the shooter. But with the palace surrounded by royal parks, it was almost impossible to make out anyone among the dense forest of trees. After a nervous wait and confident that the danger had passed, Felix pushed past the footmen and rushed to his former friend's side, lifting Percy's body to check his pulse, but his heart had stopped. Thomas Percy was dead, poisoned by whatever toxin the wooden dart had injected into his bloodstream.

Felix looked down at his peaceful face. He didn't agree with Percy's twisted beliefs or condone his actions but felt profound grief at seeing his life end so barbarically. He'd wanted the former Home Secretary to face justice in the courts and for the British judicial system to decide his punishment. That, after all, was what civilised societies did. The shock of Percy's sudden appearance and the manner of his death left Felix reeling with a renewed sense of injustice and a sinking feeling about what was yet to come.

The Brahmin

Given the weather and time of year, Green Park was incredibly busy that afternoon. The cold had done little to dampen the spirits of those who liked to frequent its rugged grounds and abundant wildlife. They had seen everything this park had thrown up over the years, the snow, the sleet, the heavy winds, and rain, but few of them had ever witnessed a sight such as Seema Sharma.

They watched in awe as she drifted elegantly through the park in her traditional silk sari, rich with bold and enticing colours. An ornate gold nose stud, matching earrings, and rows of gilded bracelets on both arms pointed to her wealth and superior caste, and the tiara in her sleek black hair sparkled with gems from the subcontinent. In one hand, she held the base of her rich garments, keeping them off the muddy floor, and in the other, a long wooden stick with images of past Indian heroes expertly carved along its frame.

Seema Sharma made her way through the park, stepping out onto Piccadilly. Parked on the roadside next to the construction site of Cesar Ritz's new hotel was a white-and-gold Rolls-Royce V-8. It was one of only three ever made and had attracted the attention of several passers-by as it sat idle, waiting for its owner. As she approached the car, Seema Sharma's steward, a tall Indian man in an elegant silk suit with the emblem of the Royal House of Jodhpur on his breast pocket, greeted her.

'Welcome back, Your Highness,' he said, opening the car door.

Seema Sharma handed him the blowpipe and stepped into the Rolls Royce.

'The Indian Embassy, Vinay,' she hissed.

Printed in Great Britain
by Amazon